COMMENTS ON CARL BROOKINS NOVELS

A Superior Mystery

Carl Brookins knows his sailing, and he also is keenly aware of how to engage the reader. His knowledge of public relations and industry is also central to the flow of the plot, and he handles these things assiduously. A Superior Mystery contains more than just a simple murder...this tale goes back in history and uses the past to make sense of the present. A delightful read. ...*Midwest Book Review*

In this second installment of Michael and Mary's adventures we once again are treated to not only a good old fashioned murder mystery but also to a wonderful time sailing around Lake Superior. With his talent for combining mystery, mayhem, and great character development with scenic descriptions that make you long to take up sailing, Brookins is definitely a must read author.... *Kathy Thomason*

Inner Passages

The title of this novel not only refers to a body of water, but also to the personal journey Michael Tanner must make as he looks for a way out of the storm surrounding his interrupted life. Carl Brookins shows his well versed knowledge of sailing, while the plot and characterizations stay strong and inviting. Inner Passages delivers a well written, satisfying story with unrelenting tension.... *The Charlotte Austin Review*

Brookins has found the range...a tight story and a wonderful sense of place. Batten down for a force eight chase rife with northwest cedar air, cold salt spray, and the chilling rumble of diesels through the fog. You'll feel this one....*Richard Barre, author of Blackheart Highway*

OLD SILVER

OLD SILVER

BY

CARL BROOKINS

Carl Brookins
March 31, 2006

Top Publications, Ltd. Co.
Dallas, Texas

DEDICATION

To all the men of the sea who have lost their lives while toiling on the great lakes and on the oceans of this world, and to their grieving families.

ACKNOWLEDGMENTS

None of the people who appear in this novel is real, although they appear to live in a real world, and real institutions are incorporated in the narrative. Few of the events depicted actually happened, although similar activities could and do occur. A great many individuals and representatives of several institutions extended a helping hand during the creation of this story. To all of them, my heartfelt thanks for answering questions, providing information I didn't know I needed, and for keeping me on track. Errors are mine, not theirs.

Old Silver

A Top Publications Paperback

First Edition

Top Publications, Ltd. Co.
12221 Merit Drive, Suite 750
Dallas, Texas 75251

ALL RIGHTS RESERVED
Copyright 2005
Carl Brookins
ISBN1-929976-32-1
Library of Congress #2004117716

Printed in the United States of America

CHAPTER 1

Ethel Jandrice looked at the heavy pages she clutched and realized two things. Her gloved fingers were smudged with the grime of decades, and her hands were trembling slightly.

She heard someone walking somewhere among the tall storage racks, racks so high they almost disappeared into the dimness of the high-ceilinged room. The sound of those footsteps carried down the long aisles. Earlier they were merely footsteps, now they sounded menacing, dangerous. In another part of the special, climate-controlled warehouse, a worker pushed one of the wheeled stack ladders used to get to the higher shelves. The clatter of the wheels bounced around the cavernous space. When the noise from the ladder stopped, Ethel heard her heart pounding. She flinched and thrust the pages back into the box in front of her. The clatter came again, then stopped and she heard footsteps receding. A heavy door slammed shut and all she heard then was her pulse.

She looked around. Long rows of gray steel shelves stretched away in either direction into brown dimness. The special hanging fluorescent light fixtures focused their harsh white glare downward, concealing the ceiling. This was her working world; shelves stacked high overhead, extending above the lights, shelves filled with records of bygone dreams, failures and successes. Papers of the dead. Her world, one of grays and browns and concrete, like the hard floor beneath her stool. It was a pale quiet world, much like Ethel herself.

It's hard to believe, she thought. I've been cataloguing collections here for nearly twenty years. I've almost never asked for a specific assignment. Now, because of Tommy, I ask for this one and look what's happened. I've heard about interesting finds other people stumble over, but it never happens to me.

But now, maybe it had. Ethel had to think about it, this letter she had discovered stuck in an unrelated file folder. She leaned forward and rested her damp forehead on her wrist. Then she again reached into the box for the letter after automatically exchanging her soiled gloves for clean ones to protect the documents. There were three thick creamy-white pages of sprawling script in heavy, black, ink. There was no salutation. It appeared that the first page was missing. This was not an ordinary letter between business associates. This letter spoke of cheating, of corruption, of blackmail.

Her day had started out in ordinary fashion, just as her days had for almost all of Ethel Jandrice's working life. She arose at six in the pale dawn and made her singular, sparse breakfast, just as she had for ten thousand or so previous mornings. She dressed in her plain, simple, blue, work dress that almost matched the color of her eyes and she combed out her short curly faded-blonde hair. The fresh summer morning didn't interest her much on the short walk to the bus stop, although since Tommy had entered her life she was becoming more aware of such things. She was glad to get to the climate-controlled storage center, located on a short quiet street on the east side of St. Paul, before the predicted heat of the day arrived.

Work took her attention, work, Tommy, and sometimes poetry readings. Ethel Jandrice was a cataloguer. She was responsible for general cataloguing and organizing new collections that were donated to the Minnesota Historical Society for safe-keeping. They never knew, when a truck pulled up to the huge delivery entrance with its steel overhead door at the document storage center, exactly what to expect. The records came in untidy, usually musty-smelling, often dusty, stacks of wood or cardboard boxes.

A very circumscribed life lived Ethel Jandrice, at least before Tommy. Work and home and the streets in between were almost her entire physical world. If she explored other horizons, it was through the records she handled, the television she occasionally watched and poetry.

Most of the boxes trucked into the records center, Ethel knew, contained ordinary business records, sometimes in the most appalling condition. She had found mice, alive and dead, and feathers and dirt, always dirt. Today she had discovered something else, something that should not have been included among the business records of ... she glanced again at the box label to be sure. It read deVole Corporation, Chicago, Illinois--1890-1910. The three heavy pieces of stationery appeared to be a personal letter from a "Tony." Was that Anthony deVole? It was written to someone called "Wally" who lived at that time in Duluth. Who, she wondered, was "Wally?" The answer was of more than passing interest. The letter indicated that something illegal had been planned between those two around the beginning of the twentieth century. Had the plan been carried out? Was it still a secret? Tommy might know. To find out, Ethel decided to commit a crime.

CHAPTER 2

Two hundred miles north of St. Paul, Michael Tanner watched Mary Whitney roll onto her side and bend her left knee. He thought the cold was getting to her, but she wasn't ready to admit it. With a quick flip, she scooped a gout of frigid Lake Superior water over the edge of the dinghy and caught him square in the chest. The shock of that icy water wiped the grin clean off his face.

"Hand me my mask and tube," she said. "I've asked three times now. You're just stalling 'cause you want to get back to the boat."

Tanner had agreed a few minutes earlier to go along in the dinghy so Mary could swim around the caves on the northeast edge of Devils Island, below the old lighthouse tower. The water was just about warm enough for a swim, although a full wet suit might have been more appropriate. Lake Superior is one of the coldest lakes in the states. Tanner figured she also wanted to try out her new swimsuit. This was their second trip to Northern Wisconsin.

Last year, when Mary accompanied Tanner to Chequamegon Bay on Lake Superior, she'd formed an immediate attachment to the lake at some psychic level Tanner didn't fully understand. Now they were back, vacationing with another couple for a week of sailing among the Apostle Islands. Their companions, Vance Jordan and his wife Ella, being of softer or saner stuff, had declined the opportunity to join Mary in the icy lake.

Tanner handed over her mask and breathing tube. She slipped them on, rolled over, and paddled away. Tanner thought Mary looked quite fetching in her emerald-green one-piece suit. He rowed with her, easily keeping pace in the dinghy.

They were in the second of a ten-day sailing trip on the

Jordan's thirty-five-foot Hunter. The Jordans berthed their boat *Carefree* at the Bayfield Marina, not far from the Apostle Islands at the head of Chequamegon Bay.

The weather so far had been fine, good breezes for sailing and warm air temperatures with substantial sunlight. Just now, brisk breezes from the northeast stirred the surface of the big lake and gave the sun high overhead a chance to project a million diamond-like sparkles off the blue wavelets. Tanner stroked the stubby oars and looked over his shoulder at the shadows on the overhanging rock of the island. The weather-worn, reddish caves of Devils Island looked dark and empty in the cool shadows. Occasionally a larger than usual roller would lift the dinghy and then slap against one of the lower cave openings. Those rollers often created the sonorous, mysterious-sounding, boom that probably gave the island its name.

Tanner maneuvered the dinghy so he could follow Mary's progress without twisting around. Every so often her finned feet stopped while she floated on the surface and examined something far below that had caught her eye. Her breath came noisily from the snorkel tube. This went on for several minutes then while floating quietly on the water, she raised her head and called, "I'm going down. I see something."

Without waiting to hear his surprised response, she gulped a lungful of air and jackknifed, aiming almost straight down. Her fins and powerful legs drove her through the water until all Tanner could see, hanging precariously over the side of the dinghy with his face close to the surface, was an occasional flash of light reflected from her silver fins.

He lost sight of her completely, then she surfaced with a rush and a loud whoop on the opposite side of the little inflatable. She held one hand high over her head. When she reached the dinghy, Mary dropped a flat piece of metal onto the floorboards at Tanner's feet. Then she shoved the mask up on her forehead and grabbed the gunwale.

"What is it? I found it wedged in a crack on a little rock ledge about twelve feet down right beside a really dark hole. The sun was just right...bounced off it. I almost missed it. What do you think it is?" She panted to regain her breath.

Tanner picked up the heavy object. It was rectangular with rounded corners and a large hole in the center and almost fit into the palm of his hand. Two ears stood out on opposite sides. One was pierced with a small hole. The other ear had a notch in it. Stamped or cast on the surface was the word AMADOR. After that were the two letters dV.

"Dunno, mermaid mine." Tanner rubbed his nose. Perry Barstowe, one of Tanner's partners in their Seattle public relations firm had once told Mary that it was an unconscious habit of Tanner's, so she could always tell when he was puzzled. "You're the amateur historian. Looks like it might have been part of an engine. Off a boiler maybe?"

"Can I keep it? It would look nice mounted on a piece of polished wood. Like a plaque."

"We'll ask Vance and Ella," Tanner smiled.

"Tow me back, will you? I'm getting cold."

"Ah, perhaps you'd like a bit of a rub to warm you up?"

Mary grinned and gestured toward the sailboat anchored a hundred yards away. "Home, my good man."

Back aboard Mary scuttled below to dry and dress. Tanner handed her find to Vance, who peered at it, rubbing his blunt finger over the dull surface. Vance was the perfect sailing companion, capable, competent, unswervingly cheerful. He was a geographer at the University of Minnesota in Minneapolis whom Mary had met quite by chance at a conference in Seattle. He'd spoken on the lumbering industry in the Northwest. He turned the piece over, running a finger around the outside edge. After a moment he shrugged and held it out to Ella, an American Studies professor. She looked at it for a moment and then said, "Vance, darling, move your thumb." He did so.

"Oh look, AMADOR."

Vance blinked and looked again. "Hunh," he said. "Sounds familiar, somehow."

"Really?" asked Mary. She'd changed into her gray sweats and returned to the cockpit, vigorously rubbing her hair with a large towel. Tanner glanced at her with appreciation. He could tell the way her body moved in the baggy sweats she wasn't wearing any underwear. She smiled at Tanner's gaze and awareness.

"Yeah. Ellie, don't we have that book on Lake Superior shipwrecks aboard?" Vance dug at the edge of the piece with his thumbnail.

Ella slipped below and they heard her sliding open cabinet doors. "Yes," she called, "here it is." She handed it up to her husband and said, "Snacks and drinks coming."

"Ah, here we are, let's see now," said Vance. He leaned back against the raised side of the main cabin, legs stretched out along the cockpit bench seat opposite Tanner and Mary Whitney and consulted the index. Then he flipped the pages.

"Around 1900, there was a lot of shipping through the lakes between Milwaukee, Duluth and Chicago. Dry goods, building materials, lots of items they didn't have up here in the hinterlands, that sort of thing. And of course they were shipping ore from the mines down to Chicago and on east to the steel mills." Vance waved expansively at the trees and gently rolling blue water.

"Would one of you give me a hand down here?" Ella's voice floated up through the hatch from the galley. Tanner grunted a quick affirmative and slipped below.

Vance raised his voice slightly so he could be heard in the cabin. "Anyway, it says here a Chicago family, the deVoles, owned a small fleet of cargo ships, one of which was named the *Amador*. The *Amador* didn't live very long. It sank in a violent storm in late 1905, somewhere off Sand Island. Apparently everybody aboard was drowned. They never found the wreck or the cargo and it's assumed the ship broke up completely."

"Anything else?" asked Mary, tracing the raised outline of the letters on the brass plate with one slender finger.

"Well, there's a story or legend about the cargo, too," Vance went on. "Some family heirlooms supposedly were lost, and maybe a relative of the deVoles was aboard. At least that's the story they put out. The company tried very hard to find the wreck, but in those days, diving was a lot more chancy than today. And the water was just as cold then as now."

Tanner stuck his head up the companionway and said. "Didn't you just tell us the ship was lost off Sand Island?"

"Yes," said Ella behind him.

"This isn't Sand. Sand is quite a way southwest of us. Am I right?"

"Yes, you are," nodded Ella, handing him two tall glasses filled with ice, generous dollops of gin and fizzing tonic, the whole garnished with thin slices of lime. "Sand is just about the westernmost of the Apostles."

"The last radio communication from the *Amador* said they were trying to get into Squaw Bay, which is west of Sand." Vance was reading more.

Tanner handed up the glasses as Vance said, "Drag out the charts above the nav table, will you?" When a chart of the Apostle Islands was unrolled on the cockpit table, he pointed out Sand and Devils Islands.

"The water is only seventy to 100 feet deep there," Mary remarked, leaning over the chart. "I'd think they wouldn't have too tough a time locating a wreck in those waters, even with the primitive diving equipment they had then. And the water, I can't believe how clear it is."

"According to the book, the company tried to find the *Amador*," chimed in Ella, "but they never even found pieces of wreckage. Some of the stories are in the book." She handed up two more glasses and then a tray with an assortment of cheese and fruit.

"This author quotes from newspapers of the time. According to this," Vance continued, "they speculated on why the company tried so hard to find the ship, but they couldn't get any answers from the deVoles."

Mary picked up a plastic plate and turned to the tray of food, saying, "Then how'd that thing get way over here? Unless it was attached to a piece of wood that floated around? Or maybe someone found it near Sand and later lost it in the water near Devils Island."

Tanner climbed to the cockpit after Ella and shook his head. "Seems unlikely."

"That thing wasn't attached to any wood, either," said Vance, bluntly. He pointed a heavy finger. "That looks like an inspection port off a boiler. It was bolted to a large and heavy part of the engine. When *Amador* went down, this went right to the bottom. Pretty quickly, I should imagine."

Tanner said, "If that's what it is, why would it have the name of the freighter on it?"

"Several possibilities. The boiler manufacturer might have done it specially for the deVole Company. A goodwill perk, if you will. Or the company might have allowed an engineer in the crew to personalize his workspace," Vance said.

"Well, you're the marine engine expert, at least on this boat, so I'll accept your explanation." The quartet fell into thoughtful silence.

The sun fled toward the western horizon, sending long slanting streams of hot light glancing off the placid waters of Lake Superior. They polished off the snacks. Mary looked around at the island and the lake. Their sloop was alone for the moment on the inland sea.

Tanner glanced at Mary. She looked back at him and smiled widely. "Then it's possible," she said slowly, "that the *Amador* was somewhere else when it sank, maybe here, off Devils Island!" Excitement rose in her voice.

"But how could that be?" Tanner responded. "I mean, they knew navigation, and they had a radio. You did say the wireless operator reported their position didn't you?"

"Yes, that's right," said Vance. "I can't explain the possible navigation error, but radio. Well. Wireless was pretty crude in those days. It was new and it was only in code, remember. There wasn't any voice chatter like we get on that thing." He pointed at the yacht's VHF radio.

"Well," Mary said after another pause. "It's intriguing, isn't it?"

"And even if it turns out to be a perfectly ordinary piece of brass, with no connection to that *Amador*," Ella remarked, "it's fun to speculate about where it came from. Unfortunately, now that the islands are a national park, you can't keep it. Technically, you shouldn't even have brought it up without a permit. We'll turn it in when we get back to Bayfield. I don't know what they'll do with it, probably bring it back out here and drop it in the water."

Mary stretched. "I'm going to take pictures of it. Something to keep as a memento." Tanner looked at her thoughtfully. There was that tone in her voice. He'd heard it before. When she glanced at him he smiled, gazing into her dark eyes.

"I know that look," he said. "I hear questions. You're starting to play what if."

Vance looked up.

"Just imagine." Mary said, leaning toward Tanner. "What if *Amador* went down somewhere else? What if we were to find the wreck? Wouldn't that be exciting?"

Tanner laughed. "Oh boy. Here we go again."

"There's a cloud line coming. Looks like we might get a little rain," said Ella, glancing over Mary's shoulder to the western sky. "We ought to listen to weather radio, although they don't always get it right."

"I'll do that," Vance said, stepping down into the cabin. "It's also time to move to a better anchorage for the night. Crank 'er up, Ellie." He emerged a minute later saying, "Nothing about rain and the wind is expected to hold overnight. Hang on, I'll get the anchor."

"Those clouds don't look too serious," remarked Mary, squinting at the sky.

Vance smiled as he went forward. "Look at the book. Quite a few shipwrecks over the years."

"Yes, but..."

"Remember the Edmund Fitzgerald?" said Ella while she eased the boat forward to slack the anchor line. "This lake has many moods and can be most unforgiving. It sometimes creates its own weather and storms. They come up quickly, out of the clear blue, so to speak." She waved at the serene sky above.

Mary looked at the book of shipwrecks and nodded thoughtfully. Although she was the most experienced sailor of the four of them, Lake Superior was a new sailing venue for her. She'd read about the sudden weather changes the lake could generate and she knew ocean sailors who had gotten seasick for the first time when sailing on Lake Superior. She took the book and the brass plate from the *Amador* below and stowed them carefully. Mary returned to the deck as Ella turned the big wheel to point *Carefree* toward their night anchorage off South Twin Island while Vance and Tanner set the sails. She looked at the water and she wondered about the *Amador* and the men who had been lost in the water under the keel.

CHAPTER 3

When Ethel Jandrice walked calmly out of the cavernous Collections Warehouse of the Historical Society that afternoon, she had no idea what she was setting in motion. Tiny beads of perspiration popped out at her hairline, even though she knew she didn't have to worry about being stopped by a security guard. It had never happened. A long-time trusted employee of the society, no one would take her for a thief. She started across the dusty parking lot toward her bus stop on the next street in the brassy, late afternoon sun, paying scant attention to her footing. She stumbled over one of the many ruts and almost fell. For a moment her nervousness almost betrayed her. Ethel was sure she could hear the faint rustling of the heavy sheets of paper concealed under the bodice of her blue dress, and so would anyone who came near.

The bus ride home was excruciating. Every time the bus swayed, or she moved, Ethel was sure someone would see the edges of the pages sticking out against her dress. Even though the bus was air conditioned, her skin was clammy and her arm stuck to the vinyl arm rest. Just before she reached the stop she wanted, one page shifted a little and a corner began to prick her chest. Heart pounding, she almost reached up to touch it, then realized she shouldn't. The library came into sight and she pulled the cord to signal a stop. The driver, who knew Ethel Jandrice by sight, looked at her in mild surprise as she left the bus. It wasn't Ethel's usual stop.

In the cool library, heart still pounding, she paid the three quarters necessary to copy the letter she had stolen, the letter from Anthony deVole to his cousin and close confidant, Wallace Edmond Mayhew. Then she walked the rest of the way home in the late afternoon heat.

Punctually at eight her friend, Thomas Callender, arrived for their planned evening of relaxed conversation. Perhaps he'd read a new poem, or they'd watch a little television if there was anything interesting on PBS, and they'd have a nice glass or two of inexpensive white wine. When they were settled, quietly sipping their first glass, Ethel looked at 'her Tommy' and spoke words that would change their lives forever.

"I found the most fascinating letter today."

Tommy Callender looked a question at his companion. He was a tall, slender man with a soft voice and a hard body. He worked out of doors, and he was brown, burned by the sun and the wind. Beside him, the pale, diminutive Ethel took on doll-like characteristics. They didn't appear to be at all suited to one another. Ethel was a shy, bookish, introspective history buff and professional cataloguer, Thomas was blunt and street-wise. He had an excellent mind, but had never had a formal education to develop and take advantage of his abilities. He'd compensated by developing a voracious appetite for reading.

Callender was the product of a brief union between his mother, Sarah Mayhew, and a Finn from the Iron Range named Piers Callender. Sarah met Callender while they were students at the University of Minnesota in Duluth.

Sarah was the youngest daughter of Anthony Mayhew. Mayhew and his wife Barbara died in a traffic accident when she was only a year old. Their three daughters were taken in by their grandfather, John Mayhew.

John Mayhew was known around town, first as Black Jack Mayhew, and later as Old Black Jack, neither an affectionate nickname. The labels came from those who'd gone toe to toe with him over some business or civic deal and lost. He was considered to be a cold man, emotionless, always grabbing for an advantage. When Sarah got pregnant, her grandfather erupted. It was a family crisis. It became clear to Sarah and subsequently to her family that marriage wasn't in Callender's plans. Mayhew never forgave Piers Callender for what he had done to 'his' Sarah. Her pregnancy forced John Mayhew to accept the reality that it was long since too late to order her about the way he did his company managers and more subservient members of his family. Sarah was headstrong and forthright and she'd always been her grandfather's favorite and she would do what she would do.

****

"Letter?" said Tommy now, turning to gaze at her over the rim of his wine glass. He wondered again what attracted him to this woman. Ethel certainly was no beauty, never had been. Not that she was plain, she was just....ordinary. That night a few months ago at the bookstore, Tommy had been startled to hear her asking the identical question of the visiting poet that he had just formed in his own head. He thought she sounded bright so he started a conversation. Their mutual attraction grew. They got along well, made few demands on each other, and became comfortable together. Tommy guessed they were a lot alike, intelligence in ordinary packages. He often made her laugh, something he instinctively felt she hadn't done much of. She was a little older, but he didn't care. He was fond of Ethel.

"Tell me about this mysterious letter," he said softly, settling deeper into the comfortable old sofa and stretching out his booted feet.

Ethel drew one short, slim, leg up on the sofa between them and picked up the stolen pages from an end table. "Remember, Tommy? After I learned that the deVole family papers were coming to the society, I asked to do the cataloguing?"

"Sure. I mentioned to you that my mother's a Mayhew and somewhere back there one of her relatives was married to a deVole."

"I've been working on the papers all week and today I found something. This is part of a letter from a deVole in Chicago to his cousin in Duluth. It was written around 1900. There's no date, and at least one page is missing. The letter talks about a special shipment of family belongings to Duluth. And it tells that the goods will be transported on one of the family company's ships named the *Amador*."

Tommy took another sip of wine and looked alertly at Ethel. "Where," he wondered aloud, "is this going?"

Ethel grinned a sly grin. "Oh, I know you, Tommy, I know what you're thinking, but just be patient. This isn't some more dry family history."

"I don't know much of anything about the deVoles," said

Tommy.

"They had business and other interests in Chicago for a long time. They were quite wealthy and successful. And they had some kind of connection to northern Minnesota, buying timber and investing in mining. They also owned cargo ships on the Great Lakes. Anyway, Tommy, the man who wrote this letter said he was sending some information and some important family belongings to his cousin in Duluth. His name was Anthony deVole."

A faint pulse began to beat in Tommy Callender's forehead. Ethel took a sip of wine and resumed her story.

"Anthony deVole says here that he's shipping the goods, he underlines that, heavily, see here? He writes that the goods will be in a special trunk inside a packing crate. Then he gives the markings on the crate so that his relative will easily recognize it. The rest of the letter is also strange. He uses funny language and underlines odd words." Ethel showed Tommy the places she meant.

"I see what you mean. Every time he writes the goods, he underlines the words."

Ethel smiled. She knew Tommy would understand. "That ship, the *Amador*, sailed from Chicago, but never got to Duluth. It sank in a terrible storm near the Apostle Islands on Lake Superior. Everybody on board was killed.

"Now the delicious part is this." Ethel laid the paper in her lap and raised her eyes to Tommy's. "I think this deVole was using a sort of code. He says the targets have to be approached carefully so's not to spook them. First approaches have to be carefully planned and on the q.t. Then he gives some examples without actually saying what he did or who he's talking about. He seems to be telling his cousin that he bribed certain city officials in Chicago, and they gave him the names of people in Duluth who could be corrupted, bought. Those names were on a list in the special trunk, the one that's packed inside the crate he mentions. See here? He refers to an important list of clients."

Tommy sat staring at the flowered wallpaper on the living room wall. The pulse in his forehead beat faster.

He turned his head and looked hard at her. "What," he said, "is the name of the person deVole wrote to?"

"Oh," said Ethel. "It was his cousin, Wallace, at least he addresses him as 'cousin Wally' a couple of times. And I looked up the name. He must be referring to Wallace Mayhew, of the Duluth Mayhews."

"Oh, yes, Ethel," said Tommy, "they were cousins, all right. And you're probably exactly right about what was in that crate. Why'd you bring this letter home?" In the past, when she had wanted to regale Tommy with some interesting sidelight on the people whose papers she was cataloguing, she would just tell him the story. This was the first time she had ever brought something home to show him.

"Well, you know I asked to be the cataloguer because of your family connection to the Mayhews. You come from an important family, Tommy. Why, Duluth has had a Mayhew in the state Senate, and they have that big mansion up on the North Shore. Anyway, I think this Anthony deVole was telling his cousin who he could corrupt to get some kind of business advantages in northern Minnesota. And I thought you could help me figure out what's missing."

"Why are you so interested, Ethel?"

"Oh, well, every so often I hear about somebody who has a job like mine who makes some important discovery, and then that person gets a little publicity and it's exciting. I thought if you can help me understand the letter better, maybe when I tell what I found, I could get a little publicity, that's all. I mean, it sounds like this deVole and Mayhew were planning some big deal. It could be kind of exciting. But Tommy, if it makes you uncomfortable to learn something bad about your family, I'll understand. But it was a long time ago.

"Besides, they couldn't have done what they planned, because the boat sank. Unless there was another shipment later. I just thought that we could do a little research before I tell the director. Otherwise they'll just give it to some historian to examine. Then they'll do the research and get to tell the story, if there is one. I thought it would be fun for us to do this together. Don't you think so?" She smiled ingenuously into Tommy's eyes. It was a long speech for Ethel. Now she waited for Tommy's reaction, still smiling.

Thomas Callender slowly placed his wine glass on the table in front of the couch and stood up. He took two paces away from the couch and turned to look down at Ethel. She stared up at him, a look of consternation growing on her face.

"Ethel, I never told you all that much about my family, did I?"

"No. Mostly that they didn't treat your mother very well and you didn't get along with them."

"That's right. I think the Wally referred to in that letter is Wallace Mayhew, my great great grandfather. He was the man who made the really big Mayhew fortunes. And I'll tell you something else. I'm pretty sure he was married to a deVole." Tommy took two paces across the living room and back. "This isn't a new story you've just told me. I've heard it more than once from my mother, and from some of my Mayhew cousins, only with a few important changes. The story I heard was that deVole was sending a lot of family silver to Mayhew, that the trunk was filled with heirlooms. They'd be worth a lot of money today. But you want to know what I think now?" Ethel nodded.

"I think "Big Tony" deVole--that's what they called him you know--I think Big Tony was sending money to his cousin to run some scheme they'd cooked up. Wallace Mayhew must have been planning to buy off certain people and there was cash in that crate to help him do that.

"Ethel, honey, that letter could be worth a whole lot of money to us. You keep it real safe."

"I've already made this copy and I'm going to put the original back in the file tomorrow."

"Where did you say you found it?"

"In an ordinary business file among some old invoices. This letter was never mailed to Wallace Mayhew. I have no idea how it got into the box I'm working on. Maybe it fell off a desk into the box and nobody noticed."

"Yeah, and didn't you say people in Chicago were upset because somebody at deVole headquarters thought they should go through the papers before they were sent up here?"

Ethel giggled nervously, watching Tommy stride back and forth in front of her. "Yes, that's right."

"I'll bet that letter is one of the reasons they were so interested in going through the records before anybody else took a look at them. Somehow deVole found out that his letter never got to Duluth." He nodded and said, "Honey, that information could be dynamite. I don't know about the deVoles, but there's never been any real scandal about the precious Mayhews. This could change things. A whole lot." There was a mixture of contempt and greed in his tone.

"Tommy, what are you thinking?" Ethel's voice betrayed a growing alarm. She had never seen him so agitated.

"I don't know yet, but that letter could be dynamite. Don't put it back yet. Okay? And keep the copy some place safe. I want to check it out. Just wait for a few days, Okay?" Without even saying goodbye, he rushed out, leaving a stunned Ethel sitting on her couch staring at the front door.

CHAPTER 4

"Michael? Are you home?" Mary called out as she came through the door.

"Yes, I'm in the bedroom. How'd you make out?"

"Not well." She strolled down the short hall to the room where Tanner was holding a note pad and staring out the window of their bedroom. He glanced around at her, smiled and made a note on his pad.

"Sorry to hear that. Come on, we'll have tea and you can tell me about it."

"I think the people at the library are beginning to believe I'm off my rocker, or at least becoming obsessive. I tied up the resource librarian for at least an hour before we found even the little they had available."

"Librarians must be used to all sorts of requests. What did you learn?"

"I—they located one old book about Midwestern business that indicates there was a fleet of lake steamers on the Great Lakes controlled or owned by the deVole Shipping Company from Chicago, but its all very general. I'm assuming it's the same deVole. It didn't specifically mention the *Amador*. The librarian said they could get the book on Lake Superior wrecks through interlibrary loan, but I've seen that one too. She suggested the Minnesota Historical Society as a good place to check. I think I have to go back to the Twin Cities."

"Now that I do find a little obsessive." Tanner grinned. "However, anticipating such a possibility, your need and your frustration at having to do long-distance research, I have made some arrangements."

"You have." Mary Whitney smiled and touched Tanner's cheek. "I might have known."

"I have arranged my schedule to take some time away from the office, and I checked with Edmund at the foundation."

"What did the estimable Mr. Hochstein have to say?"

"He allowed as how he thinks they'll get along just fine without you for a while."

"And so? Put that tea strainer in the sink, I'll wash up later."

"And so I have booked two e-tickets on Northwest to Minneapolis for the day after tomorrow. And I called Vance to find us a place to stay in the Twin Cities."

Mary clapped her hands softly. "Excellent! I knew I'd found a winner when I latched onto you up in Desolation Sound."

****

The doorknob rattled and Tommy came through. He leaned over Ethel and gave her a sound kiss on her cheek. He looked energized.

Ethel smiled and touched her cheek. "Why Tommy, you're early. Didn't you have to work today?"

"I took the afternoon off. Things were a little slow today. The electrical contractor didn't deliver the materials they need right now. At least the truck didn't. So we couldn't start on the paneling." Tommy was working as a laborer on a new office building going up in Bloomington, a suburb of Minneapolis. "So I took the afternoon off and went to the library."

Although Tommy Callender had always worked as a laborer for various employers, Ethel wasn't surprised to learn he spent time in the library. His mother had seen to that. Sarah Mayhew had remained unmarried. She appropriated Tommy's father's family name and soon after he was born, took her son away from the hospital. Then she sank below the surface of Duluth society and out of sight. Other than Tommy's great grandfather, John Mayhew, Sarah's family thought little about her and her son Thomas through the years he was growing up. But the old man did. He kept quiet track of his favorite granddaughter and her bastard son.

Tommy inherited Callender's aggressiveness along with the

Mayhew intelligence. His mother gave him an appreciation of fine art, fine literature and fine spirits, but he was able to conceal all that through most of his twenty-six years as a roustabout and common laborer around northern Minnesota. Then he moved to St. Paul looking for better paying jobs and soon after that met Ethel Jandrice.

"I'll just get you a glass of lemonade," she said.

Tommy nodded. "Okay. Thanks." He would have preferred a beer, but he knew that other than an occasional glass of wine, Ethel didn't approve of spirits.

Ethel went across the small living room with its lacy white curtains and around the dining table. The small oak table had been her mother's. In fact, nearly all the furniture in the house had belonged to Ethel's parents. It was old-fashioned and showing its age, but it was still serviceable so Ethel didn't replace it.

In the kitchen, barely large enough for two people standing side by side, she opened a white metal cabinet over the stove and took down two tall plastic glasses. From the refrigerator she retrieved a big pitcher of pale lemonade she'd made the night before. The metal ice-cube tray was stuck in the freezer compartment so she took a table knife to chip away the frost.

"What's the holdup?" Tommy called. I have something to discuss with you."

"I need to defrost the refrigerator and the ice tray is stuck. I'll just be a minute," she called back.

"I wish you'd let me buy you a new one," Tommy groused.

A minute later, Ethel deposited one of the tall glasses of lemonade in Tommy's hand. "Now, Tommy," she said, "what did you learn at the library?"

"I went to the MHS library, you know? I found a book about shipwrecks on Lake Superior and it had quite a bit of information. There are two key points. First, after the *Amador* went down they couldn't find the wreck. They looked hard, too, that summer. The second thing is that according to the Chicago newspaper stories, the deVoles were really upset and accused the authorities of not looking hard enough. So the next year they paid for a second search."

"I can understand that," said Ethel thoughtfully. "If you're right about the shipment of cash, the deVoles would have had trouble explaining it if someone else found the money, don't you think? So they must have been anxious to locate the wreck."

"Yeah, especially if the stories about a shipment of money and information are true."

CHAPTER 5

"I'm going to run over to the Historical Society this morning and see if they can tell me anything more about that brass plate. It's Saturday and they're only open until noon." Mary could hear Tanner moving their luggage around. They'd arrived in Minneapolis from their home in Seattle late the previous night and hadn't fully unpacked.

"Don't you at least want a cup of this new coffee before you go?" Tanner came out of the bedroom with a copy of the *St. Paul Pioneer Press* in one hand and a foil bag of coffee beans in the other. He often searched out new varieties of coffee to try. He always tried to make the first pots of a new variety with the most rigorous care possible, so they could evaluate the bean and decide if they wanted to buy more. Sunlight streamed in the window.

Mary shook her head. "I've already made coffee. We can try your new find tomorrow, and I'll get a snack at the History Center. I understand they have a good restaurant in the building. Figure out what we should do about dinner and I'll see you later this afternoon. Oh, and would you call a florist? Send a plant or a really nice bouquet of flowers to the Jordans. This is just such a great place they found for us."

"I will, and I agree. I like this location and I haven't even been in all the bedrooms yet." Tanner grinned at Mary as she swept by, collecting her purse and briefcase.

"While you're gone I'll look over the contracts I brought along and email the office. Then..." Tanner looked up and realized he was talking to Mary's back. She was already on her way out the door. It closed with a soft click on Tanner's last words. He shook his head and went back to his laptop.

Mary drove across town to St. Paul holding detailed directions on her lap. Even on this early Saturday morning, several people were in the library; some reading, others clicking through screens on computers terminals. A few sat poring over documents or books at long tables. The air smelled faintly of wax and musty paper. She walked up to the counter that partitioned off one end of the big light room. The young woman seated on a stool behind the counter was examining a large tattered volume. She looked up and smiled.

"Pardon me," Mary said in a low voice, "perhaps you can help me?"

The woman nodded encouragingly.

"I'm a visitor. From Seattle. A few weeks ago while I was sailing in the Apostle Islands, I found a brass plate. Now I'm curious about its origins. Can you recommend a book or something that will give me some background on the ship this piece came from?" She placed a color photograph of the brass plate in the young woman's hands. The woman brought it closer to her face and examined it closely. Then she looked up at Mary.

"You know there are rules about taking things from the national park."

Mary nodded. "Yes, we took the piece to park headquarters"

The woman looked more closely at the picture. "*Amador*. Oh yes," she said softly. "We know about the tragedy of this freighter. One of the biggest in terms of loss of life. It belonged to the deVole company and sailed on the Great Lakes. It's a Chicago company, you know. The family recently donated the corporate papers to the Society, did you know that?" She smiled brightly.

"No," said Mary. "That's interesting, though. I know the *Amador* was a Great Lakes freighter, I read about it in a book about Great Lakes shipwrecks, but I wonder if you have any books about that period or a history of the family, something that goes into a little more detail?"

"Yes, we have a couple of books here that should help." She started to turn away and then turned her head back to look squarely at Mary. "It's odd, you know. Just recently, last week it might have been, a man was in here asking about the same ship, and about the deVole family. Isn't that interesting? I mean, two requests about the same family and the same ship in such a short time? And right after the deVole corporate papers arrived at our warehouse." She smiled brightly once more and showed Mary how to request the books she needed. One was about Minnesota in the late nineteenth century and the other was about Great Lakes shipping. Mary took them to a table and sat down with a notebook and pencil. She realized almost immediately that there was a great deal of information to go through. Since the deVole shipping line had been active around 1900, Mary also saw references to her great grandfather and the Whitney logging business.

When she turned to the newspaper files, she found several vivid accounts of the tragedy. In one paper an artist had provided a drawing of the scene aboard the freighter moments before the doomed ship had disappeared.

****

The wind was a living monster. She was standing, clutching a rough hemp line that ran from a stanchion at the base of the forward cabin and pilot house down the center of the ship to a heavy stanchion near the aft superstructure that covered the engine. Smoke from the tall stack blew sidewise down the starboard side of the struggling ship. The moaning, howling wind out of the northeast that November day tore resentfully at her hooded cloak and picked at loose lines anywhere on the ship itself. The steel deck beneath her feet vibrated with the rhythm of the straining engine and the waves that rose again and again over the stern. The sickly gray water seemed to hang there, far above the deck, waiting against an equally gray sky. She thought the wave must be seeking a weak spot, a place where its terrible power could flail down on the ship and pound it straight to the bottom of the lake. It was almost as if Superior resented that puny man could float across the surface of the great cold lake with few consequences. The temperature had grown colder. Her feet slid dangerously on the slick deck. Ice was forming on the superstructure. Looking behind her, toward the pilot cabin and the crew quarters at the bow of the 200-foot freighter, she could see ice on the side and the deck railings and stanchions. Ice. Except for fire, ice was one of the most dangerous conditions sailing the lake this late in the season. Ice could add thousands of pounds to the weight of the vessel, driving it still lower into the water. And the forty-foot waves sent thousands of gallons of water aboard, water the pumps in *Amador*'s hull were struggling to eject.

The rain beat down so hard her shoulders were starting to feel bruised. She raised her voice to shout into the wind and couldn't hear it. She turned back, away from the stern, step by step, trying to reach the door in the cabin's structure where she'd foolishly exited onto the main deck. It grew darker and the wind's voice seemed louder, moaning and now screaming, grinding against her and against the *Amador*. Her cold fingers touched the latch and she pulled on the handle, slowly forcing the door outward against the pressure of the wind. Stumbling over the coaming, she staggered inside. The hard wooden sides of the passageway magnified the crashing sounds from without but now she could hear groaning complaining rumbles as the long hull flexed again and again under the uncertain rhythms of the lake.

The freighter suddenly seemed to slew sideways under a rogue wave. It rolled and righted itself, bow down, then up, fighting the enormous waves. Above the main deck in the forward steering station, water sheeted down the windows and the compass swung wildly around and around. It was impossible to see the ship's course or anything else.

Wave after wave smashed down on the cabin. Higher and higher they rose as *Amador* valiantly struggled to raise her plunging bow out of the waves. But the waves were too great that November day, the wind too strong. She saw the cabin windows disappear and the cabin itself begin to fly apart. Suddenly the deck beneath her feet disappeared and she was floating out through the cabin roof. Looking down she saw the *Amador* fading, sinking in the gray thrashing fog and water. There was no land to be seen anywhere.

****

"Miss? Excuse me, Ma'am?"

Mary realized with a start someone was talking to her.

"I'm—Oh, excuse me, did you want something?"

"Yes, I'm sorry to disturb you but we're closing in a few minutes."

Mary smiled at the young woman and rose, collected her purse from the locker and looked at her watch. Two hours had passed in what seemed to be mere moments.

CHAPTER 6

Later that same evening at a quiet Minneapolis restaurant, Mary told Tanner what she had learned. "Naturally a lot of it was unhelpful. I don't really care how many tons of goods they shipped to Duluth between 1899 and 1910, and I didn't need to learn about the amount of ore coming out of the iron range then, at least not right now. Maybe tomorrow. There were several references to my Whitney ancestors, which might help us fill in the family history at some point." She took a sip of scotch and gazed down at her notes.

"But you did find out more about the *Amador*?" Tanner picked up his menu.

"You bet, sailor," she continued. "The *Amador* was a standard sort of lake freighter, about 120 feet long with a coal-fired boiler. It didn't carry ore. It carried lumber, furniture and packaged goods, cases of machinery, sometimes private stuff for people moving to Duluth.

"What does that mean, private stuff?"

"Not commercial stuff. Crates of belongings shipped between family members. It also carried stock for retail stores in northern Minnesota. There were factories and warehouses in Chicago and they shipped up the lakes. They carried almost anything except loose cargo like iron ore or coal."

"I suppose the roads were still pretty primitive those years. Why didn't they use the train? Even today, ship traffic isn't what you'd call swift. And there must have been a rail line to Duluth by then."

"Don't know, Michael. Maybe it was just a whole lot cheaper."

"Was she an old ship?" Tanner asked. He put the menu down and sipped his single malt.

"They told me at the society that there are probably

documents in the deVole collection that will provide even more details about the Amador, and about their other ships too. But the collection was only received this summer and it will take months of organizing before anybody can actually look at the papers. Right now they don't even have an index. Did you know there's a township in Chisago County in Minnesota with the same name as the freighter?"

"Does that belong to the deVoles too?" Tanner beckoned the waiter.

"No, silly," Mary laughed, "it's just another odd bit I picked up while I was doing research."

"Here's our waiter. Have you decided what you want to eat?"

"Oh, 'scuse,'" said Mary. "Just a minute." While Tanner and the waiter watched, Mary scanned the menu and chose a baked salmon with beurre blanc, a shallot-flavored butter sauce. Tanner selected Lake Superior lake trout on a bed of wild rice. The waiter approved their choices and left.

"Anyway," Mary picked up her thread. "The Amador was only a couple of years old and it went from Chicago to Milwaukee to Green Bay and then Duluth. It was on a regular circuit. Freighters often stopped in Bayfield in those days, or in Washburn, but not this one. So, somewhere north of Ontonagan, the ship ran into this big storm and after several hours fighting the waves and rough water, it sank. Everybody drowned, apparently, just like Vance said. I looked at microfilm of newspaper reports from the time. Newspapers speculated that the end came suddenly, after hours of fighting the storm, and that's why no lifeboats were launched. Or the lifeboats sank."

Mary's voice trailed off and she and Tanner were quiet, imagining what it might have been like that day aboard the Amador. As experienced sailors, they sometimes encountered stormy weather while sailing and although they tried to avoid such dangers, it hadn't always been possible.

"I can't figure out how that piece of brass you found got to Devils Island," Tanner muttered. "That inspection port must have been tossed ashore or somebody found it years ago and then dropped again where you found it."

"I'm still wondering about that too. I asked the people at the MHS if there was any way to check for another boat with the same name. They told me the Coast Guard would probably know, something I should have thought of myself. Maybe deVole built a new boat sometime later with the same name, but that would be unusual and I couldn't find any evidence of another *Amador*. I looked at some Chicago newspapers that told about the grief and anxiety in the company right after the sinking. They put an expedition together to try to find the *Amador* after the authorities quit looking. Apparently they weren't satisfied with the official efforts. I didn't find anything specific about a family member being aboard, though."

"If no family member was lost in the sinking, it seems like an overreaction." Tanner finished his scotch as Mary nodded.

The waiter brought their dinners and they concentrated for several minutes on the excellent food.

"The Chicago papers wondered about the cargo. A deVole representative was quoted as saying they didn't talk about the cargo they carried, the owners would do that."

"But they wouldn't say who owned the cargo, right?" Mary nodded and Tanner chuckled. "Dead end for the reporter."

Mary smiled and went on, "There was speculation that the reason the deVoles made another attempt to find the wreck was because there were some expensive goods aboard for an important Duluth family."

"You said you have a theory," probed Tanner, sitting back from his plate and fondling his wine glass. "First, coffee?"

"Yes, please, black." Mary smiled. "About the place *Amador* went down. This comes after I read all the newspaper accounts, both here and from Chicago. I couldn't find a definite statement that the *Amador* was actually near Sand Island. The wireless operator sent messages saying they were trying to slip into Squaw Bay which is west of Sand. That would be logical, because the storm was a Nor'easter. The *Bayfield Bugle* quoted the text of one message. The story interpreted the message to mean that *Amador* was north and a little west of Sand. But according to everything I've read so far, the ship never radioed its exact latitude and longitude."

"That could be because they didn't know it, so they could very well have been north or east of Devils Island," said Tanner nodding.

"Exactly!" Mary gestured sharply with one hand and then took a swallow of coffee. "This wasn't all that unusual, you know. Other ships on the Great Lakes have gone unreported and never been found."

Tanner grinned. "But occasionally found many years later, I'll bet."

Mary grinned back, nodding. "I was surprised they even had radio aboard. It was still so new then. Morse code was their only recourse and in that storm I suppose some of the messages could have been garbled."

"I wonder why the story got around that a family member was aboard. Maybe because the deVoles were upset and paid for another search. How many people drowned?"

"I don't know; one story said fifteen, another said nineteen. The papers didn't all agree. Whichever is right makes it a pretty big tragedy."

"Do you know anything about the officers?"

"Like what?" Mary recognized Tanner's probes. He had a talent for getting at important questions, honed from years of working with uncertain clients. Even questions that at first seemed irrelevant always had a point.

"What about the crew? Were they competent? Experienced? This was a fairly new ship, I gather. Was this a new crew or an experienced one? Was the captain new to the lakes or not? Was there any suggestion of panic?"

"No answers at the moment, but interesting questions I shall explore at a future time." Mary smiled across the table at her companion. "Naturally," she said and her subdued tone made Tanner look up. "I had a small revelation while I was at the library."

Tanner nodded. "I knew something had happened, from the way you were acting when you got home."

"Really. I thought I was dissembling quite well."

"Yes, but I know your moods. I didn't ask because I figured you'd tell me when the time was right."

Mary reached across the table and folded Tanner's idle hand in her own. I had a daydream while I was at the History Center. It went on for quite a while."

Tanner sipped his coffee and waited.

"I was reading about other shipwrecks near the Apostles and about the *Amador* and I kind of went there."

"You mean you dreamed yourself aboard the *Amador?*"

Mary nodded. "Yes, just at the last part of the voyage. I think I got a clue as to what happened. In my daydream I couldn't see anything at all off the ship. I know there are lighthouses on some of the islands, but not in my dream. The waves and the rain were too much. The sky was filled with water. It was everywhere, the water. When I was on the bridge just before she broke in two and sank, the compass was going mad. That's the only way to describe it. There was no way the crew could have known exactly where they were or even what their course was. I think that's why the wreck has never been located. The *Amador* isn't the only one, you know. It's common enough along shipping lanes, not just in the Great Lakes, but on the Inside Passage, for example, pretty much everywhere there's ship traffic. Ships just disappear."

Tanner smiled and squeezed Mary's fingers. "This *Amador* thing has got you really hooked."

"Finding that brass plate has given me some kind of connection to the *Amador*, and to the lake."

Three hours later, as they got ready for bed in the apartment overlooking St. Anthony Falls, the subject of the *Amador* returned. From his place in the king-sized bed, Tanner watched Mary hang her slacks on the back of a chair. He said "The more I think about what you said, the more I think I agree with your theory that they didn't know where they were. After hours of fighting the storm and not seeing land or a lighthouse on the islands, it must have been very confusing, especially if their compass was out of whack."

"That's right." Mary squinted at the ceiling, trying to recall the words from one of the newspaper reports. "'Several hours apparently elapsed since the ship reported their last sighting of a beacon,' something like that."

"Wireless wasn't the greatest in those days and if they hadn't seen a beacon for several hours and if their compass wasn't working properly, you're likely right, the ship wasn't west of Sand at all, but maybe a little east and north of Devils."

"Boy, that's a lot of ifs and maybes."

"Sure, but it's a possible explanation why you found the plate where you did."

Mary got into bed, reached out, and flicked off the bedside lamp. "But when was the last time you saw a compass go out of whack?"

"I know, I know, it's rare. Maybe everybody just looked in the wrong place all those years ago. Here's another possibility. What if the wireless operator got the message wrong? If he was seasick or scared out of his wits, or some jittery sailor wrote down the position wrong, wrote west of Sand when he really mean east? Just think about it."

Mary sighed. "Okay, I'll think about it, but no more tonight, all right?" She looked at his lean tanned body as she slid down under the sheet and questions about the *Amador* faded away.

Tanner stretched out a long arm and turned off the other lamp, plunging the room into darkness. He rolled closer.

CHAPTER 7

Tanner pulled down the slat of a blind in their bedroom and squinted at the morning. The day gave every sign of becoming a Minnesota heater. The sun shown out of a pale blue sky, already soiled by pollution rising from the city. In spite of the cool blue ribbon of the Mississippi at his feet, shimmering heat waves pulsed above the air conditioning exhausts on the roof of the building across the street. Even though he was a visitor to Minnesota, he remembered the hot July days of their previous visit with their soaring humidity, the air so thick and heavy it became an effort just to cross the burning street. He went to the desk in the corner of the living room and opened the *Pioneer Press*. The news was mostly about worsening relations with the Middle East while more UN representatives raised questions about sanctions and the possibility of war.

Tanner scanned the local news pages as well as the national. It was his habit. Wherever he was, if the local newspaper was available, he read everything in it, except the classified section, and sometimes even that. It gave him a sense of the community, he said, a snapshot of the place. He heard the sound of running water from the bathroom and knew that Mary was awake. A short item caught his eye. It wasn't much of a story. In life, Ethel Jandrice hadn't been important in St. Paul society. In death, even though hers was violent and untimely, she rated only a couple of inches near the bottom of an inside page of the Metro section.

Jandrice had been struck on the side of her head by a blow hard enough to break her neck. According to the story she was found by a fellow staffer from the Minnesota Historical Society, who had expected to meet Ms. Jandrice for a working breakfast before they went on to the society's collections warehouse. When she missed the appointment and then didn't show up for work the entire morning, the unnamed co-worker went to Ethel's neat little Frogtown bungalow and found her there, dead on the living room floor amid a scene of incredible wreckage. Police had no leads, or weren't saying so if they did. The reporter suggested that police might be pursuing theories that Ethel Jandrice had surprised a burglar. As an afterthought, the news item noted that Ms. Jandrice's current project at the Historical Society had been a preliminary cataloguing of the recently acquired deVole company papers.

"Well," Tanner mused, "violence in the city." The item promptly slipped into the recesses of his mind. It came back to center stage sometime later. Vance and Ella Jordan were having lunch that day with a close friend and had invited Mary and Tanner to join them.

They met at noon in a Minneapolis restaurant near City College with the college's recently installed president, Anton Marshall. Marshall and Tanner were acquainted from their days as undergraduates at the University of Washington.

City College, being a dispersed institution without a formal campus, leased space for classrooms and offices throughout the Twin Cities, but the college was in the process of associating with a nearby campus-based Community College in Minneapolis and building an Administration building.

"I hope the women won't be long, I'm hungry," said Marshall. He glanced at Tanner. "I'm looking forward to meeting your wife."

Tanner knew immediately that President Marshall had been briefed that Mary Whitney was associated with a substantial foundation in Seattle, a West Coast philanthropic organization with ties to Minnesota and Wisconsin.

The men seated themselves at the table in an alcove off the main dining room of the restaurant. Tanner looked up a few minutes later and watched with pleasure as Mary Whitney and Ella Jordan wove their way through the tables toward them. Ella paused briefly to acknowledge a greeting from a colleague at another table.

"Michael, Vance. President Marshall. Sorry to be late."

After introductions, the hovering waiter took their orders.

"I had a last minute walk-in," said Ella. With an advanced

degree in psychology, she worked part time as a counselor to troubled students at City College.

"Some kind of emergency?" Marshall's eyebrows went up. He was an active, engaged president who wanted to be kept apprised of even small incidents affecting his institution.

Ella shook her head. "No, she's a student I've known for about a year, but not in a professional capacity." She paused and took a sip of water. "You know her; Marsh, you met her after the opening of *Enemy of the People* last year at the opening night party."

"Oh, right. Beth Taylor," Marshall said.

"Well, anyway, Beth has—had an aunt living in St. Paul. She was found murdered, just the other day, and Beth dropped in to talk about it. It wasn't a formal session."

"I think I just read something about that," said Tanner. What was the aunt's name?"

"Ethel Jandrice," said Ella.

"Right," Tanner said. "I saw the story in the newspaper. Tough break. We have enough trouble dealing with the death of family in general, but when it's homicide, it must be even harder."

Ella nodded. "That's right. The police don't tell her anything, of course, except that they want to talk to her boyfriend."

"Beth's?" asked Marsh, taking another bite of his salad.

"No, Ethel Jandrice's boyfriend. Somebody named Tommy Callender. They can't seem to find him."

There was a moment of silence while the party at the table each in their own way contemplated the awfulness of sudden violent death.

"Any vacation plans for you this summer, Vance?" President Marshall broke the silence. His big mocha-colored hands made the table utensils look like children's playthings. When he knuckled his short curly hair, the muscles in his shoulders bunched and rolled, straining the fabric of his crisp white shirt. Beside him, the other men looked almost puny.

Vance watched Marshall shove another forkful of salad in his mouth. "How can you eat that stuff with such relish? I eat it, but I usually have to load it up with lots of dressing."

"It happens I like salads, and it's a good thing, with my everlasting weight problem. But you, you're the gourmet cook."

"Not salads, thank you very much. Vacation. Well. Ella and I went sailing for a week last month, with Mary and Tanner, as you know. I'm not sure what we'll be able to do the rest of the summer. We'll at least try to sandwich in a couple of long weekends before Fall Semester runup starts."

"How 'bout racquetball tomorrow? Help you burn off some of that grease." Marshall glanced at Vance's big shiny hamburger and winked across the table at Tanner. Vance shrugged, his mouth too full to respond.

They listened to Marshall relate the latest troubles at the construction site. It appeared the architects had inadvertently left some crucial wiring for the college computer system out of two floors. The diagrams were wrong and various sub-contractors were busy pointing fingers at each other, directing blame away from their firms. "Enough about our troubles. I understand you're one of the famous Whitneys who have that very successful lumbering and shipping company in Seattle," said Marsh, turning his high wattage smile on Mary.

Mary laughed and shook her head. "I'm not sure about the famous part. But yes, I am one of those Whitneys who got their start years ago cutting trees not all that far from here in Northern Minnesota and Wisconsin." She stopped and looked expectantly at President Marshall.

He leaned toward her slightly. "You're a board member of the Whitney Foundation, the Seattle Ballet and you're involved with a couple of small art galleries, and you're an accomplished bluewater sailor. Last year, when you were in Bayfield examining a small logging company for possible investment, you were attacked and survived a long swim to shore in Lake Superior."

Mary's amusement was evident. "You've done your homework. What next?"

"I'd like to offer you the opportunity to consider two interesting proposals. But not here and not now. Sometime while you are in town, if you wouldn't mind spending a little time with me."

"I'm sure it would be interesting. I've heard a bit about you too, President Marshall. I'll call your office for an appointment. But I warn you, Michael and I are here on a combination vacation and research project. A personal research project. I don't intend to spend a lot of time dealing with grant proposals and the like."

Marshall tipped his head in a slight nod of understanding. "I understand completely. I promise not to even attempt to monopolize your time. Now, changing the subject, can you explain a little about your project?"

"My family was involved in the logging business in Northern Wisconsin during the late 1800s. So I'm interested in learning more about that history. Plus, I happened to find this piece of brass near one of the Apostle Islands a few weeks ago. There seems to be some mystery attached."

Marshall nodded again.

"When Mary discovers a puzzle like this she often follows it to the very end," interjected Tanner.

"A Chicago firm of some importance in the Nineteenth Century shipped a cargo to Duluth. Enroute the ship sank somewhere in or near the Apostle Islands. The wreck has never been located. Rumor has it that part of the cargo was extremely valuable. Now, purely by chance, I may have a lead, tenuous though it is, to the location of the ship. Let's just say my curiosity is piqued. More than piqued."

"I see. The name of the Chicago connection is…"

"deVole," said Mary. "Is the name familiar?"

Marshall glanced at his table companions. "As a matter of fact it is. The deVole corporation has a foundation and City College has received grants from them."

"Really."

"Yes, even though we're a small state college, we aren't hesitant about going after foundation money wherever we can find it."

"Since you're interested in the freighter," said Ella, "and her aunt was involved with the deVole papers, would you like to talk with Beth?"

"Good idea," said Tanner. "Maybe the aunt talked with her

about the foundation or about the company itself."

"Of course," said Ella. "Mary, if you can come with me after lunch we'll see what can be arranged."

Later that afternoon Tanner lay on the couch, the telephone stuck to one ear. He was listening to Mary relate her plans for the evening.

"We were lucky. Ella's student, Beth Taylor, was available this afternoon for a few minutes. Long enough for me to persuade her to come for supper tonight."

"Okay."

"So I need you to find a good grocery and pick up some supplies. Got a pencil?"

"Sure. Go."

Mary rattled off a short list of groceries and then said, "I have to pick up some material that's ready for me at the History Center so I'm counting on you to put together the sauce for the spaghetti."

"Not a problem. I'll see you when you get here. Oh, when's Beth expected?"

"About six. Thanks, you're a sweetie."

****

Beth was waiting outside the apartment building when Tanner drove up from his second trip to a store, this time for wine. He produced a key and opened the outer door, then followed her dark curls and plump form into the hall. He considered the empty apartment waiting upstairs.

"Beth, Mary isn't here yet, although it shouldn't be long. Would you feel more comfortable if we wait out here?"

She turned large dark eyes on Tanner and smiled. "Thanks for thinking of that, but it's okay. You can just go in first and I'll sit near the door until your wife gets here."

They reached the landing together when Mary opened the outside door and came in behind them.

Tanner produced a tray of snacks and gave Beth a drink of wine while Mary checked the sauce Tanner had started an hour earlier and whipped up a green salad. After supper, they took chairs on the small balcony with the last of the wine. The sun, an enormous red ball, sat malevolently on the western horizon, as if refusing to let go and allow the temperature to fall to a comfortable level. It had dropped a few degrees and on the second floor balcony, there was the faintest suggestion of a breeze. It caused Beth Taylor's light curls to wave gently around her ears. She sighed softly and stared out toward the river and the treetops lining the shore.

"I guess I should just stop worrying and assume the cops will find whoever did it. I don't know." Her voice trailed off. "I don't even understand why I'm so upset. I mean, we weren't terribly close, or anything."

"But she was part of your family. Beth, did she ever tell you much about her work? Did your aunt ever say anything about odd happenings at the society?" Mary's voice was gentle and firm, carrying sympathy and understanding.

"No. I don't see how it could have anything to do with her job. I mean, what could be more boring? She was a cataloguer." Beth's voice grew listless in the darkening twilight. "Her work wasn't dangerous, unless a box fell on you or you slipped on a ladder. She spent all her time grubbing around in cartons of old papers and company records. Ugh! We hardly saw each other, you know? Talked on the phone every month or so, is all."

"What about her boyfriend, Tommy?" Tanner asked. "Did you ever meet him?"

"Once or twice. He seemed nice. Aunt Ethel met him at a poetry reading about a year ago. Tommy's from Duluth. A detective told me she might have surprised a burglar."

"Why do they think that?" Mary asked

"They said the place looked as if someone had been searching for something."

"Tell us about Tommy," Tanner suggested.

She shrugged. "What's to tell? He was big. Tall, I mean. Taller than you, I think, and heavier. Nice, but not good looking. But he seemed in good shape." She sighed again.

Tanner listened carefully and watched Beth's body language. She seemed restless and out of sorts, but the questions didn't appear to make her nervous.

Mary brought out the picture of the brass plate she had found and explained to Beth that it probably had belonged on a ship owned by the same family whose papers her aunt Ethel had been working on. Beth looked at the photograph, but she appeared uninterested in the plate or its history.

"What do you think?" Mary asked after Beth had gone.

"Unless she's a helluvan actress, she's just what she appears to be. Whatever is going on with Ethel Jandrice, her niece isn't involved."

"I agree. But it's still odd. I find a brass plate which is probably linked to the Amador, a ship owned by the deVoles. When I go to the Historical Society here to do some research, I learn that somebody else—a man—has been asking some of the same questions I have. I wonder if that could have been Tommy Callender?"

"Why would this Callender be interested in the Amador right at this particular time?"

"Maybe because the woman he's been seeing, Ethel Jandrice, is the lead cataloguer of the deVole papers. Now she's murdered and maybe somebody searched her home."

"Something's going on, that's for sure. But whatever it is doesn't involve this young woman—Beth."

CHAPTER 8

Tanner watched Mary wander to the living room window, coffee cup in hand. Her peignoir acted as a thin screen leaving her slender form in silhouette. She leaned against the window frame, parted the glass curtain, and gazed out. Tanner could tell she was looking down at the river four stories below.

He folded the newspaper and said, "I bet you're looking at that sailboat anchored down there." The sloop in question had arrived Saturday, the day after they'd moved in and had been anchored there ever since. They'd seen no signs of human activity aboard her.

Mary turned her head and nodded. "How did you know?"

"I'm pretty well tuned in to most of my lady's moods. I have a suggestion. Why don't we interrupt this phase of your exploration and go sailing?"

Mary's smile widened. "I can see I'm going to have to do something out of character pretty soon, or you'll become entirely too sure of me and my moods." She crossed to where Tanner was sitting and leaned over to peck his cheek. Her robe fell open.

"Hmm," said Tanner, "now what was I saying? Your charms are distracting me." He leaned toward her.

Straightening, Mary wrapped her robe tightly around her. "Pooh. Can you get away from your computer for a while?"

"I have to do a little more polishing on this proposal the guys emailed me and then I'll be entirely at your disposal for a few days at least."

"Great. I'll call Vance and see if they're available." Mary whirled about and ran into the bedroom to the telephone.

It turned out neither of the Jordans was available for several days, but they generously offered their Hunter *Carefree* for Mary and Tanner's use. Tanner drove to the Jordan's home to pick up the boat manual, keys and advice on where to shop for supplies. Meanwhile, Mary packed clothes for the two of them and called Seattle to leave messages regarding their plans.

Tanner returned and they headed north in their rental on I-35. Tanner drove while Mary studied the boat manual.

****

"That's the last of the groceries. I'm ready for a brief break before we take off. What do you say?" Tanner straightened and wiped his face with the bottom of his t-shirt and gazed around the sun-washed marina.

"How 'bout a cool beer?" Mary popped the cap on a longneck and handed it up to Tanner who had stepped up into the cockpit. After a long swig that finished off half the contents, he leaned over the grill that was hung outboard of the stern rail to one side. He took the blue cloth cover off and began to examine the piece of equipment.

"Nice little grill we have here. It doesn't appear to have had much use. I didn't have charcoal on the list."

"I found a bag of briquettes behind the engine compartment. Do you want 'em?"

"Nope." Tanner replaced the cloth cover and turned away. He picked up his beer and took a drink. There was a sudden twang of metal on metal and a splash. "What the heck?"

"It fell off!" Somebody shouted.

Tanner turned back to see the gimbal clamp where the grill had been was suddenly empty.

"Quick! It's floating in the water." The voice came from another boat docked behind *Carefree* across the water. Tanner looked over the side to see the grill, held up by a bubble of air under the blue cloth cover, sinking slowly into the lake, just inches out of reach. He grabbed a boat hook, but he was too late. There was nothing to do but watch the grill sink slowly, tantalizingly, into the murky water of the harbor. Peering down, Tanner thought he could see it resting on the bottom, but he wasn't sure.

By this time Mary had come to the cockpit, shaking her

head and frowning at Tanner. "Now what? We have to get it back." She twisted and glanced at the instrument panel. "It's only twelve feet deep here. One of us can dive down there."

"One of us?" Tanner raised his eyebrows and grinned. "I think I'm elected. I was closest to the damn thing when it went over the side."

"What were you doing to it?"

"Now isn't that just like a woman? Assuming this is my fault?" He ducked Mary's mock swing with the boat hook, laughing.

"Get your goggles and your suit while I drag the dinghy down here," Mary decided. "There's nothing for it but to jump in, sweetie."

By now, several nearby boat owners, were offering good natured advice and the loan of their own inadequate boat hooks. None offered to jump into the chilly water to retrieve the fallen equipment. Finally, a sailor on a nearby boat popped up out of his cabin and hailed Mary.

"There's a twenty-footer hanging up by the office."

While Mary and Henry Morgan walked down the dock to get the long pole, Tanner clambered into the dinghy and with goggles in place, stuck his head in the cold water. He could just make out the blue cloth cover attached to the barbeque grill lying in the silt and bottom growth to the right of the piling that marked the side of their slip.

With Henry supporting the long pole from the cabin top, Tanner leaned into the water over the dinghy's gunwale up to his elbows. He carefully maneuvered the pole until he felt it touch the grill. After several tries, he managed to edge the hook under the cover.

"I hope the knot on the laces stays in place," muttered Tanner. "There's nothing else to hook onto." He signaled and the two men slowly raised the pole until Tanner could reach down and grasp the clamp on the underside and bring the errant grill dripping out of the lake. Mary grabbed her camera and took a couple of snaps of the activity. When he raised the wet grill overhead, there was faint applause and a cheer from the watching crowd.

Mary and Tanner returned the pole to its place and

examined the clamp on the grill. "Nothing's broken," said Mary. "Looks like the bolt that holds the grill on the clamp just vibrated loose. We're lucky it fell off here in the slip instead of out on the lake somewhere."

Tanner changed his wet shirt then went to the bow to loose the dock lines. With Mary at the wheel, he heaved on *Carefree's* bow, pushing her back toward the open water behind their slip. *Carefree* puttered smoothly along the waterway, headed toward the gap in the Bayfield Marina rock breakwater. By the time they'd made a hundred yards into the North Channel beyond the ferry track between Madeline Island and Bayfield, Tanner had the fenders stowed and the mainsail run up the mast.

"Ready for the jib?" asked Mary.

"Aye aye, Cap'n."

Grinning with satisfaction, Mary luffed up into the wind and Tanner smartly unfurled the sail from his seat in the cockpit. *Carefree's* jib was permanently attached to rigging that ran from the top of the mast to the bow. When not in use the sail was rolled tightly around the forestay. This roller furling system of wires and lines allowed sailors to conveniently control the size of the jib from the cockpit, without the need to crawl forward. Changing a sail at the bow in rough weather could be a dicey proposition.

Because the jib was always in the weather, it required a heavier trim to slow down deterioration brought on by the sun. The trim edge affected performance of the sail, particularly in light air. Some sailors insisted roller furling was lazy. Like many aspects of recreational sailing, divergence of opinions was wide.

"With this nice north breeze, we should zip right up the channel to Stockton," remarked Tanner, neatly coiling the jib sheets.

"Look, up in the sky," said Mary, pointing above the masthead. "Isn't that a bald eagle?"

Tanner fished the bright yellow binocs out of a cubby and trained them on the bird soaring high overhead. "I do believe you're right."

"Tighten up that main, will you? Let's see what this boat will do."

The wind blew steadily from the north and *Carefree* danced northeast, holding to the middle of the channel while Basswood Island on the left hand and Madeline on the right, slowly unreeled. Looking back, Tanner watched the disappearing wake, straight as a steel rail. With the wind, the sun, sparkling waves and a fine woman next to him, he felt good, without a care in the world.

A little later, Tanner relieved Mary at the wheel and looked ahead as Stockton Island grew larger on their horizon.

"I can see the bluff that marks the north side of the bay," said Mary, peering through the binoculars.

"No trees on it."

Closer, on their left hand, the heavy green trees and underbrush of Hermit Island that covered the land right down to the water's edge, concealed a long-closed quarry. "You look at that now and it's hard to realize that less than a hundred years ago the island's trees were logged off and a big crew of men and machines were cutting big chunks of brownstone out of the ground."

"Lots more traffic hereabouts in those days. Right now I can see ten or fifteen sailboats." Tanner said, glancing around their horizon.

"I was reading a history of the area," said Mary, opening a cold beer and handing it to her husband. "In the 1890's practically everybody who lived here had a sailboat of some kind. On a good Sunday, the writer said, Chequamegon Bay was covered with white sails."

"Must have been a lot more people up here then."

"These islands seem widely spaced, don't they? It occurred to me that commercial traffic, like a freighter such as the *Amador*, would be big enough to make these channels seem pretty crowded."

Soon *Carefree* rode easily at anchor in twelve feet of clear water over the smooth sand bottom of Quarry Bay, her sails doused and neatly covered. As dusk arrived, Tanner fussed with the CNG stove in *Carefree's* galley and they successfully completed supper.

Tanner looked around the peaceful little bay and said, "Do you feel like stretching your legs?"

Mary nodded and said, "Just let me get my light jacket and I'll help you put the dinghy in the water. Tanner fished two bright orange life vests, or PFDs as they were officially known, out of the cockpit lazzaret and laid them on the deck beside the oars.

"Do we really need those?" asked Mary, coming back on deck. "No, but park regulations require 'em."

Mary shrugged and said, "I've switched on the anchor light, and I'm leaving the bow and stern lights on as well while we're gone. It'll be easier to find our way back in the dark that way."

"Good idea," said Tanner. It was the work of a moment to hoist the inflatable into the water. Mary clambered down the boarding ladder at the stern and took the oars. She settled onto the single thwart and with a few strong strokes of the little plastic oars, pushed the dinghy around the yacht. She raised her head and sniffed the scent of the land, heat, dust and growing things.

Ashore, they walked hand in hand to the dock, then turned up the path to a pole in the grassy area that carried the Park Service bulletin board. Tanner used his penlight to check the posted weather report. As they walked the gravel path, they could hear excited voices of children still too restless to sleep, coming from tents pitched beyond the low screen of bushes a little farther inland.

After a short stroll to stretch their legs, they returned to the water's edge. Mary knelt where the wavelets nibbled at the beach and dipped her fingers in the cold water. Tanner looked at Mary's bent head, then raised his gaze to the dozen boats of every description riding at anchor in the cooling night, their masthead lights making lazy circles in the moonless dark. "Cold," she murmured. She raised her fingers to her face. "But it smells clean." She glanced up at Tanner. "Are you looking for something?"

"No, I was just thinking about these people out here, comfortable, trusting that their expensive boats will protect them while they sleep."

Mary smiled and tugged his hand toward the dinghy. They put it in the water and rowed back to the yacht. Tanner stood on deck, raised his arms overhead and stretched, looking up at the open sky where millions of stars gleamed and pulsed above the masthead. "How 'bout a little brandy?" he said softly.

"Sounds nice," said Mary. "A small one."

In the main cabin Tanner reached into the small locker

above and outboard of the cushioned bench seat. He selected a flask of Courvoisier. From the galley he took two acrylic tumblers and into each poured a splash of the good brandy, timing his move against the gentle rocking of the boat from the long smooth rollers surging under the hull. Replacing the bottle, Tanner carried the drinks to the dark cockpit. He sat down on a cushion, his mind traveling back in time to two years earlier when he'd been a heavy drinker and had nearly succumbed to a perpetual alcoholic haze. It was just after he'd lost his beloved first wife, Beth, to a killer on the waters of the Inside Passage off the coast of British Columbia.

With the help of good friends and his partners, plus his own force of will, Tanner had put the heavy drinking behind him. Mary knew about his struggle to bring himself out of that deep depression and relegate alcohol to an insignificant part of his life. As he settled back on the seat, he handed Mary her glass with a smile and slid closer.

"Well, what shall we drink to? I know. Here's to a pleasant and successful exploration of these Apostle Islands."

Mary nodded and added softly, "and to absent friends, and lovers."

Tanner nodded in acknowledgement. He looked at Mary's profile in the glow from the cabin light and murmured, "Beth would have liked you."

Mary turned and gazed into Tanner's eyes. "Yes, and I'm sure I would have liked her." Tanner sipped again and cocked his head. "How did you happen to think of her just now?"

Mary took Tanner's free hand. "Because it's the first evening of this particular voyage. I've noticed a pattern from you at the beginning of every sail we take. After we reach our first anchorage, you get a little quiet. Not morose or sad, just quiet. I think that subconsciously, at least, you're thinking about Beth and the only sail you and she experienced together. On the Inside Passage."

Tanner considered her words and then smiled. "I guess I wouldn't disagree."

"She will always occupy a very special place in your heart. And that's good. I certainly hope for a similar place, should that ever become necessary."

"You're a remarkable woman, Mary Whitney." Tanner leaned toward her, but she fended him off.

"Oh, pshaw, sir, now you'll be tryin' to take advantage of me. Usin' your silver tongue to work your wiles. My daddy and my gran'daddy warned me about city slickers like you, sir. I vote we go to bed."

Laughing contentedly they drained their glasses and went below. Tanner closed the hatch above their heads and doused the cabin lights. Together they went forward, shedding clothes as they did so.

CHAPTER 9

At two a.m. by Tanner's wristwatch, he was awakened by a loud banging in the galley. He rolled out of the double bed in *Carefree's* forward cabin hissing when his bare feet touched down on the cold deck. He reached for a handhold and quietly started toward the door. Mary snuffled quietly and rolled over, her bare arm reaching for the warmth of Tanner's body. He stopped to see if she would awaken and when her breathing regained its peaceful rhythm, he walked silently into the main cabin. In the galley he discovered an unsecured cabinet door was swinging back and forth as the boat rolled with the increased waves sliding under the hull. He went to the hatch thinking that as long as he was up, he'd take a look around.

He was naked but he figured nobody would be watching. On deck, he found himself in the midst of a raucous night. The wind blew in strong, fitful gusts across the deck, while waves from the lake rolled through the bay sloshing and growling on the beach behind him. The number of dancing masthead lights had doubled since they'd hit the sack hours earlier. Tanner skipped forward to check the lashing on the roller furler and peered down at the anchor line, bar-taut over the bow chock. The sliver of crescent moon, high overhead, rode through a cloudless sky, dimming all but the brightest stars in the Milky Way.

As he returned to the cockpit, he heard a snort from the nearest boat. Glancing over, he saw the dim glow from a cigarette but he couldn't make out the smoker. Oh, well, he thought, and waved at the unseen watcher. In the main cabin he opened a drawer and slid out the pair of military specification night binoculars Mary had presented to him in celebration of Tanner and Associates signing a big contract. The firm had been intensely immersed in trying to win West Coast Manufacturing for several months and the contract represented a major victory. He opened the hatch again and stood on the lowest step, slowly scanned the bay, pausing briefly on each boat within range. Apparently the silent smoker had gone below.

There was nothing unusual to see. Tanner wondered why he was up. After a few minutes he slid below into the warmer confines of the cabin, satisfied that nothing short of pirates would disturb *Carefree* the rest of the night.

Dawn broke on a restless lake. After breakfast in the cabin, Tanner raised the anchor and they let the wind push them southwest until they cleared Stockton. Then they sailed west and a little north, past Oak and on to Little Manitou where they dinghied ashore to visit an old 1920s fishing camp. Not long after lunch they rounded Otter Island and headed due north, Bear Island on their left and Devils Island dead ahead on their horizon.

"You were up last night," Mary said.

"Sorry, did I disturb you?"

"No. Did something happen?"

"I just wanted to look at the anchorage. Being cautious," Tanner said, wondering if that was all it was.

"Let's run up the west side of Devils and circle back," said Mary. A big wind-driven plume of cold spray came aboard just then, wetting the deck and Mary's back. She flinched when the icy droplets spattered against her thin blouse.

"Ouch. I think a jacket is called for. Michael?"

"I'm okay for now." He widened his stance behind the big wheel as *Carefree* plunged through another breaking wave. More waves came aboard and cold water sluiced down the deck and gurgled through the cockpit drain. *Carefree* heeled, her bow wave chuckling. "We're really moving."

Mary returned to the cockpit and used the yellow binocs to scan the western side of the island as they slashed out into the wider lake. Tanner took them well beyond the northern tip of Devils Island and then turned through the wind to head south along its eastern side.

Except for the navigation light on its tall steel tower, and the rusting black ring bolts still protruding from some of the reddish flat rocks on the near shore, there was little in the brush and scrubby trees to attract much interest. The depth finder had been steadily registering water of fifty or sixty feet in depth, except when they crossed the Devils Island shoal which was only eleven feet below their keel.

With the wind finally dying late that afternoon and the sun losing strength behind a thickening canopy of high clouds, Tanner and Mary, tired and relaxed after a long day of exhilarating sailing, aimed their sailboat toward the sheltering bulge of South Twin Island.

The new dawn found *Carefree* heading northeast toward Outer Island. Following their plan hatched at a breakfast of fresh fruit, toast and several cups of coffee, the couple decided to sail into the lake, north of the Apostle Islands. Then they would turn about and try to imagine what it might have been like nearly 100 years earlier aboard the doomed *Amador* as it ran for cover behind Sand Island.

The wind out of the east had freshened and when they left the shelter of Outer Island, *Carefree* found a boisterous lake full of long rollers and sharp wind-blown whitecaps. After an hour, Tanner stood up at the wheel and looked around the sunny, bright blue but empty lake. "Where are we?" he asked.

Mary consulted the GPS unit and replied, "45 degrees, fifteen minutes north latitude."

"What say we head for Sand Island."

"Right. Make your course 230 degrees. With leeway from this easterly, we should run right by the northern tip of Devils Island."

"I'm going to bear off rather than coming about, so if you'd lend a hand to the main, I'd appreciate it."

As they were then on a beam reach, there wasn't a lot for Mary to do other than check the boom as they swung 'round and took the wind on the left hand side of the boat. Now on a broad reach with the wind coming from slightly behind, *Carefree* picked up speed and they bounded through the water at an exhilarating pace.

Mary replaced Tanner at the wheel of the yacht,

commenting, "Nice sailing we have here. Would you rub a little more sunscreen on my left shoulder?"

Half an hour later, Tanner had just gone below to bring up cold fresh water from the refrigerator when Mary shouted, "Whoa! What's happening here?"

Tanner stuck his head up the hatch. "What?"

"Check out the compass. This one just went crazy." Mary was staring at the compass mounted on the instrument panel in the cockpit.

Tanner picked up the bearing compass he habitually wore on a lanyard around his neck when they were under way and examined it. The card looked steady. But as he watched, it suddenly flickered, then steadied down. "Huh. That's odd, isn't it? Would have missed it entirely if you hadn't been looking at it."

"We were just speculating the other night about the possibility of compass error being a contributing factor to the death of the *Amador*. I don't know much about compass technology in those days, but I bet things weren't as stable as today."

"True, said Tanner. "Remember you daydreamed an erratic compass on the *Amador*? Well, a compass can be used to find studs behind a plaster wall. A large piece of ferrous metal nearby can affect a compass reading. We're not that far from that huge ore deposit up north there called the Iron Range. For another thing, we're passing near the Devils Island shoal. It's only about 11 feet deep."

"Interesting. Would you tend the sheets? The wind has shifted a wee bit," said Mary. Tanner set down a plastic bottle of water and turned to the winch holding the jib and tweaked the main sheet. Their speed picked up. Tanner looked at the chart of the Apostle Islands and said, "We're sailing right down a trench that's over a hundred feet deep. Lots of room to lose a ship. And the Devils Island shoal is only half a mile or so east of the island. What if the *Amador* hit the shoal?"

"What's the depth south of the shoal?"

Tanner consulted the chart again. "It varies from fifty to ninety-five feet."

"That's a lot of water, and if the storm was really violent the ship could have broken up and been scattered all over the bottom of the lake." Mary had changed their direction slightly. She carved a long steady arc in the water and they gradually altered course to run south on the western side of the island. In the shadow of the island the waves flattened out and they rode smoothly down to the southern end.

"I'd like to stay out here for a week or so, but if we're going back to Minneapolis tomorrow we ought to be in the marina early so we don't have to drive back in the dark."

"Okay, the weather report says we can anchor at the tail of Cat Island. If we leave there at dawn we should have plenty of time."

CHAPTER 10

The hot sun had disappeared but there was still light in the western sky when Tanner wheeled into their assigned underground parking space in Riverview Terrace.

Mary yawned mightily as she hefted her duffel and a box of supplies left over from their trip. Tanner, similarly burdened, struggled to fish keys out of the pocket of his shorts. When they reached their apartment door, Tanner dropped his duffel and juggled the box to his other hand while he pointed the key at the deadbolt. He put the key in the lock and turned it, then he stopped. He stepped back and looked at the lock.

"Michael?" said Mary

"It doesn't feel quite right. Hang on." He set down the box and tried a little pressure on the key but it refused to turn. Mary took the knob and turned it, pulling the door toward her. This time the latch gave and the bolt clicked back. Tanner gave a little push and the door swung partway open. They didn't enter.

"Do you smell that?" Tanner said in a low voice. He put a hand gently on Mary's shoulder and they stepped aside, standing close to the wall beside the door. As Mary moved, her foot crunched on the carpet. She looked down and pointed to some sparkles of broken glass in the thick fibers. Tanner frowned and leaned across Mary to push the door farther open. There was no sound from inside the dark apartment. He heard Mary take a sudden breath. He glanced to see her raise one foot. She slammed her foot against the door and kicked it open.

Silence.

Tanner reached around the door frame. When he found it he flipped the light switch and the ceiling light came on. There was still dead silence. Hot air brushed their faces. The air conditioning was off. They looked at each other. A sick odor of rot emanating from the door became stronger. Tanner bent from the waist and risked a quick look.

"Oh shit!" His uncharacteristic expletive was sharp and hard. He straightened. Mary stepped past him and stopped, stunned. Someone had destroyed the apartment. The furniture was broken, ripped and upended against the walls. At first glance nothing seemed untouched. Mary stared at Tanner. He looked back, a hard expression on his face. Mary swayed, put out a hand, steadied herself with a touch on the wall. Tanner moved closer, wrapped one arm around her shoulders. He gazed at the wreckage. His stomach churned.

Even though it was a rented apartment, it was their space and the belongings had been put in their safe keeping for the term of the lease. They felt just as violated as if the ruined furniture had been their own. Ketchup had been splashed on the walls by the door to the kitchen.

Tanner didn't know how he looked, but he felt the blood draining from his face. His pulse pounded in his head. His muscles seemed to lock up and it became difficult to move. Sound faded but for a rhythmic roaring in his ears. Mary started to tremble ever so slightly. Tanner reached to pull her closer but she shrugged off his arm and walked away to stop in the entrance to the kitchen, dodging debris as she went.

Tanner went around Mary into the kitchen, first righting a floor lamp which was lying on its side, its dented, torn shade barely hanging to the frame by a single grommet. Mary followed and looked in after him. Things were no better there.

The refrigerator door hung open, held there by the overturned step stool. The light was burned out. Or broken.

Whoever was responsible had cleared the cabinet shelves by the simple expedient of sweeping everything onto the floor. One door was hanging by a single hinge. Tanner leaned into the refrigerator. He discovered that the odor was coming from a container of cottage cheese that had been dropped to splatter on the floor. The sick-sweet odor said the damage had happened hours earlier. Other food was spoiling as well. Canisters were open and the floor was gritty with spilled sugar. Flour dust lay on the counter tops.

"Mary." Tanner raised his voice. "Call 911. Let's get the cops here right now." She went to the phone. Tanner pivoted and went down the short hall to their bed room. He heard Mary explaining the situation. She gave their address.

"She wants me to stay on the phone," Mary called after reporting the situation.

"Whatever, there's no one else here now." Tanner's muffled voice came from the back bedroom. Mary reported that to the operator and then hung up the telephone. The bedrooms were a repeat of the other rooms.

Total carnage.

"The bastards were thorough," Tanner muttered. In the master bedroom the bed was upended and the mattress bottom had been sliced into with a sharp object. Stuffing protruded from the slashes, but it didn't appear as if the springs had been dislodged. Clothes from the closets were dumped on the floor and the chests of drawers had been emptied of their contents, then the drawers themselves had been tossed into the middle of the room.

"They certainly had their fun," Mary said. Her voice was flat and heavy. Tanner looked into the bathroom. "Not much mess in here," he said. "The towels are all pulled out of the linen closet, though. I don't think they even opened the cabinet. God Damn! Should we wait for the patrol car before we start cleaning up?"

"I suppose," Mary said. She ran her hand through her hair, eyes bright with unshed tears.

"Can you tell what's missing?" Tanner's voice was muffled. When Mary looked around, he was on his knees, peering under the bed frame.

"Too late for that," she said. "Missing! God, it'll be a week before we get this straightened out. Then just maybe we can tell what's missing."

"I wonder what they were looking for. This wasn't just a casual break-in. It's too complete, too... I don't know, methodical. That's the word." Tanner looked around, unconsciously straightening a framed print that hung askew on the wall.

"You're exactly right," Mary said, retreating back into the

hall. "They may have tossed our stuff around in an attempt to conceal their real purpose, but either they didn't get what they were looking for or we're completely misreading the situation."

Tanner heard the heat in her voice that continued to quaver.

"All this destruction." Mary sighed and took a deep breath.

He knew she was getting angrier by the moment. "Hey, babe? Are you all right?" He came up behind her beside the corner desk and slid his arms around her waist.

"No. I'm not all right. I'm—oh, shit!"

"He pressed her close, giving and getting comfort. "I know it's a mess but it's just stuff, you know? It's pretty nice stuff, but it's all replaceable. What if one of us had been here? You're not replaceable."

There was a loud, imperious rap on the jamb of the still open door. When they turned to see who it was, two uniformed police officers stood in the entrance.

Half an hour later the Minneapolis Police officers finished a preliminary report and were gone. They left with solemn assurances Mary and Tanner could clean up the apartment and begin procedures to replace the broken furnishings. They explained that it was possible to add to the list of missing items later, but they should make a list of missing items as soon as possible. They questioned Mary and Tanner closely about any potential enemies they might have.

It was clear the police were puzzled. The occupants were from out of town and hadn't been in the apartment for very long. Since the more portable expensive entertainment systems were still in place, it didn't appear to have been the work of thieves looking for something to turn into quick cash for drugs. Mary assured the pair they had no drugs of use to users and the bathroom was relatively undisturbed.

After the cops left, Mary switched on the air conditioning and took a long look around the living room. "I say we go to a hotel for the night," she announced.

"Good idea," Tanner agreed. "It's too late to call the leasing agency. I'll do that first thing tomorrow."

"Okay, I'll call the Jordans to let them know what's happened so they won't worry if they try to reach us." Mary called Vance and Ella to assure them they'd had a great time on Lake Superior and they're returned safely with no damage to *Carefree*. Then she explained they'd had a break-in while they were away and would stay at a hotel overnight.

"They didn't take the computer," commented Tanner after Mary hung up the telephone. "But it looks as if somebody searched the menus. We'll have a hell of a time trying to figure out what's missing."

"Maybe not," said Mary. She was standing by the desk, poking through the litter. "I'm sure I left my *Amador* file and the pictures right here." She raised her gaze to Tanner. "The whole file is gone."

CHAPTER 11

Tanner sat on the floor in the apartment, taking a break from cleaning up the mess they'd come home to. He dialed a number on his cell phone. "Vance, do you have any contacts at the St. Paul PD? Specifically in homicide?"

"I might," Vance's voice rattled through the receiver. There was a roaring noise in the background that seemed to rise and then wane.

"Are you on the highway?" asked Tanner.

"Yeah, I'm going down 94 to the U."

"Maybe we should wait on this. I don't like your using the telephone while you're driving."

"It's okay. There's almost no traffic right now. I might have a contact. It depends."

"On what?"

"On what you want to know about which case and whether there are any answers to be had."

"You remember Ethel Jandrice. Ella's student's aunt? The one who just died?" Tanner explained his request.

Vance sighed. "You really think the killing of Ethel Jandrice and the wrecking of your apartment are connected? Seems pretty farfetched."

"Indulge me," urged Tanner. "See if you can get one of the homicide boys to talk with me. I realize it's a long shot but they might give me some ideas."

"Okay, I'll see what I can do. No guarantees though. The man I'll try to reach is named Ed Teach. He's in homicide."

Tanner dialed the Apostle Island National Lakeshore headquarters in Bayfield. When the telephone was answered, he identified himself and said, "I have a kind of unusual request. Recently we brought you an artifact we found in the water off Devils

Island."

"Oh yes," the woman said. "The piece off the sunken freighter *Amador*."

"I was wondering if I could have someone photograph the plate and send me the film. I'll be happy to pay whatever it costs, of course. Can you recommend a photographer?"

"Oh, I think we can accommodate you. Just a moment please." Tanner heard the click when the woman put him on hold. He whistled a soundless tune and gazed out the window.

The phone was reconnected and Tanner heard a different voice. "Who is this please?"

"Michael Tanner. I was asking about the brass piece from the—"

"Yes sir. If you don't mind, would you answer a couple of questions?"

Tanner pulled the phone away from his ear and looked at it with surprise. "Excuse me?"

"This is Park Superintendent Winslow; can you provide me with some verbal identification?"

"We met, Superintendent, when my wife, Mary, turned a brass inspection plate over to you maybe a month ago. We're from Seattle. Do you remember her? Tall. Slender. Good looking, with medium-length auburn hair. She has a tiny crescent-shaped scar just below her left cheekbone. Her last name is Whitney. The two of you talked about how best to display the plate."

"Is she there? Could I speak to her?"

Tanner frowned. What was this all about? "Yes, all right. Hang on, I'll get her."

He went to the kitchen where he found Mary on her hands and knees, wiping up the last vestiges of flour dust from a cabinet. "Superintendent Winslow from Bayfield is on the line. He wants a word with you."

"Me? Okay."

Mary picked up the kitchen extension with dusty fingers. "Superintendent Winslow? Good morning." She listened. "Yes sir that's right. And we decided that you might have a small piece of nice walnut to use as a background for the thing." She listened, nodded, winked at Tanner and handed him the telephone.

"Mr. Tanner, I believe you. Sorry for the third degree, but we had a break-in over the weekend."

Tanner suddenly got a sinking feeling in his stomach.

The thief took the small amount of petty cash we had in one desk, plus one other item. That brass inspection plate from the *Amador* is missing and I'm sure it was taken at the same time."

****

"Vance and I go back a long way," Edward Teach, the St. Paul homicide detective said when Tanner tracked him down by phone later that day. "He and Ella were very helpful with my daughter when college became a problem for her. Which is the only reason I'm talking to you about the Jandrice case. And since I'm busy, let me run down what we have and what I think. But God help you if any of this turns up in the *Pioneer Press* tomorrow." He paused, apparently organizing his thoughts. "We have very little to go on. The place was pretty well trashed. She was hit a hard shot on the right side of her head. Probably by a hand. The blow was enough to break her neck, and it could have been accidental. From the location of the body and the stuff under her, I think she came in and surprised the perp. He grabbed her shoulder and slammed the heel of his other hand on the side of her head."

"You think whoever hit her didn't mean to kill her?" Tanner asked.

"Right. We aren't sure anything was stolen. Maybe she had some cash around. But the TV and the stereo were still there and there wasn't any silver or expensive jewelry to be had. She may have walked in on somebody already angry because he hadn't found anything of real value. On the other hand, there's the possibility she was killed by her boyfriend, Tommy Callender. He's a good-sized fellow and in good shape, from what we hear. But frankly our main reason for suspecting him at the moment is that he was her closest friend. We can't ask him for an alibi because we haven't found him yet. He hasn't been back to work since the day before her body was discovered."

"So your only lead at the moment is Tommy Callender. He's only under suspicion because you can't find him and someone close to the victim is usually responsible." There was a pause. Tanner could hear Teach breathing and waited patiently for a response. He'd learned long ago that he was likely to get more information by being patient, rather than pushy.

After a minute Tanner decided Teach was just as good at saying nothing. "What about his family?"

"Callender? He's from Duluth. Only a mother still living, apparently. We asked Duluth PD to send somebody around to talk with her. Sarah, her name is, but he got zilch. She's apparently related to a prominent family up there."

"Did you get a name?"

Teach sighed, "Yes, Mr. Tanner, it happens we did. It's a family named Mayhew."

"Thanks, Detective Teach. I appreciate the confidence. If I turn up anything that might help your case, I'll be sure to let you know."

Mary and Tanner concentrated on setting the apartment to rights. The owner's insurance rep had been by to have them fill out papers, as had the leasing agency contact. Mary had talked with the apartment owner who said they'd defer decisions on what to keep and what to toss after they returned to Minneapolis later in the year.

Tanner had called a furniture rental place and they were waiting for delivery of a few essential pieces.

"I've been thinking," Mary said at one point. "Since the Amador was owned by the deVoles, why don't we call them?"

"That's a good idea, but let me call."

Mary nodded. All right. See what the deVole people have to say. If you want to get involved, that is."

"Involved?" Tanner said in a sour voice. "Oh, I got involved the minute somebody trashed the apartment and stole your file."

Mary grinned, and with tongue firmly planted in one smooth cheek, retorted, "Ah, my white knight, riding to the rescue. Thanks." Then she looked thoughtful. "You might get some answers in Chicago, but maybe we should just forget the whole thing and go home."

"I've considered that, but I don't think so. Let's play this thing out a little longer. Maybe I can wangle an invitation to see somebody in Chicago. I could stick in a few needles here and there and see who bleeds."

"You'll probably only get as far as their PR people, but maybe they'll tell you a few things."

"Now, don't knock PR people, Mary. I'm not going to call from here. I'll find another phone.

Mary frowned, "Do you seriously think we need to be that cautious?"

Tanner nodded, stuffing a load of books into a two-shelf bookcase in one corner.

"Same reasoning for why I call instead of you. A few degrees of separation. We'd better be more circumspect until we find out what's going on. I think it would be a good idea if you didn't tell anybody else about your missing file or about that brass plate."

Mary nodded her agreement. "Okay. Just be sure those needles are sharp." She smiled down at him and went away to the bedroom.

It had been a rough several hours, but Tanner could see Mary was rapidly regaining her innate good humor. For himself, his stomach still felt sore. At the time they discovered the break-in, he hadn't realized how tightly he was clenching his muscles. He was still angry about the violation of their space.

After lunch Tanner went to the office of the insurance agent handling the claim for the damage to the apartment to review the paperwork and sign more forms. He took advantage of that visit to borrow an empty office. From there he called the deVole Corporation in Chicago.

After some thought, he adopted a casual feet-up-on-the-desk approach. Three times Tanner explained that his friend had found a piece of brass off a deVole freighter and he and his unnamed friend wanted to learn something about that ship. Mere curiosity, romance of the sea, all that. The first person who answered immediately assumed there were going to be lawsuits and Tanner found himself talking to the corporation's legal department. On the third transfer, he met Lou Winchell at the other end of the phone. She sounded more authoritative. He didn't catch her title but she talked like someone at a management level. Letting a touch of impatience into his voice, he mentioned the name of the ship for the first time.

"I beg your pardon." Her response was more alert. "Did you say 'Amador'?"

"That's right," Tanner replied, "The Steamship Amador."

"This is really quite interesting," she said.

"Why is that?" asked Tanner.

"I think the head of our public relations department may wish to speak with you. Hold on, please." Now he might be getting somewhere, Tanner mused silently, while waiting for someone to pick up and hearing nondescript music in the background. There was a click, the music departed and he heard the first male voice from within the deVole Corporation.

"Hello sir, this is Harold Mason, vice president for public relations. To whom am I speaking?" His voice was warm, soothing, even.

"Good afternoon, Mr. Mason. My name is Tanner, Michael Tanner. A few weeks ago a friend of mine found a brass plate from one of your ships, and—"

"Excuse me for interrupting, Mr. Tanner, where did you say you are calling from?"

The man is right on point, Tanner thought. I wonder if he's recording this. Then it also occurred that Mason probably had caller ID.

"I'm calling from Minneapolis, sir," injecting just a touch of obsequiousness. "We were sailing on Lake Superior when my friend found a brass plate, and I'm hoping to learn more about the ship the plate came from. The Amador." He stopped. Waited.

Finally, "Well, sir, I'm afraid there's not much I can tell you. The deVole Corporation goes back to the family roots in early Chicago, you know. The company has been active in shipping on the Great Lakes for many, many years. Excellent safety record too." He was slipping into the boiler plate language found in company annual reports. Talking to fill space. "DeVole has owned a significant number of ships over the years. From time to time, if they are still serviceable, but become surplus, we sell them," Mason went on.

"Well, that's interesting, but I really want to know about this one specific ship."

"*Amador*. Yes, you did say that." There came another of those pauses sometimes referred to as pregnant. Tanner could hear Mason breathing, evenly, regularly. The man did have good control. "Ummm. Why don't you try your local library? They must have books on Great Lakes shipping. Still, I suppose I could have someone look up our ship holdings for the past hundred years. If you'll just give me your name and address..." It became apparent that Mason wasn't going to tell Tanner anything he didn't have to, but he gave Tanner an impression that he knew very well the ship Tanner was asking about.

"Oh, that's really not necessary, Mr. Mason. I'm here in Minneapolis only temporarily and I don't want to put you out. I am in the public relations business myself, so I know something about the workload you must have."

"I see."

Tanner stared across the room at the office wall. It needed painting. Then he leaned back and crossed his ankles, thinking hard. Although *Amador* might be an unusual name, why would this Harold Mason seem to know immediately about a company freighter that had ceased to exist over ninety years ago? Perhaps it was the only one the company had lost. And why had the woman—Winchell—made that 'interesting' remark? The very caution both Winchell and Mason had displayed suggested to Tanner that he might be on to something serious. That there might be, he thought wryly, something under the surface. Of course there were innocent explanations. Tanner knew that reticence was a universal trait among corporate public relations managers.

"However, if you should run across any information you are willing to divulge, I'd appreciate it if you could send it on. My friend would be grateful." Tanner recited his company address in Seattle and hung up the telephone.

CHAPTER 12

While Mary and Tanner restored order to the apartment and had new locks installed, they discussed the murder and burglaries, interrupted by the building manager who appeared and wrung his hands over the breach of building security. He left, promising to find and prosecute whoever was responsible.

Tanner met Mary's eyes. "You think?"

"I think their security is good enough except when determined burglars come around."

"My feeling exactly," Tanner agreed. "It's too expensive to install foolproof security and in spite of the mess they made, I think this was a professional job. Whoever came in was looking for specific things and created the mess to try to conceal the real target."

"My file on the *Amador*."

"What I don't get is why the clean burglary in Bayfield and the messy one here. Maybe it was a deliberate attempt to separate the two incidents. Or maybe whoever is orchestrating this saw a difference between hitting a federal facility and a private apartment."

Mary raised her eyebrows. "You definitely think the burglaries are connected?"

"I do. Somehow we've provoked three burglaries and possibly a murder."

"Wait now, Michael, that's a real stretch. Think about the timing. The murder of Ethel Jandrice happened before any of the rest of this. She was killed a day after I found the brass inspection plate off the *Amador*. I can't see how someone could have gone looking for Ethel Jandrice that quickly. Besides, what's the connection?"

"You've forgotten something. Didn't you tell me that somebody at the society said Ethel Jandrice was cataloguing the deVole corporate papers?"

For a moment, Mary was speechless. "That's right! I'd forgotten in all this mess. Could she have found something in the papers she was handling? Talked indiscreetly?" She shook her head. "It's hard to imagine that, given what we know about her."

"But look here, I talked to the detective and learned that Tommy Callender is from Duluth. He's related to a prominent family named Mayhew.

Mary's eyebrows went up. "Wait a minute! That's the name that was in the newspaper! The one name the reporter got of a cargo consignee. Mayhew. In Duluth. Oh, this is way too connected to be coincidence."

Tanner looked unseeing at the living room wall. "Let me see if I have this right. There's a freighter, *Amador*. It's carrying goods to Duluth. Part of the cargo is for somebody named Mayhew in Duluth. Rumor has it it's valuable."

"Right."

Tanner raised another finger. "The freighter is owned by deVole who sent the cargo to a Mayhew in Duluth." He raised another finger. A Minnesota researcher is cataloguing the deVole papers in St. Paul. She's murdered and we now know that her boyfriend is from Duluth and may be related to the Mayhews."

"Correct again," said Mary.

Tanner held up another finger. "You find a piece of brass from the *Amador* and start research." Another finger. "Our apartment is trashed and your file is stolen. At around the same time the brass artifact is taken from the Apostle Islands Lakeshore office."

Mary nodded. "It can't all be coincidence."

"I think we ought to go to Duluth. Let's reach out and see if the people supposedly on the receiving end of some of the *Amador*'s cargo can tell us anything."

"I think that's a good idea. We should also talk to Tommy Callender's mother, Sarah."

"Good. I'll pursue the corporate types while you get in touch with Sarah. We'll try to combine the interviews into one trip to Duluth."

The telephone rang. It was Ella Jordan.

"Hi, Mary. We're going to Bayfield to sail. Thought you two might want another trip on the big lake."

"Sounds excellent," Mary responded. "But we're trying to set up some interviews in Duluth."

"How about this? We're going up on Wednesday. We have some maintenance to do that will take most of the day. After you finish in Duluth, you can just pop across Wisconsin and meet us at the marina."

"That's an excellent idea, Ella. We'd love to sail with you again and I like *Carefree*.

*****

The three-hour trip up I-35 took them through good-looking green farm fields that gave way to scrub and then to the deeper green forests of tall pine and fir. While Mary drove, Tanner read aloud from books she'd picked up at the library, history books that included information about the Mayhew family.

"Elgar Mayhew arrived in Chicago as a teenager in the 1800's with his friend, Theodore deVole. The boys' families were neighbors back east. Baltimore, according to some accounts. They had business dealings of various kinds together for years, always successful. Then they went their separate ways and Elgar moved again, this time to Duluth. He arrived there sometime in the first half of the nineteenth century, around 1860. By then he was married and had three sons, Chester, Harold and Edmond.

"The first two, Chester and Harold, were also married by the time their father moved to Minnesota." Tanner skimmed several pages, reading a line here and there.

"And the sons came along? Must have been a close-knit family," interjected Mary.

"Edmond was just a kid when they moved. He married a Duluth woman named Louise Voorhees right around the time of the Civil War. Apparently Elgar had some money, because he built a warehouse at the harbor, where the St. Louis River enters the lake. There are also references to some investments on the iron range, but not specifically mining. He soon had a sawmill and things were going well until the depression in 1893. It wiped out a lot of people and the Mayhews were pretty badly hurt.

"Anyway, the oldest son, Chester, had three children, Catherine, Edward and Wallace."

"The next generation of Mayhews."

"Right. Wallace went to Chicago, right out of high school, I guess, to college there and then to law school. This is interesting. He was introduced to the deVoles and it says here he stayed with them part of the time. He eventually married a deVole. Leah."

"Really?"

"Yep. And she must have been something else."

"Why d'you say that?"

The raucous blast of an air horn interrupted their conversation. A big blue and chrome tractor with no trailer roared by.

"Well," Tanner said, glancing up briefly from the book, "Wallace married Leah in Chicago in 1892 and they went back to Duluth to mind the Mayhew businesses which were sort of teetering along after the depression. They had four kids between 1893 and 1900 and then old Wally died. By then, according to this, he was the business head of the family, even though he had an older uncle and brother, and things had just started to turn around."

"So what about Leah 'something else' deVole-Mayhew?"

"After Wally died, it looks like widow Leah ran the business for years until her first-born, John Jeffry, was old enough and had graduated from the University of Minnesota. Then he took over the family biz. That would have been around the time of the First World War. John Jeffry, also known in these parts as 'Black Jack' Mayhew."

"Is that right? I've heard of him," Mary commented, maneuvering smoothly around a big double-bottom semi laboring up one of the several small hills on the road to northern Minnesota. "I ran across some mentions of him in my research."

"Look, there's the Lift Bridge. The Mayhew family home is up there along the North Shore somewhere." Tanner stretched, easing his cramped muscles. "Let's find Sarah Callender."

Following instructions they soon found the address. Mary alighted at the curb in front of Sarah Callender's apartment building and Tanner drove downtown to his appointment with a public relations flack at the Mayhew corporate offices. Mary and Tanner planned to meet afterward at Grandma's, a popular dining and games spot along the harbor wall near the Lift Bridge, for a late lunch before taking off to Bayfield.

Tanner had just a glimpse of a tall, slender woman, who opened the door for Mary as he drove away. Mary was a good interviewer. Tanner hoped she'd get some answers. He hoped they'd both get some answers.

CHAPTER 13

"When you called, Ms. Whitney," Sarah said, pouring two cups of tea, "you said you might have some information for me about my son. About Tommy. Has he turned up? He drops in and out of my life at random, I'm afraid, and we aren't all that close. But now, I'm a little worried, the police coming around and all. It's been quite a while since I've seen or talked to him."

"Please call me Mary. I don't have a great deal of information for you, Mrs. Callender, but perhaps if we put what I know together with what you know, we can get a little further. Did the Duluth police tell you why they're interested?" Mary gratefully sipped the strong aromatic tea.

Sarah drank her own tea, almost emptying the cup. "I'm in the habit of drinking quite a bit of tea in the morning and then tapering off as the day goes on. I know I drink too much of it but good tea seems to sustain me. About the police, no, they didn't tell me anything," Sarah said tartly. "I'm afraid my relations with our police force aren't all that cordial. That didn't sound right, did it? I just mean that my life hasn't always gone strictly by the rules and coming from such a prominent family, I had a little more, what, public attention, I guess you could say." Her mouth twisted at the memories.

"Mrs. Callender, the St. Paul police just want to talk with Tommy. I guess he's a suspect in Ethel's death, but that's mostly because they haven't been able to talk to him. If he has an alibi, I expect they'll drop their interest. Did you know his friend, the woman who was recently murdered?"

"You mean Ethel Jandrice. Tommy told me about her. They have been friends for over a year. He seemed quite happy, the few times he talked about her. It was a shock to learn she'd been killed. Tommy must be hurting."

Sarah Callender appeared most attentive when Mary told her about the brass plate from the engine of the *Amador*. But before long she grew restless. She stood up and walked to the window, parted the curtain and glanced out. At the end of Mary's narrative there was a moment of silence. Sarah turned and smoothed down her pale blue dress over her hips. The dress picked up highlights from her eyes, Mary realized, those marvelous calm, gray eyes. Mary watched the tall, handsome, almost stately woman. She had an aura about her, a presence. Somehow Mary knew that when Sarah Callender entered a room, people would know it. It was something she herself had experienced and now, looking up at Sarah Mayhew Callender, she knew that the other woman was intuitively aware of the similarities of their stations.

"So you see, Ethel was killed, our apartment was trashed and my file of notes and pictures of the plate were stolen. The plate I found was also stolen from Park Headquarters. I think there must be a connection."

"Oh, yes," Sarah replied softly. "I'm sure there is. Tommy came to see me the day Ethel was murdered." Mary's eyebrows went up involuntarily. "Ethel Jandrice had found a letter, a letter that Tommy said seems to prove some of the old deVole/Mayhew legends. Do you know about them, Ms. Whitney?" Her voice rose and a harsh note crept in. She stood tall, hands clasped at her waist, looking across the room at her visitor.

"I don't think so, except the story about a valuable treasure that was supposed to have been aboard the *Amador*. Is there more?"

"Oh yes, Ms. Whitney, much more." She took a deep breath I'll tell you that story, a story I've heard ever since I was a little girl growing up here in Duluth, on the North Shore Drive, in that big mansion."

"Please, won't you call me Mary?" Sarah smiled faintly. "Do you think Tommy might have taken my file?" Mary asked. "That would certainly explain some things. Except," she went on, "if it was Tommy, how did he learn that Michael and I found the piece from *Amador*?"

"Oh, I guess he might have taken your file, but he would never trash your apartment. He's not destructive like that. But, yes, if he knew about it, the pictures of plate, or the plate itself, could be helpful to Tommy, I suppose."

"Not to be too dramatic, although my family occasionally accused me of being a drama queen, you see, Mary, my full name is Sarah Leah Mayhew Callender. I am the granddaughter of Black Jack Mayhew and mother of Thomas Mayhew Callender. I never knew my father or my mother. They died when I was one." Mary blinked. A quick little smile came and went on Sarah's face. Then Mary realized what Sarah Callender had just told her.

"I can see it on your face. The St. Paul police know Tommy is related to the Mayhews, but not how closely. When Tommy came to see me, he wanted to hear the old stories again. He was more interested than I have ever seen him. He thought the letter could be used for blackmail, or at least to force the family to do better by him, by us." Sarah returned to the table to sit.

"Where do you think he went after he left here?"

"It's hard to say. But I expect he went to the library. Our Duluth library was built by the Carnegies you know. And the Mayhews and some others donated a lot of money, over the years. There's even a hall or something, named for my grandfather. I told Tommy he could find a lot of family history there."

"Would he find what he's looking for?"

She glanced up at Mary, a tiny beam of amusement in her eyes. "No, Ms. Whitney, I don't suppose he would. Do we ever? Find what we're really looking for, I mean?" She paused.

"So your great grandmother is—was—Leah deVole?" Mary asked to keep the flow moving.

"Ah," Sarah nodded. "So you have done a little homework. Yes, I'm named for her. That letter Tommy had could be what someone was searching for, the one Ethel Jandrice found, about links between the deVoles and the Mayhews. The letter tells about a certain business proposition between our men. Whoever killed poor Ethel probably stole the document. If she never told anyone but Tommy that she had the letter, it mightn't be apparent anything was missing."

Mary nodded agreement. "Yes, that could be what happened. But if Tommy didn't commit the burglary in

Minneapolis, someone else did and they may have known about the letter. Who could that have been?"

"Let me tell you about Tommy and me," Sarah changed the subject. It wasn't a very sordid story, and it wasn't all that unusual. A pretty, bright girl from a wealthy Duluth family insisted on going to college locally, instead of to a good eastern women's college, as her status and her grandfather's desires dictated. In her second term, Sarah fell in love with a young, ambitious, boy off the range named Piers Callender. When Sarah became pregnant, Piers, who wasn't going to be slowed down by an inconvenient wife and infant, disappeared. Sarah believed, she said, he had been helped along with money from her grandfather. The split in an already tender family relationship came when Sarah announced she would not go to the Twin Cities to stay with relatives when she began to 'show' and furthermore, that she would keep her child.

"I took Callender's name," she said, "even though we never married and it wasn't really legal. Piers disappeared and his family wouldn't have anything to do with me or with the boy. I guess they blame me for Piers going off the way he did."

"So you and Tommy have lived here in Duluth all this time? Tommy knew, of course, who his family was?"

"Oh yes. I never made any secret of our family relationships, but I'm afraid I still don't get along with my grandfather and he has never even spoken to his great grandson, so far as I know. Tommy has had some arguments with his cousins, though, and I know he resents them, or at least he resents the differences in status. My son thinks the Mayhews owe us something. There were even some fist fights years ago, but that was mostly kid stuff. I thought all that was in the past, but then Tommy came to tell me about the letter."

There was another little silence while Sarah Callender replenished their tea. Mary could tell she was struggling with her decision of how much to reveal so she just sat quietly waiting. Finally Sarah continued, "Tommy told me he thought the letter had enough specific information in it to be embarrassing to the Mayhews and he thought he could sell it."

"He was planning to blackmail his relatives?"

Sarah nodded. "I argued with him. He never has done

anything really bad and I tried to make him see it was a poor idea."
"And did you change his mind?"

"Mary, I just don't know, but I think Tommy is more likely to try to get it published in the newspaper to embarrass the Mayhews, than to try to blackmail them."

"Do you know the specifics referred to in the letter?"

"No, but here is what I do know. When Elgar Mayhew and Theodore deVole first arrived in Chicago, things were a lot different. Chicago was practically a frontier town. There are wild stories about what they sometimes did to get ahead, not all of it legal. And over the years, those... rumors crop up from time to time. There was talk about smuggling during prohibition and profiteering in World War II. You can appreciate those kinds of stories are told about most of the wealthy and powerful families all over the country. But there's never been any proven scandal in the Mayhew family background.

"Oh, you know, Aunt Minnie was mad and Great-uncle George was always coming drunk out of some old brothel or gambling house, but nothing major."

Mary realized Sarah wasn't talking about real family members or even real events. "But there has been some local talk about your grandfather, hasn't there?"

Sarah nodded and looked down at her hands. "Yes, and there still is, but it starts with his father, Wallace, and the panic of '93." She stopped and smiled. "That's 1893. I have to remember that's now over a hundred years ago. There's a whole century in between. The family fortunes and their power were at a low ebb and my great grandfather was under enormous pressure. The whole clan was—is—very success oriented. Some say that's why he died in 1901, after the *Amador* sank and before things began to get better.

"Anyway, the story is that Leah wrote to her brother, Anthony deVole, and asked for help. There were a series of letters, all lost, I guess."

"Or destroyed?"

Sarah nodded slowly, "Or destroyed. And then in '99 it was arranged that Anthony deVole would provide some help, in return for some business concessions."

"What kind of help?"

"Wait, Mary, let me tell this as I have come to know it so I don't leave out anything important. The help was to come in two forms. One was to be easily negotiable. Some say it was cash, others say silver or gold or bearer bonds.

"The other help was to be some explicit instructions and some names. A list of names. Here again, some say one thing, some say another. Supposedly, Anthony deVole was sending a list of corruptible Duluth and Minnesota officials, people who could be bribed, or already had been, or it was some kind of inside information about the important holdings of other businessmen in this area. Perhaps the list included names of private individuals who could be influenced because of damaging information from Chicago."

She laughed softly. "Don't you see how bizarre this is?" Mary waited, silent, listening to Sarah spin out her story, not wanting to disturb a fragile web that blended folk legends with truth. Sarah's voice softened and took on a dreamy quality as she continued.

"Where was I? Oh yes, those old stories also say there was enough information in the documents to implicate the deVoles in illegal activities in Chicago, and maybe some other prominent Chicagoans as well.

"It seems to me that if deVole had shipped gold or silver, there would have to be some record of it. The same thing would be true of bearer bonds. I don't see how they could hide enough money to do my family any good, no matter how the deVoles acquired it. And as far as I have ever heard, there aren't any such records. Apparently that's why the stories persist. It's hard to prove a negative. So here's another version. Suppose the cash or the bonds carried on the *Amador* were counterfeit?"

"Counterfeit? If that was true, there certainly wouldn't be any records," Mary responded.

"So, you see, the stories vary and no proof one way or the other has ever been found. The only certain thing is, whatever was aboard the *Amador* never got here. Great grandfather Wallace, supported and probably driven by my great grandmother, struggled ahead. Then Wallace died and Leah carried on. Did better, too. In about 1925 my grandfather took over the business and things continued to improve. But that's another story. Don't you wonder how my grandfather came to be nick-named "Black Jack?"

"Well," Mary admitted, "I expect it's an interesting story, but I really want to stick with the *Amador*."

"The *Amador* was one of several cargo steamers owned by the deVole Shipping Company. In August 1900, it went to Milwaukee, then to Green Bay, and then up through the locks at Sault Ste. Marie and into Lake Superior. Early in September, it was steaming along through the lake, heading for Duluth. Are you familiar with Lake Superior, Mary? The Keeweenaw peninsula sticks up into the lake quite a way from the south shore and ships use it as a reference point. It's a lovely place, incidentally. They used to mine copper there.

"Anyway, from the end of the peninsula you can draw a straight line to Duluth and you'll pass north of the Apostle Islands."

"Yes, I know, I've sailed in the islands."

Sarah nodded. "Yes. From Bayfield, I suppose. It's a nice little town. A nor'easter came up. It was a big one and it blew the *Amador* off course and into the islands." Sarah shrugged and gestured gracefully. "They didn't have radar in those days of course, and maybe there were other problems. I don't know about that, but I know the *Amador* sank and everybody aboard was lost."

She stopped and raised her eyes again to Mary's. "You said you found a brass plate from the ship, is that right?"

"Yes, Sarah, I did. We think it's probably a brass inspection plate for a boiler. It weighs about four pounds. About so big." Mary held her hands apart to show the size. "I found it in twelve feet of water on the northeastern edge of the Apostle Islands."

Sarah Callender stared at the other woman. "That isn't right, you know," she finally said.

"Yes, I do know," Mary responded, leaning forward. "We were with some people who had a book about Great Lakes shipwrecks. You've probably read it. According to the book, the wireless operator reported they were trying to get into Squaw Bay, which is southwest of Devils Island. But we were nowhere near Squaw Bay where I found that plate, Sarah. It couldn't have floated away from where the *Amador* is supposed to have gone down. We think now it's possible the captain and his navigator made a mistake, or the wireless operator did, or the transmission was unclear and the man at the receiver misread the message. That doesn't matter now, but maybe we've stumbled across the location where the *Amador* actually sank."

"Oh, if you've actually located the *Amador*, it may matter a lot," Sarah said with some heat. "If that special crate was aboard and somebody finds it, even after all these years, it will be worth a lot of money, and it could ruin any number of reputations, depending on which of the stories is true and what may actually be in the crate."

"Yes, but is that kind of scandal enough to kill for? After all these years? Especially if there isn't any hard evidence that the special cargo actually existed?"

"I don't know, you tell me, Mary. Besides, who says there isn't hard evidence, maybe in Chicago, that a crate of valuables was put on board that ship? There's one thing for sure. Somebody killed Tommy's friend and somebody stole the information from you, and when he came to see me, Tommy was sure the letter was solid evidence that crate really existed. He thought it was worth something. A lot."

The two women sat in silence for a few minutes, each busy with private thoughts. Finally Mary rose to her feet. "Thank you for seeing me, Mrs. Callender. May I use your phone to call a cab?"

Sarah nodded and pointed toward the instrument. The dispatcher said five minutes and Mary returned to her chair. Tension had steadily risen in the apartment during their talk, but now they were finished and both women sensed it. Mary had a strong sense of relief, and she suspected Sarah Callender felt much the same. But under the tension was another feeling. Sarah Callender and Mary Whitney had established a tenuous connection, a bond. Instinctively Mary knew she liked this tall independent woman, and she thought Sarah Callender was beginning to reciprocate.

The two women talked about inconsequentials for a few minutes and then a car slowed and stopped in front of the apartment. The cabbie sounded his horn. Mary collected her purse and turned to go when Sarah touched her arm. "Tell Tommy to call me, Ms. Whitney," she said. Mary nodded and left her there, a proud, lonely woman, standing at the door to the apartment watching as Mary went briskly down the walk and into the waiting vehicle. As the cab pulled away, Mary waved, wondering what would become of Sarah Callender.

CHAPTER 14

"Tanner?" queried the guard, consulting a small video screen built into his desk console. "Yes, sir. Just take any one of the elevators to the fourth floor." He'd just explained his presence in the lobby of Mayhew Enterprises; an appointment with Roger Watt, corporate director of community relations. Watt's office was in Mayhew Towers, a bright new high rise with lots of glass and shiny steel sparkling in the morning sun. It was in the center of the business district of downtown Duluth, one of two buildings in the block that housed the Mayhew corporate offices. The lobby was not over large, but made the point, with murals and Lucite-cased displays, that Mayhew Enterprises were involved in most aspects of commerce in Duluth and in St. Louis county, which covered a large section of Minnesota. It was clear that in the twenty-first century, Mayhew Enterprises had a global reach.

When the elevator doors whooshed quietly open again, Tanner was presented with a scene of complete corporate calm. A large bone-white and chrome desk stood squarely in front of the elevator doors a mere three steps away. A tawny-walled corridor carpeted in beige led in either direction at right angles to the elevator door and the desk. At the desk, an elegantly turned out middle-aged woman sat half turned away from the elevator, typing at a computer work station. Apart from a small telephone and a smaller white ceramic pot of pale blue flowers, there was nothing on the polished surface of the desk.

She looked up out of eyes that matched the flowers and said evenly, "Mr. Tanner?" He admitted she was correct.

She looked back at her terminal and tapped a few keys. Whatever the response was apparently satisfied her because she nodded at the screen and said, "Mr. Watt will see you in just a moment. There is a small lounge at the end of the corridor." She gestured gracefully in the direction she wanted him to go. "If you will walk down there, Mr. Watt will send for you. May we offer you some coffee?"

Tanner declined with thanks and went down the corridor to a corner of the building where the thick carpet gave way to oak parquet, and dark brown leather and oak furniture. The decor was at noticeable odds with the building facade. What appeared to be several original hunting prints expensively framed in warm earth tones, hung neatly on the walls. The big leather sofa was creased, and like the chairs and other furniture, had seen years of careful use. And, since they were good quality pieces to begin with, they had only turned more comfortable and somehow comforting, instead of shabby. It was a peaceful room. There was no television or radio and there was no reading material to clutter the satiny polished surfaces of the tables. The air conditioning was well modulated. It didn't make Tanner feel as if he'd entered the walk-in cooler at a local cold storage plant. There was a discreet cough. He turned to find a younger, broad shouldered sandy-haired man, impeccably attired in a dark three-piece suit over a white shirt and dark tie. Tanner smiled, nodded and endured a quiet once-over. He wondered how long the man had been there, watching him through his round steel-rimmed glasses. He decided not to inquire.

"Mr. Tanner? I'm Roger Watt. Shall we sit down?" With one nicely manicured hand he gestured minimally to the chairs beside a small occasional table in one corner of the lounge. Tanner nodded, minimally, and both men sat. Watt took a moment to carefully ease the fabric of his well-tailored trousers so they wouldn't stretch and bag at the knees.

"How may I help you?"

"I appreciate your willingness to see me this morning." No reaction. Tanner waited. Watt's mouth twitched in what Tanner took to be a smile. His unlined brow furrowed with an interrogatory look.

"I'm doing a bit of research on the Mayhew family as the result of two incidents that I'll describe in a moment. My particular focus is the panic of 1893 and subsequent—"

"Ahhh. Perhaps you'll be kind enough to provide me with

ahhh, the name of your principal?" Watt's interruption was abrupt
and Tanner stopped to consider it for a moment. The tone hadn't
been exactly hostile, but there was something there, something
other than polite curiosity. Tanner had encountered it before. He
labeled it corporate arrogance.

Tanner waited a beat and said, "I beg your pardon?"

"It's a straightforward question, Mr. Tanner. Ahhh. Every
so often we get someone like you in here, poking about, asking
questions, trying to disturb the even tenor of our normal routine,
although I must admit you are better dressed than most of those
who... ahhh... find their way to these umm, precincts." Watt raised
one hand off his knee to indicate the room and whatever lay beyond.

"I'm afraid," Tanner said, "I don't follow you."

Watt looked at Tanner calmly, raised his eyebrows and then
said, "Mr. Tanner. I'll ahhh, elucidate. I've made, umm, inquiries,
you see. I know who you are, and some of your employers, you see.
But this query is obviously not within the purview of your regular
duties. Surely not. None of your present clientele have any current
interest in the Mayhew Corporation, except as a possible donor, I
suppose. I admit the possibility that you are acting as sort of an
advance man for the, ahhh, the Whitney Foundation. Therefore, I
have to assume you are here today, ummm, attempting to discover
some scandal about the Mayhews for someone else. It is hardly
possible your research is connected with the University of
Minnesota here in Duluth. Are you free-lancing, perhaps? In any
case Mr. Tanner, I can assure you, we know, we know how to deal
with you people." He went on like that, intermittently twitching
that smile at Tanner, like a fitful strobe. His voice never lost its
even tone of mild superciliousness.

"Excuse me, Mr. Watt. I think you're under some
misapprehension here. I do not write free-lance articles for some
sleazy tabloid, nor am I fronting for someone. Anyone. This is a
simple private inquiry." Watt blinked at Tanner and didn't respond
for once so he went right on.

"I'm here today because of two possibly unrelated recent
incidents, one involving a friend of mine, the other in which a
relative of an acquaintance was killed." At this, Watt's attention

sharpened noticeably.

"Are you aware," Tanner continued in an even, neutral tone, "that the woman who was working on the deVole papers at the Minnesota Historical Society was murdered a few days ago? And that an artifact connected to the deVoles was stolen from the Apostle Islands Lakeshore headquarters?" He watched carefully, but Watt had himself totally under control. Any external reaction was non-existent, except for that restless hand that rose and fell from his knee when he talked.

"Poor, unfortunate woman. But I, ahhh, I fail to see what that has to do with Mayhew enterprises. What was stolen?"

"A brass plate, an inspection port possibly from a boiler with the word *Amador* cast on its surface, and a file on the ship by that name."

"I beg your pardon?"

Ah, Tanner thought, got your attention now, I have. "A lake freighter. The *Amador*."

"The *Amador*. How, ahhh, interesting. If your brass plate is authentic, it's the first concrete evidence of that wreck to come to light in about a hundred years. Do you realize that? Goodness, information about that piece might be, ahhh, valuable to us. Yes, valuable." Now he was nodding, on the verge of rubbing his hands together, Tanner thought.

"I believe I have some understanding of the value of the piece. We've done enough research to be satisfied it's authentic, and perhaps its value will be enhanced if we can develop a more complete picture of the circumstances surrounding its deposit in Lake Superior. That's why I'm here." Tanner found himself about to gesture as Watt had, but restrained himself.

"What is it you, ahhh, wish to learn from us?" asked Watt.

"I'm not entirely sure, frankly, but it would help if you can give me some background on Anthony deVole and his relationship to the Mayhews."

Watt twitched his smile again. "I'm afraid you are in the wrong city. The deVoles are a Chicago family you see, and their corporate offices are also in Chicago, a not illogical location. The *Amador*, ahhh, was one of their freighters and it was coming here,

but there are no records, of which I am aware, to indicate she was
carrying cargo consigned to the Mayhew Corporation."

"You've looked?" Watt didn't answer. He wasn't giving
anything away he didn't have to, although he'd already told Tanner
more than he had probably intended. "What about private goods?"
Watt's eyebrows went up slightly in a question.

"Maybe something was shipped personally by a member of
the deVole family, Anthony deVole perhaps, to a particular member
of the Mayhew family?"

Watt shrugged and said in a flat voice, "Ahhh. Same
answer, I'm afraid. As I said, there are no records. And such a
possibility is doubtful in any case."

"All right. What can you tell me about Edward Mayhew or
his wife, Eileen? Her maiden name was Jarowsky, I believe."

He twitched again. "Try the library. Our local library has
some quite excellent and detailed histories of the family. Other than
suggesting that, ahhh, I don't see how I can be of any assistance in
this matter."

Tanner, irritated by Watt's superciliousness, pushed just a
little. "All right, Mr. Watt, let me lay this out for you. I think
whoever murdered Ethel Jandrice in St. Paul took something from
her house, something that was connected to that sunken freighter.
And I'm damn sure that brass plate that was stolen from the Park
Service in Bayfield is connected."

"Yes, your brass inspection plate. My, my. Most distressing.
I fail to see the connection, however. Where did you say you found
the plate?"

"I didn't, but it wasn't in Squaw Bay." That got a reaction.
Watt went very still and stared at Tanner, full lips slightly parted.
Tanner imagined he could hear gears meshing behind the man's
smooth forehead.

"I see. I see. Now, let me try to respond in an adequate
manner." He glanced at his gold wristwatch. "There is nothing we
can tell you. Those old, ahhh, stories of bullion or silver or
whatever, are just that, stories, endless stories, part of the folklore of
the family. There is no evidence to support them. You'd do well to,
ahhh, forget this whole dreary affair. Yes, that's my advice, Mr.

Tanner, just forget about it. Go back to Seattle and your firm, Mr. Tanner. I'm sure that will be far more rewarding than this, ahhh, wild treasure hunt." He stood up, signaling that the interview was over. Tanner automatically grasped Watt's partially extended hand. His hand was dry and his grip was missing.

"Thank you, Mr. Watt. It has been entirely disappointing, if not entirely surprising." With that Tanner turned and left the room without looking back. Talk about enigmatic statements, he mused, what did I mean by that last sally? Frustrated, Tanner had a niggling feeling that if he'd been more skillful, he might have been more successful. It was the kind of interview he needed to replay for Mary. It had only been a day since Tanner had called for the appointment and he was impressed by the depth of the background knowledge they'd developed so quickly.

CHAPTER 15

Tanner left the Mayhew building and drove across town to the harbor and Grandma's restaurant, a popular place, where he found Mary waiting.

"You certainly have had an interesting if not entirely productive time," said Mary after he finished telling her about his foray into Mayhew enterprises, "or have you?"

"Watt seemed like an odd type to have his position. I felt ... I dunno, like I wanted to wash my hands after I left." Mary nodded her understanding.

They were sitting in the second-floor art-deco bar of Grandma's having a pre-lunch drink. Even on a Thursday noon the place was crowded. Outside, enthusiastic youngsters carried on a hot, sweaty, swim-suited game of volleyball on the sunny, sand court. They could hear the shouts of the small crowd through the windows. The temperature was still climbing, in spite of the leavening effect of the big lake that spread its deep blue carpet to the eastern horizon.

"One of his interesting responses was when I mentioned Anthony deVole. There was no question he knew who I was talking about. He didn't even try to misunderstand me. Both of us knew right away I meant Tony D," Tanner said. He dragged an onion ring through a puddle of dark red hot sauce.

"And don't forget his research on you. I seriously doubt they do that about everyone who calls. I wouldn't be surprised if he also knew about Ethel Jandrice."

I considered asking that. "Could Sarah have called him?"

"She didn't make any calls while I was in her apartment, and I can't imagine why she would."

"Enough of oily Watt. What about Sarah Callender?"

A voice on the public address system called Tanner's name

and they descended the stairs to the bedlam of the high-ceilinged main floor, a series of semi-open rooms and alcoves, crowded with tables, chairs and booths. Hot, harassed waiters and waitresses rushed in controlled frenzy between customers, kitchen and bar, carrying trays laden with drinks and food. They dodged pillars and bus boys carrying high-heaped trays of the detritus of previous servings on their way to their tables.

The lunch crowd of Duluthians and tourists was a mixed bag of several generations, some in suits and ties, some in ripped jeans and t-shirts, and every other kind of costume in between. There were singles, couples, groups at noisy, crowded tables sharing foaming pitchers of beer, and family groups with wide-eyed and occasionally squalling infants.

Nearly every available bit of wall space and many of the windows were crowded with examples of bygone commercial display art, in the form of advertising signs for every conceivable establishment and product. Fine examples of stained glass ad art hung in the windows. Over all, was the pervasive odor of cooking grease and grilled food. It was wonderful.

While they ate, Mary related her interview of Sarah Callender and efficiently sketched out what she had learned. "Impressions?" Tanner asked, polishing off yet another succulent deep-fried onion ring.

"Proud, decent, intelligent, lonely and worried about her son Tommy."

"We've done some work with an ad guy who lives here in Duluth. I feel a bit of an obligation to at least drop by and say hello. I called him and he's expecting me in an hour or so. He knows we're just passing through so it shouldn't take too long."

Mary looked thoughtful. "Knowing you and your business meetings, we might not get to Bayfield until after dark. I better call the Jordans and let them know." Mary fished out her cell phone and dialed the Port Superior Marina to leave a message. Tanner had paid the bill and they were leaving Grandma's when Mary's cell phone buzzed. She glanced at Tanner and flipped the unit open.

"Ella! Hi," she exclaimed. Then she listened nodding once. "Okay. Thanks. I'll see you soon." She took the phone away from her ear and said, "They've invited a third guest. His name's Bill Taggert and he lives here in Duluth. Ella suggests that we try to reach him. Maybe he can bring me to Bayfield while you see your acquaintance. If I can get a ride from this Taggert, I'll take our gear and we'll be all set to shove off when you get there."

Tanner shrugged. "Sounds okay to me."

Mary dialed the number Ella had given her. While she talked, Tanner opened the car doors to let out some of the hot air. Standing in the parking lot, Tanner surveyed the busy scene. Behind him there was a long mournful sound from a ship and he turned to glimpse a big freighter sliding by on its way under the Lift Bridge into the harbor.

"All right," Mary said, closing up her phone. "Bill Taggert is on his way. I caught him in his car. He said he'll be happy for the company across Wisconsin."

A silver Porsche Spyder roared into the lot moments later with a theatrical series of downshifts.

Bill Taggert pulled up smartly beside the couple, waving enthusiastically.

Tanner smiled. "This Taggert must be okay. He drives a Porsche." Taggert jumped out, revealing a tall, hard body in shorts a striped polo shirt and sockless top-sider deck shoes. He ran around the car and grabbed Tanner's hand in a strong grip.

"I'm Bill Taggert and it's sure nice to meet you two." He took Mary's hand and gave her an appreciative once over. "Be glad for your company across the state. But I'm afraid there's not much room for your gear."

"That's all right, just let me get this one small bag and I'm all set."

With a flourish, Taggert handed Mary into the Porsche and hopped around to the driver's seat. "Never fear, Michael Tanner, I promise to drive conservatively and put no bumps or bruises on fair lady." Taggert waggled his eyebrows rapidly up and down, and grinned.

Mary fastened her seat belt and winked at her husband. Taggert shifted into gear and they roared off, spitting loose gravel.

CHAPTER 16

Tanner consulted his watch and saw he still had over an hour before his business meeting. He took a chance and drove to the big Mayhew mansion on the North Shore at the eastern edge of Duluth. At least, he thought, he'd see what the place looked like. And just maybe there'd be somebody he could talk to.

The house was barely visible from the street. Large trees grew thickly on the grounds, obscuring all but the occasional turret, a flash of sunlight off a high window, a grim stone wall. A heavy wrought-iron gate hung in the break between high granite walls that stretched off for a considerable distance in both directions along the street. The gate was closed and locked. After a few moments of searching, Tanner found a small speaker phone and pressed the buzzer. A tinny voice, barely intelligible, asked him to state his business. He was told to wait and a few minutes later, a small white golf cart with a pale yellow awning appeared, coming down the winding driveway. It stopped on the other side of the bars. The driver looked like a gardener or maintenance man of some sort. He dismounted and walked to the gate. "Mr. Tanner, I'm instructed to tell you that no one in the family is available now. They don't usually have uninvited folks in, anyway."

Tanner smiled his understanding, handed the man his business card and turned away. In downtown Duluth the sun was making its considerable presence known. His courtesy meeting with the Duluth ad executive took place in a dark, pleasant bar in the same building where the man had his office. Tanner drank iced tea.

Now he was finally on his way to Bayfield. Heat from the late afternoon sun shimmered on the asphalt as he drove southeast across the sprawling harbor on freeway bridge I-535 to the city of Superior. From the highway he looked down on a complex scene of ships, grain and other terminals, myriad railroad switching tracks, and spurs and water. Tall gantry cranes stood idle in the sun, their glinting steel superstructures flashing obscure messages at passing motorists. Traffic was moderate.

In Superior, Tanner headed east on US 2. The air conditioner seemed to be taking a vacation and trickles of sweat meandered down his sides. Tanner pushed a cassette into the tape player and punched up Jethro Tull. He hummed along in his indifferent baritone.

"Damn, it's hot," he muttered, wishing Mary was there to share his discomfort. An image rose in his mind of Mary in her green swimsuit reclining on the deck of Vance's boat with a drooling Taggert hanging over her. He grinned at the thought. On his left, long low Minnesota Point, a narrow finger of land, ran right out and almost touched Wisconsin Point coming from the other direction. Through the rear window of the car, the sun blazed down. Road houses, small convenience stores interspersed with aging, once-grand mansions, stood on the landward side. Past Barkers Island and its huge and growing marina of sailing and power yachts, his path turned inland. He approached the base of Wisconsin Point. There, in the high grass on his left, lay the rusting remnants of an earlier time when ore from the range fed the superheated blast furnaces of Pittsburgh and Bethlehem; when the busy trains ran night and day on these spurs and trestles, loading a constantly renewed string of ore boats. Two world wars had sucked out all the high-grade ore and the iron mining industry was mired in hard times. Now what remained was rusting, unused track, and sagging, rotted bridge pilings.

As he drove east, he reviewed what he was coming to think of as the Amador question. The Mayhew Corporation was not interested in cooperating; they were apparently tired of scandal seekers trying to dredge up dirt about them, which suggested to Tanner that he might be following a well-trod path. If so, why? Was it just that the Mayhews were important people, or was there a persistent hint of scandal?

The clot of traffic around him moved steadily along. On a whim, he turned due east just before Amnicom Falls onto old Highway 13, a narrow two-lane asphalt road that took him east, then north and east again in a series of jogs closer to the lake. The road followed the bluffs along the south shore of Superior, giving him glimpses through the forest of the still lake gleaming quietly blue in the failing sunlight. The fields were dusty green. Tanner met few cars on this route. He crossed the Amnicom, the Brule and then the Iron River. His route took him down a long hill through cutover scrub forest, among small groves of popple and aspen and into Port Wing. The town had a small cafe, a gas station and a marina where yachts making the long passage along the south shore could shelter for a night, or until an adverse weather system blew through.

The next town was Cornucopia, on Sisqwit Bay, home to another small marina. Dusk had arrived as he steered the vehicle along the down slope to Bark Point Bay, just west of town. Tanner leaned forward and switched on his lights.

There was an enormous blast from a close-by air horn. He heard the frightening blast at the same instant a big rig slammed into his right rear fender. Tanner felt the shock in his teeth and his stomach clenched while he fought to bring the car back under control. What the Hell had happened? The shiny chromed front end of the big tractor filled the rear view mirror when he glanced up. Tanner tromped on the accelerator. Desperately he tried to pull ahead and save himself, but it was hopeless. The horn sounded again, a long blast, and Tanner felt the surge from the big diesel as the other driver jammed the throttle home. His now tenuous control of the car's steering deserted him. Even when he jammed the brake pedal down and felt the tires begin to skid along the pavement, the big rig behind him was irresistible. There was a rising scream of tortured metal and that peculiar cracking, snapping sound made by splintering fiberglass.

Suddenly, instead of asphalt roadway, all Tanner could see was a blur of green grass, saplings and, oddly, a fence post with wire strands still attached that reared up in his path. The post slammed into the windshield. After that he was blind. The headlights went and he felt the car flipping end for end. The noise was horrendous. The car went airborne, slamming into the earth on its rear, front end high in the air. It landed on its top, skidding across the grass and then flipped again. Tanner's head banged back against the headrest. The vehicle twisted, snapping his head forward. With another great crash it landed on its wheels, the top smashed down toward the seats. Apparently the tires hadn't blown because the car started to roll, faster and faster down the hill. The engine died and Tanner could hear weeds and long grass swishing against the sides. With the engine dead, the power brakes and steering were gone. Tanner wondered how far it was to the sheer drop-off at the edge of the lake. He tried to restart the engine but nothing happened when he twisted the key. A front wheel dropped into a hole and the vehicle slewed abruptly to the right and rolled over. The motion slammed Tanner against the side of the car and he blacked out.

When he regained some sensibility his head ached unbearably and he felt a lump growing on his forehead. He'd bashed into the steering wheel during his wild ride. There was no way to tell how long he'd been unconscious. He felt for his wristwatch. It was impossible; his left arm was pinned between the door and the seat. It was very quiet. Mixed odors of spilt gas and oil and fresh earth tested Tanner's nostrils. He cautiously wiggled his arms and legs. They hurt. Everything hurt. He felt shooting pains from bruises, muscle strains, scrapes and hits. The fingers of his left hand were numb and there was more numbness in his brain. He leaned left but he couldn't get the door open. The smell of gas grew stronger. He suddenly realized there was an awful possibility of a fire. God! His mouth went dry. He started to pant. To survive the crash and then be trapped in burning wreckage seemed impossibly ironic.

His struggles grew frantic. He had an almost irresistible urge to cry out, to scream. As in a dream, he began to see himself from a little distance, a frenzied pitiable mortal, desperately struggling and banging about ineffectually. Exhausted, he stopped. Took deep breaths. Forced his mind toward calm. Physical exhaustion helped, but Tanner returned to his rational self and began to use his mind, began to think logically. He knew he had to get free of his iron prison before it was barbecue time. Every time he moved or flexed a muscle his headache exploded in throbbing pain.

Tanner needed some slack, some room to maneuver. Even with one arm pinned, he discovered he could roll a bit from side to side. The motion caused the car to sway and creak. He started to rock his body from side to side, gradually building up a rhythm. More creaking. The smell of gas fumes increased and sickened him. Tanner forced down the gag reflex and continued to roll from side to side with greater force.

With a suddenness that left him gasping and sprawled across the interior, the front seat tore free and dropped down to land against the rear bench seat. Its mounting bolts had apparently torn completely away from the frame. His arm was released and he unhooked the seat belt which had gone slack. He already knew the driver's door was jammed; he reached across the width of the car and pushed the other door. It moved an inch with screech and protest, and then refused to budge further.

When Tanner raised his head he saw his escape path in plain if fuzzy view. The windshield had disappeared. Using the steering wheel as a hand hold, he dragged himself up to the frame and thrust head and shoulders into the opening. There weren't any pieces of windshield to worry about, the whole thing was gone. Now he could see the sky, pale gray, with a few stars winking placidly down. There came a metallic, screeching groan, like the death rattle of some mechanical monster. Tanner's shifting weight had overbalanced the station wagon where it lay against a small tree. Groaning, the car rolled to the left while he clung frantically to the steering column, legs flailing. Then the car slid down the trunk until the front wheels touched the ground. In the pale sky light of early night, Tanner slithered across the buckled hood and fell groaning into the soft grass of the field. The shock of landing sent renewed spasms of pain through his shoulders and throbbing head. The night sky pinwheeled overhead. He figured he had a concussion.

Tanner rested in the grass for a minute, or perhaps an hour, until the horizon steadied. Then he cautiously rose to one knee. His new slacks were badly torn, dark smudges and streaks of soil and blood decorated his shirt. There was still no fire, not even any smoke. The car was a complete mess. Tanner rose carefully to his knees, anxiously scanning the empty field. Was the driver of the truck that forced him off the road out there somewhere in the growing darkness watching to see if Tanner had survived? Perhaps he had already checked. Maybe it was too risky for him to hang around. Tanner had no doubt the trucker had deliberately run him off the road. But why?

A swinging bloom of light sprayed quickly across the trees and was gone with a muted hum. Tanner flinched and then realized it had been headlights from a passing car. He looked up the hill toward the highway. It seemed an impossible distance. There wasn't much traffic, but if he could make it to the highway, someone would come along and take him to Cornucopia and a phone. And a doctor. He started out, slowly, groaning occasionally, stumbling through the thick grass, using the car for support. His legs trembled and his left ankle sent shooting pains up his leg when he tested it. By now he was overdue at the marina in Bayfield and Mary and the others would start to worry.

He glanced at the wreck. The trunk had popped open and then crumpled against a back fender. He considered retrieving their gear, then decided the pain and aggravation wasn't worth it. Dragging the bags fifty yards up the grassy slope to the highway was impossible. His trembling grew markedly. Every movement increased Tanner's agony. He had so many bumps and muscle strains, he couldn't decide where his greatest injury was. It didn't feel as though anything was broken. It hurt to breathe, but not with the jagged pain of broken ribs. He'd had those years ago as a kid when he'd fallen off a garage roof.

It seemed to take hours to get back to the highway. Sometimes the steepening slope defeated him and he slid back a few feet, falling almost prone, tearing handfuls of grass from the turf. Finally, he changed tactics. He began to angle across the hill. His path was longer but not so steep. His crabbing about on the grassy slope may have saved his life. He was just below the level of the highway and about to pop his head up when a trick of the wind brought the sound of a heavy diesel engine idling on the road a short distance away. It sounded as if it was parked across the highway, about thirty yards from where he had finally reached the road. The engine had that low bass rumble of a big machine, big enough to have been the one that forced Tanner over the edge. He crouched in the damp grass, breath coming in gasps, pain shooting through his muscles. He dropped his jaw and breathed through his mouth to reduce the noise he was making. Voices from the edge of the road came and went in the breeze. He rocked forward until his head touched the grass. It smelled damp and sweet. If whoever it was stayed there long enough Tanner knew his strength and determination would fail. He was close to passing out again. An oncoming car slowed, tooted its horn once and he heard tires biting the gravel edge of the roadway. A voice called out,

"Evert'ing okay? You fellas need some help?"

"Nope. We're okay." The voice was big and robust sounding.

"We jus' stopped for a smoke." Hell, there were two of them.

The three men exchanged a few more words, but the wind and noise of the engines carried away their conversation. The car revved up and departed, and a moment later, Tanner heard doors slam and the big diesel wound up. Its huge tires clattered in the gravel and then whined away to the west, away from Cornucopia.

Breathing heavily with relief and pain, Tanner dragged himself up on the edge of the highway and sprawled full-length on the hard knobby gravel of the roadside. Moments later, headlights swept over his prone body and a car screeched to a halt. Careful hands rolled him over and in halting phrases he explained about the car wreck and that he needed a doctor and a phone. Then he passed out.

CHAPTER 17

The next awareness Tanner had was the pulsing murmur of voices in the background and a dim light swaying somewhere above his head. Cautiously, he flexed his right arm. It worked but the movement provoked sharp pain in his elbow. His other arm was tied down, he found, to a bed rail with a tube running from the back of his hand to a plastic bag suspended on a stand. He lay on a bed under a soft blanket. Tanner became aware that someone else was in the room, watching him. The figure shifted at the edge of his vision and a shadow blocked out most of what little light there was.

An unfamiliar male voice said, "Doctor, he seems to be waking up." Since he had always assumed angels were female, Tanner decided he wasn't dead. The pulsing in his head faded and the light steadied.

"Well, sir, you've had a bit of a bang." Another unfamiliar voice. Hands gently touched his face and a strong light shone briefly in his eyes.

"I need to make a call." Tanner's voice didn't sound right and his throat stung with the effort of speech.

"In a moment, son." A third voice, this one deep and hoarse. Tanner tried to sit up then, but the pain screamed at him and he abandoned the effort.

"Mr. Tanner," said the hoarse voice. "I'm a deputy sheriff hereabouts. When Ed Peabody there picked you up outside of town, he drove in and called me. I notified the doctor and we're all here now, in our town clinic. Doc says he wants to keep you here overnight, most of which is already gone, I guess."

"You're pretty lucky," broke in the other voice, from the man Tanner now knew to be a doctor. "Your seat belt kept you from banging around too much when you went down the hill. Probably saved your life. Fortunately the car didn't catch fire. There doesn't appear to be anything broken, but you've got a lot of bumps and bruises, a few contusions and several abrasions. Plenty of muscle strain, possibly a light concussion."

Tanner groaned as a lance-like skewer of pain shot through his gut. The doctor went on, unperturbed.

"I'm injecting a sedative to keep you as comfortable as possible. It will probably put you out for the night. There's some muscle relaxant for tomorrow. You'll be pretty uncomfortable for several days, but you're healthy so you'll be back in shape before too long. Call your own doctor when you get back to Minneapolis and have a thorough checkup."

"Sheriff, doctor, people are expecting me in Bayfield and I'm overdue. They'll worry. I need to call them right away." The deputy nodded, handed him the phone. The doctor turned away to get out some packets of pills and pack up his bag.

There was no answer at the marina office, which Tanner had expected, so he dialed the pay phone that hung on the wall outside the office, common practice when one wanted to call a boater after the office closed. There always seemed to be people passing to and from boats and showers at all hours. After it rang a long time, a woman answered and he gave her a message for Vance Jordan's boat, *Carefree*. Tanner didn't mention the wreck, just asked her to give Vance, whom she knew slightly, the message, with the phone number of the clinic.

Ten minutes later, a worried-sounding Mary called. "Hey, love. What's happened? I would have called sooner but Ella and I were up talking to the police when Vance got your message. We were getting really worried. I tried to find out if they had reports of an accident."

"I had a little accident," he said. "Totalled the car."

"My God!" she cried. "Are you all right? Where are you?"

"Right now, I'm in the clinic at Cornucopia. Nothing's broken. I'll tell you the rest after you get here. Right now, the doc wants me." An agitated Mary broke the connection saying she'd get Taggert or Vance to drive her to Cornucopia immediately.

Tanner handed the phone to the deputy and sagged back in bed. "I didn't want to tell her it was a hit and run."

"You didn't happen to get a good look at that truck, did you? Driving through those trees, if you'd made it all the way, you'da had quite a fall down the bluff." The deputy was making notes.

Tanner started to shake his head and the throbbing increased. It hurt. "I remember switching on my lights. Then I looked up and lost control." The frightening surge of power he'd felt when the semi driver had accelerated after the truck made contact, rekindled in his mind. "Obviously I have no proof it wasn't an accident."

"But you're sure this trucker tried to run you off the road. Why'd he wanna do that?" Tanner didn't know and said so.

"Was the truck a big blue and white job with no box? Man in town reported a rig like that sideswiped a car after your little set-to."

"What time was that?" Tanner asked.

"'Well, we're not too sure, but it musta been around nine. Coupla other citizens reported their parked vehicles were damaged in sideswipes and from the damage, it could be a big tractor. We got some white paint off one car, in case we run across a possible. Also heard from people live up on the bluff behind where you went off the highway. They reported hearin' a diesel horn right about the time you musta gone through the fence. People don't usually report such, but it's a small town an' ever'body knew pretty quick we was lookin' for a tractor." He smiled briefly.

The recollection of that big chrome bumper filling the rear view mirror and the raucous sound of the diesel's air horn came back in a rush. The deputy grinned again at the expression that played over his battered face

"Somethin' just come back to you?"

"I do remember something. That big diesel had a chrome bumper. Clean. Not banged up. I have some flashes of white or blue paint, but I can't be sure. When I glanced up, he was right on my tail and I really jumped when he hit the horn."

The deputy sheriff nodded. The doctor removed the drip and taped down the connection on Tanner's hand. Moving carefully, like a fragile, elderly person, Tanner removed the rest of his clothes and eased back into bed between the sheets to wait for

Mary. The doctor had arranged for Mary to be allowed to stay in the other bed in the clinic. Unless, he amended, there was another accident. Mary stormed in to the clinic a short time later, took a look at Tanner's battered form and sagged into a nearby chair. She recovered a few minutes later and with tears trickling down her cheeks, helped Tanner to the bathroom. Two of the doctor's little white pills soon put him into dreamless sleep.

CHAPTER 18

The next morning, a long hot shower and Mary's assistance temporarily eased Tanner's aches. Bill Taggert had brought her to the clinic and then returned to Bayfield. He'd be back to drive them to the Duluth airport, she said.

Already, ugly black and blue bruises were showing up on nearly every part of Tanner's body. Mary's murmurs of concern as she helped him dry the unreachable parts without painful twisting, testified to the battering he had sustained. When he glanced in the mirror, a stranger with two black eyes and a swollen misshapen jaw looked back. The lump on his forehead at his hairline throbbed angrily whenever he moved his head too suddenly. He was fortunate he hadn't bitten his tongue. He was fortunate to be alive.

A nurse who worked at the clinic when needed, dropped in to see how he was doing. She suggested a light breakfast would be a good idea and encouraged Mary and Tanner to go to the local tavern for a meal. Together they hobbled across the road to the Village Inn, a small restaurant tucked just out of sight of the highway on the edge of Cornucopia. Tanner ordered soft scrambled eggs, a slice of fried ham he couldn't manage with his sore jaw, and a glass of milk, together with several cups of hot black coffee. He was surprisingly hungry. He chewed the eggs slowly, since he discovered even the act of eating was painful that morning. They intercepted several wary glances at Tanner's battered face from other patrons, but neither detected any unusual interest.

"Gee," grinned Mary, "I'm glad you didn't break your nose again."

"T'sa good thing nobody's being aggressive," he mumbled, "I couldn't protect myself from an attack by a three-year-old with a feather."

By ten, Mary had arranged to have the car towed to a local

garage. Tanner doubted it would ever run again. When Bill Taggert returned from Bayfield, Tanner was dozing in the sun in a chair beside the clinic door. The sun, already getting hot, felt good on his painful strains and bruises. The doctor had come by to check on his patient and declared Tanner able to travel so long as he took it easy.

"Sorry to spoil your sailing weekend," Tanner greeted Taggert.

He shrugged. "Don't give it another thought. We're just awfully glad you aren't seriously hurt, although looking at you now, it's a little hard to believe you're not flat on your back in a hospital bed."

Taggert went cheerfully off to load the gear. He'd borrowed the Jordan's vehicle for the occasion. They'd retrieve their car at Taggert's in Duluth. The trio drove west toward Superior, Tanner planted in the back seat amongst pillows, blankets and the overflow of luggage.

Two state patrol cars, a wrecker and a county sheriff's car stood on the side of the road near the wreck. Tanner recognized the deputy sheriff who had interviewed him the previous night. The wrecker crew had hooked a long cable from the truck onto the rear axle of the car and the driver stood by the controls watching over the back of the wrecker. Taggert pulled off and stopped so they could observe. The man at the wrecker looked up and nodded once.

"Your wreck?" he called. "Total mess. We'll haul 'er in on the flatbed. Here's our card." The smudged white card had an imprint in raised black ink that said JENS WRECKING/GARAGE SERVICE and in smaller lettering in one corner, 24 hours and a phone number.

"Tell your insurance guy to give us a call." He glanced back at the wreck. "I wish they'd hurry up whatever they're doin'."

Two patrolmen and the deputy sheriff were clustered at the rear of the car, closely examining the right fender.

"What's going on?" Mary asked.

The man shrugged. "Got me, lady. I was about to haul it outa there when all three of those guys showed up and made me wait. It's been near an hour."

The uniforms separated. The two state police walked

together at an angle away from the wrecker, following tire tracks across the ground towards the place Tanner had wiped out the fence.

The deputy came straight up the incline and said, "Okay, Fred, you can have her now." The garage man's helper stepped to one side of the wreck and waved. Fred Jens cleared the watchers on the highway well away from the side of the truck and the cable. He touched his controls and the engine took on a different note when the winch clutch grabbed hold. The cable tautened and smoothly dragged the wreck across the grassy slope and up the bank onto the gravel beside the highway. The flat tires left a fresh set of gouges in the soft green pasture.

Tanner watched the two state police officers walk slowly along the highway close together, looking at the ground. They were talking quietly to each other. The stocky woman gestured at the ground and the other officer spoke into a small black tape recorder in his hand.

The deputy sheriff came over. "Mr. Tanner, we're pretty sure it was a blue and white tractor, possibly a Kenilworth, that hit you. I got no reason for you to stay here. We'll be in touch if we need you to come back up. If we find the tractor and can tie a driver to this incident. Frankly, unless we get a break, there's not much to go on."

"How are you classifying this?" Mary asked him.

"Hit and run, ma'm," he said.

Taggert got back behind the wheel and they drove slowly west, leaving the scene of Tanner's wreck. He shuddered once, realizing again how close to death he had been. Mary turned and put her hand on Tanner's leg, gently squeezing in sympathy.

****

In Duluth, Mary and Tanner caught a late Saturday flight back to the Twin Cities. They talked again about Tanner's interview with Roger Watt. The more they examined the timing, the more convinced Tanner became there was a connection between the wreck and that interview. "I didn't say anything to the deputy about talking to Watt because at the time it hadn't occurred to me there was a connection."

Mary shook her head slowly. "I don't see how Watt could have gotten someone so quickly to follow you to Cornucopia and try to stage that accident. Surely the Mayhews don't have killers sitting around waiting for a call. And how did they find you? How many people use 13 to go from Superior to Bayfield? I bet not even ten percent. And you don't even know for sure you mentioned going on to Bayfield."

Tanner admitted there were many questions, "but the more I think about it, the surer I am it was deliberate, so it's got to be tied to the *Amador* and the Mayhew Corporation. Who else wants me dead? Taggert?"

Mary just looked at Tanner.

"We're going to be even more careful from now on."

They sat in silence for a time, listening to the steady drone of the turbines as the airliner closed on the Twin Cities. Tanner swallowed another pain pill.

"I just thought of one way they could have found you," Mary said abruptly, turning to look at Tanner's drooping eyes.

"Hmmmm?"

"Don't nod off yet. Suppose that truck was with us since you dropped me at Sarah Callender's? Or maybe picked us up at Grandma's? Or," she paused, "or suppose it came from here in Minneapolis?"

Tanner dozed off, nodding. "Why not?" He didn't feel the plane land at Twin Cities International and Mary had to shake him awake when the plane reached the gate. They waited until everyone else was up and moving out before he unbuckled and slowly stood. Weary and in pain, he stumbled a little from the drugs. Mary half-supported him across the terminal. "I probably look drunk," he mumbled, offering her a lopsided smile. No one paid more than casual attention, so far as they could tell. Tanner shuffled slowly toward the cab stand while Mary went to retrieve the luggage.

"Wow, man. I'd hate to see the other guy," the starter chivvied. "You better sit here. We'll get you a cab quick."

"Wait," Tanner said. "My wife is getting our luggage. It was an auto accident," he said unnecessarily. The starter was already walking swiftly away signaling the next cab in line. The cabbie helped Tanner into the back seat and they waited while a porter brought Mary and their duffels to the cab.

"So much for our sailing weekend," Tanner commented ruefully.

Once in their apartment, Mary made tea and he shucked his clothes, then climbed carefully into bed.

"What you said on the plane. You could be right," he mumbled. "Maybe they were tagging us to Duluth and decided, after we saw Sarah and Watt, that we might be getting too close."

"But too close to what? That's what's so exasperating." Mary waved her hand in irritation. "We really don't know anything more than anyone else, do we?"

"I don't think so, except we've got new pieces to go with old stories. Jandrice, the letter, the brass plate and Beth. Don't forget Beth."

"Do you think Beth had something to do with the truck?"

"Unlikely but possible. The only thing I'm sure of right now is that it's become a lot more dangerous than we ever imagined. Mary, honey, I have to sleep. No more." Tanner's tongue was thickening and he could hear his voice slurring. It was hard to focus. Random thoughts slid carelessly through his viscous consciousness.

"But... Oh, go to sleep." Her voice sounded ethereal.

Once again, a thick black blanket of nothing descended.

CHAPTER 19

Tanner did as little as possible for the next several days to avoid distracting his body from its principal job of recovery. He slept a lot and while awake spent time on the telephone with his partners in Seattle and on his laptop computer.

"My friend," said Mary Whitney, entering the room with a laden bed tray, "the doctor tells me I ought to limit your computer and telephone activities." She smiled and placed the tray with a dish of soft scrambled eggs, a banana, milk and coffee on Tanner's lap.

"Hmmm, I could get used to this treatment." Tanner reached out a hand and held Mary's wrist, wincing as he did so. "But I'm going crazy with my lack of mobility." He pulled her toward him and planted a kiss on her warm palm. "I miss you too, sweetie."

He picked up the fork and put a small bite of eggs in his mouth, chewed slowly. He still had some tenderness from the knot on his jaw. "I think that doctor set me back a few days with all his poking and prodding."

"The doc thinks you ought to visit a shrink," Mary said. "So do I, to help ease you over a reaction to the trauma of the wreck."

Tanner nodded. "I'll go along with that. Every so often I have a flashback. Or I wake up sweating in the night, remembering as much as I do about going down that slope toward the cliff and the lake. Jesus."

"The president of City College called. Marshall? I'm going to have lunch with him today. I might as well get it over while you're laid up."

"Makes sense to me. But you be careful. Regardless of what the police in Cornucopia or anybody else says, that truck driver was trying to wipe me out. I mean, he came back, for God's sake."

"You didn't actually see the same truck parked on the highway, did you."

"No, I already told you that. What's your point?"

"Michael, it's not that I don't believe you, of course I do. I'm just reminding you that we don't have any way to identify either the truck or the driver."

"Yeah, I know. Dammit. Leave me be, woman, I feel a pout comin' on."

Mary bussed Tanner on his unbruised cheek. She hoped that by the time she returned, his natural optimism would have reasserted itself.

****

When Mary got back from her lunch with Anton Marshall, she found Tanner dozing in a chair near the window overlooking the river.

He woke when she put her cool hand on his neck. Stretching his arms overhead, he winced and then smiled. "See, I am getting better. How was lunch?"

Mary shrugged. The usual. I met some of President Marshall's administrators, we talked about several projects that might be right for the foundation, I went window shopping at Marshall Fields, and here I am."

"And?"

"And nothing. I did pay attention. I can't be absolutely certain, of course, being untrained in the subtle arts of sussing out spies and surveillors, but I don't think anybody paid the slightest untoward attention to me."

"Good. I'm glad to hear it. What's for dinner?"

"Oh, I see. Getting our appetite back are we? Good. Oh, President Marshall offered you the use of his extensive and elaborate health club. He'll get you an unlimited guest membership. They have whirlpools, machines of various description, racquetball and handball courts, and I don't know whatall. And I've invited Ethel Jandrice's niece, Beth, to supper."

"I see."

"The poor girl is having a tough time coping with her aunt's estate and all the details of the legal process. I offered to help her with it."

****

After dinner, Tanner resumed his seat in the living room recliner while Beth and Mary sat at the dining table and went through the documents and inventory sheets from Ethel Jandrice's estate.

"Gee," Beth said at one point. "I've been through everything in Aunt Ethel's place, packing, you know. I still don't know if anything was taken. And the police say they've been through her desk and stuff at the society. I guess nobody there knows anything either. Except, they keep saying Ethel was really respected and they're so sorry to lose her. There is one funny thing."

"What's that?"

"Well, I found this receipt in her desk." Beth pulled out a small piece of white paper. "My aunt kept everything, all her receipts and records of stuff she bought. I just thought this was another one of those."

Mary plucked the paper from Beth's fingers. "It's a dated receipt for three copies. Seventy-five cents for copying. The date is the same day that your aunt started working on the deVole papers." Mary looked over at Tanner who was listening from his easy chair.

"The thing is," Beth said, "Aunt Ethel was really careful with money. They have all kinds of copy machines at the society. Why would she pay for copies?" She shrugged and watched Mary write down the information from the receipt. She put it back in the brown envelope. A little later, carrying a new list of places to call and things to check out, she left. Mary returned to the living room and sat near Tanner on the sofa.

"Well."

"I think the receipt probably means Ethel copied something that has nothing to do with her work, so she didn't want to use the machines at the society."

"Or she had already stolen the letter Sarah mentioned and wanted to copy it so she could put it back where it came from," Mary said.

"I'd like to know where that receipt came from," said Tanner. He rose slowly from the chair and shuffled toward the bedroom.

"I think I may be able to find out," Mary said. "Anyway it's worth a shot."

Tanner looked at her.

"Beth says her aunt never went anywhere except to occasional poetry readings, to work and to the library. There's a number on the receipt. I copied it and if I can figure out where she might have gone to make the copies, that will help."

"There is something about all this," Tanner said, crawling carefully into bed, "that is so helter skelter, so random."

"I wonder where Sarah Callender has got to," mused Mary. "I've tried to call her since my visit, but there's never any answer."

Tanner lowered his head to the pillow and looked up at Mary through slitted eyes. "I think I ought to go to Chicago and interview some of the deVoles," he said.

Mary sighed. "You don't think we should just run for cover? Forget this whole thing?"

"Do you? Personally, I'm too involved. We triggered things we don't yet understand when you found that brass piece. Now we've been burgled and I've been run down. I can't just walk away at this point."

Mary sighed. "I've never known you to step aside from this kind of challenge, so I guess I'm stuck with you and the *Amador*. Okay, I think you should start with whatsisname, the lawyer who made the deal with the society for their papers."

The next morning, Tanner planned his trip to Illinois. He decided he would go first to Champaign to see Harry deVole, the seventy-year-old attorney who made the actual transfer of the corporate records to the Minnesota Historical Society. From there he'd go back to Chicago and try to see whomever the corporate and family mechanisms might allow. Busy on the telephone, the hours fled and lunch time passed unnoticed. He was reaching for the telephone again when it rang.

"I've got something, but it may not mean much," Mary said in his ear. "I've also got a lot of stuff about the deVoles I'll bring home. I'll see you in half an hour. Oh, and eat something, will you?"

Tanner grinned. He went to the kitchen and fixed a thick turkey breast sandwich. His jaw was improving by the minute.

Mary arrived looking hot and distracted.

"Here are my notes on the deVoles." She handed Tanner her notebook. "I found the copy machine Ethel used."

"You did!"

She smiled. "Maybe I'll take up a new profession as a private eye."

Tanner smiled back. "But you hate guns."

"That's true. Anyway. First I thought, where would Ethel go to get copies that was convenient? So I parked the car and rode the bus she always took. On the way back from the warehouse, I saw a library about three blocks from her house. So I went in and found a librarian. She told me it's an unusual machine that spits out a receipt if you want one. I put a quarter in the machine and got one." Mary handed it to Tanner.

"Same number that's on the receipt Beth turned up," he said.

"Exactly. Judging by the amount, she must have copied three pages. It must have been the letter Sarah told me about, the one Tommy Callender had."

Tanner looked thoughtful and then said. "Since neither original nor copy showed up in the inventory of Jandrice's place, either Tommy took both or the burglar who killed Ethel did."

"Seems like a reasonable assumption to me," agreed Mary. "But the timing is really tight. She took the letter and one day later was murdered."

"Which may mean someone was already on the trail, even before the letter surfaced." Tanner furrowed his brow. "Let's just think about that for a while. Let me take a look at the deVole information."

"Old Harry deVole was a direct descendant of "Tony D,"
Harry's grandfather, the main man in recent deVole history. Harry
was the second child of George. George was Tony's youngest of
three, apparently the favorite and the one who had the best business
sense. Tony and son George had focused their energies on growing
the many enterprises of the corporation and making Harry the heir
apparent to corporate leadership.

"Then, when Harry wanted to go to law school like his
father, no one could really object. After law school and a short time
in the legal arm of the family, he was positioned for the top job. But
he never got there. Wonder why not." Tanner wriggled his
shoulders.

Mary had dragged home the official deVole family history.
It wasn't clear why Harry deVole had never become chairman of the
board and CEO. And that made even more intriguing the question,
did Harry fully understand what he was doing when he made the
donation? And why to Minnesota?

CHAPTER 20

The Boeing 737 settled with a small bounce on the runway and shuddered as the pilot engaged deflectors that sent the tornado-force exhausts down and forward to help slow the aircraft. It was raining at Midway Airport. Tanner deplaned and found the gate where the flight for Champaign/Urbana waited. He made it with only a little time to spare, and was one of the last aboard before they closed the door and pulled away from the gate. He still wasn't moving very fast without pain.

The hundred mile flight was over almost before the passengers were settled. With no encumbering luggage, Tanner quickly found a cab and started back the way he had come, the airport lying several miles south of the city. The man Tanner was on his way to see, Harry deVole, was directly in line in that wing of the family which now controlled the deVole business empire but had been passed over. Tanner wondered what deVole was like, as he gazed out at the sunny countryside. The trip into the city took only a few minutes, so he had time to spare before his luncheon with deVole at the local country club.

"Take me into Lincolnshire," he directed the driver. "I'm looking at the possibility of relocating and Lincolnshire Fields was recommended." The cabbie drove through the quiet neighborhoods. Tall, stately elms that had survived the plague of Dutch elm disease, mixed with ancient oaks, nicely set off the streets of pleasant homes. The architecture was mixed; the houses were all eighty to one hundred years old, well maintained with perfectly manicured, spacious lawns. Lincolnshire was an enclave of wealthy professional families. Tanner assumed that the homes had been built by lawyers, doctors and important business men, many of whom would have close ties to both the University of Illinois in Champaign and to Chicago.

Harry deVole's home, as they drove slowly by, appeared neither more nor less pretentious than its neighbors. It sat on two lots, with good-sized lawns separating it from the houses on either side. At the rear, Tanner caught a glimpse of a small barn that probably served as a garage.

The country club, apparently rebuilt in more recent times, was a long, one-story rambling affair. It was formed of a series of boxes joined at different angles. When one walked along the deck or porch which surrounded the place, one was frequently confronted with the odd line of a wall going off in an unexpected direction. The parking lot consisted of a series of small four- and six-car spaces, separated by narrow driveways and grassy verges.

The cab circled three sides of the building, then turned left off the driveway and drove to the canopied entrance, depositing Tanner precisely on the deep burgundy runner. The near lot was filled mostly with dark colored late-model Cadillacs, Mercedes Benzes and BMWs. Two young uniformed attendants, looking slightly uncomfortable in their slacks, white shirts, dark red vests and dove-grey gloves, waited beside the big intricately carved wooden doors. It was still relatively cool under the canopy, but Tanner could feel the rising heat from the open parking areas, giving promise of becoming even hotter before the day was over. One of the young men stepped up and opened the door as Tanner approached.

"Thank you," Tanner said and passed into the cool, flagstoned lobby. Directly ahead, through a set of open sliding double doors, a corridor led straight through to the other side of the building. At the far end, light filtered through a draped window. At a large desk to one side a few steps inside the main entrance, sat a heavy black-clad woman. She appeared to Tanner to be in her early fifties. Apart from a telephone, also black, there was nothing on the polished surface of the desk except her lightly clasped hands. She looked up and smiled a professional, perfunctory welcome.

"Good morning. My name is Michael Tanner. I have an engagement with Harry deVole."

"Of course, sir. Your table is ready in the club dining room. Through that door," she gestured to her left, "then take the first right. The dining room will be directly ahead of you at the end of the corridor."

Tanner followed her directions and found himself at the

entrance to a small room with floor to ceiling windows on nearly three sides. Light colored draperies had been drawn back on the two glass walls that were no longer in the sun so members and their guests could gaze out on the sun-washed, rolling sea of uncrowded greens and fairways. The maitre'd in a black tuxedo approached and led Tanner to a table set for two in the window corner. It was cool and very quiet. Only one other table was occupied, a small one on the other side of the room. There weren't many tables, he noted, and they were widely separated so that conversations, unless they became boisterous, would remain private.

As he held the chair, the maitre'd murmured in Tanner's ear, "Mr. deVole offers his apologies, sir. He is unavoidably detained but will be along directly. He suggests you have a drink while you wait." The chair into which Tanner sank was heavy and wooden with a finely padded cushion.

"Good. What do you suggest?"

"At this time of day, might I suggest a Bloody Mary? Ours are considered to be of exceptional taste, sir."

Tanner agreed and the fat heavy glass of dark red liquid appeared so quickly, he wondered if it had been prepared ahead of time. The drink was excellent, mixed just the way he liked it, with enough spices to bring a noticeable tingle to his lips and tongue.

Tanner had only time for two leisurely swallows when a tall distinguished looking, elderly man in a dark, well-fitting suit, appeared in the doorway. He and the three men at the other table nodded brief greetings. Then the newcomer made his confident way toward Tanner. The man was well over six feet, Tanner realized as he rose to greet his host.

"I do apologize, Mr. Tanner. I should have been here to greet you." They seated themselves and Tanner felt the appraising gaze of the other. From across the table, he made his own polite assessment. Their handshake had been brief, just a shade more than perfunctory. DeVole's hand was warm and dry, his grip neither strong nor weak. He was thin to the point of emaciation, but he appeared vigorous, tall and straight.

"Well, sir," deVole said with the barest hint of a smile, "I have awaited this meeting with some anticipation. You have no idea, the consternation in certain quarters, since I made the bequest of deVole papers and then actually saw that they were delivered to St. Paul." His lips twitched from some inner amusement. His voice was soft and precise, laced with echoes of Ivy League schooling.

"I appreciate your willingness to see me, Mr. deVole. As I mentioned on the telephone, I'm interested in learning the background that led to your decision to donate the collection to Minnesota," Tanner said. Mary had suggested that Tanner not be totally forthcoming with all his reasons for requesting the appointment. A waiter appeared at deVole's elbow. The men ordered quickly and resumed their conversation.

"I am happy to cooperate, Mr. Tanner. Do you know the family structure? No? Then let me give you some relevant family history.

"Theodore deVole and Elgar Mayhew laid the foundation for the family fortune in Chicago during the mid 1800s." He smiled. "Chicago was hardly more than a collection of rude shacks when they arrived. Some time later Elgar moved to Minnesota and started over, after the two had made several bold and successful moves. Even after the separation, the close ties between the two families continued through several generations. Indeed, there are such ties today. Theodore's granddaughter, Leah, married Wallace Mayhew. Her brother, Anthony, sometimes called Tony, became the titular head of our family. I am a direct descendent of that Anthony, my grandfather." Harry deVole sipped a glass of water while Tanner watched him closely. He hadn't ordered a drink. The waiter brought salads.

Why is he telling me all this? Tanner wondered. He must know it was all, or mostly in the history books. Wouldn't he assume I'd have done some research? Maybe he's playing at being totally cooperative to keep me from raising topics he'd rather not discuss.

"My grand uncle Henry inherited the dominant role of supervising the family business. He was good at it. When he died in 1957, with no sons to inherit, control passed to my father, his nephew. As the eldest son of that generation, the company, still a family corporation, I would normally become the CEO. However, since I had already established an active law practice, and at the time of my father's death was in the final, rather delicate, phases of acquiring a larger, prestigious, law firm in Chicago, I declined the honor. The family then turned to my brother Theodore. He is the current chairman. The board was and is dominated by deVoles and close relatives, so naturally, they agreed with that decision."

"How large is the board?" Tanner interjected, as he finished his salad.

"Family members in addition to myself, include my brother Ted, my son Robert, his sister Elaine, Ted's two children, Melvin and James, and my sister's two sons, Theodore and Perry Miller."

The Millers are the offspring of my sister Elissa's son David and his wife. They are attorneys in the banking business in Minneapolis. They are two of four out-of-towners on our board."

"The others are John Mayhew, who, as you may know, is elderly and never comes to meetings. The other is his son-in-law, David Watt, who at present heads the Mayhew Corporation in Duluth. It is an overly large board, I'm afraid. The family branches consider it important to have representation."

"How did you come to have control of the family records, if that isn't too impertinent a question?" Tanner asked.

DeVole smiled. "Not at all. Since earliest times, the family has had a perhaps inflated sense of its importance to the commerce and the history of this region. The founder kept every conceivable record and his will stipulated similar record keeping in succeeding generations. The family has always taken such directives most seriously and a tradition was born, fueled, no doubt, by a sense of having influenced important events. Thus, you see, over the years, our archives grew enormously. In fact, most original records were shipped to a company warehouse with necessary copies kept in the corporate offices. It is not a normal way of doing business. However, there are other idiosyncrasies within our family.

"I've always been interested in history," deVole continued. "My undergraduate degree is in American history. It might interest you to know that I was partway through a graduate degree in history at Northwestern, when family pressures and, to be fair, my own waning interest, led me to abandon the formal study of history for the law."

"Your interest in history must have been seen by the family as a natural fit, so you became the custodian of the family archives." The old man nodded thoughtfully. For a moment, he gazed out the window at the sun-blasted golf course, then resumed his narrative. "Yes. My law practice flourished and that plus general family activities and, of course, the growth of the family business, all conspired against any real custodial activities. Ah, but I can assure you, Mr. Tanner, it was always there, at the edge of my consciousness. I would have given up part of my practice, if I could have been assured of time to spend with the deVole papers."

"But you weren't able to, and the collection continued to grow, didn't it?"

DeVole nodded his assent. "The best I could do was protect the materials and try to insure they were stored chronologically. Then about five years ago, I believe it was, I realized I was retired but I still hadn't begun to really examine and collate the papers. I wanted to write a book about the deVoles, you see, but it became clear to me I never would."

"How did you decide to donate the papers to Minnesota?"

Harry deVole smiled again and nodded in recollection. "Ah. That decision I owe in large measure to my wife Susan, bless her heart. She shared, to some degree, my interest in history. She has—had, the man is dead—a distant relative who was on the staff of your state historical society. Through them, I came to know how professional and how highly regarded, nationally, the Minnesota Historical Society is, which includes its collections and research staff. Besides, there are the Mayhews there in Duluth. And the deVole Corporation has many interests in your state. So it isn't particularly unusual, in my view, that Minnesota should receive the papers.

"There are, or were, two aspects of the situation which could be considered unusual," deVole went on. "First, I decided that the papers needed to be under the care of professional archivists and historians. I believe the papers should be available to the public for research. Corporate records are invaluable resources when studying various aspects of our national development. I made the decision to donate the papers at that time because of...certain...shall I say, negative attitudes among some board members toward the expense of maintaining the collection."

"Was there any particular reaction by the board when you announced your decision?" Tanner asked. "I assume you had to get board approval for the donation."

"Not so. By longstanding regulation of the corporation, and provisions in the wills of both Theodore and Anthony, the custodian has absolute authority over such decisions. The board and the operating officer can hamper the custodian by refusing to allocate adequate funds, but I had the right to do anything except deliberately destroy the records.

"You asked about the reaction. I should characterize the initial reactions as relief, a little surprise, and a certain satisfaction that the matter, frequently on the agenda of board meetings, was finally to be put to rest. This all happened five years ago, you understand."

Tanner nodded.

"There was some surprise and a few questions when I announced the recipient of the papers, since everybody assumed, I suppose, they would go to the state of Illinois. But with the help of the Society's director and Susan, we made a persuasive presentation. A week later, the board affirmed the decision and I thought, there, that's that."

"Something must have happened," Tanner said, "because, as I understand it, there are stories of threatened lawsuits and a few rather insulting and public comments from some members of the family. Is that right?"

"Yes, your research is accurate. However, there is one incident which didn't get any publicity. Someone tried to destroy the collection." Harry deVole said it in a calm matter-of-fact tone, consistent with the rest of his narrative.

"What?" Tanner leaned forward, startled.

"Indeed. The papers were stored in a warehouse here in Champaign, a community in which I have a certain level of influence. A deliberately set fire was discovered, fortunately, before it could do any significant damage. The perpetrator was never found." He stopped again. It was another of those momentary silences in the conversation.

A cold finger unseen by any in that room touched Tanner's psyche. "I gather you think it may have been an inside job?" Tanner raised his eyebrows in question.

"Quite right, Mr. Tanner. I was able to keep most of the story and all of my suspicions out of the media."

"Suspicions? Are you saying you think you know who set the fire?" DeVole merely gazed calmly at Tanner. Then he went on.

"The questions and threats of lawsuits came from the corporation, not the family, but we never determined who really initiated the actions. The question turned on whether there were sensitive corporate papers co-mingled with family records and other, more routine corporate records. The corporation took the position they should be able to purge the files before they were turned over to Minnesota."

"I see. You took the position that the corporation had had nearly a hundred years to do that and hadn't, and what were they afraid of, anyway. Do I have that right?"

"You are essentially correct." DeVole smiled a wintry smile across the table. "Ultimately the problem was resolved by inserting in the conveyances a restrictive clause limiting access to the papers and a requirement that nothing directly attributable to the family or to the corporate enterprises be published for at least twenty years."

Harry deVole fastidiously patted his lips with the white linen napkin. He fixed Tanner with an intense look. Tanner felt the power. "Naturally, the corporation was quite correct." DeVole's voice had deepened and roughened.

He must have been a hell of a trial lawyer in his prime, Tanner thought. "I beg your pardon."

"I am quite sure there are indeed sensitive papers among the collection, but not in the usual corporate meaning of that word."

"I'm afraid I don't follow you," Tanner said.

DeVole smiled again and his voice changed once more. "If you believe some or all of the myths and stories surrounding the family and the corporation, and if you assume that powerful people are sometimes careless in their efforts to tidy up after themselves, then you should also assume that tucked away in that mass of records there are likely to be some papers that reveal the truth or falsehood of some of those stories. What exactly was the family business in Chicago at the turn of the century? Were they profiteering during the World Wars? What was the cargo of the *Amador*? Are there links to Chicago's organized crime figures?" DeVole stopped, watching Tanner.

Tanner looked back, saying nothing. How had he known about the *Amador*?

"I am not naive, Mr. Tanner, and I pay attention to media stories about the family, a family I still wish to protect. But I am an ethical man and if deVoles are involved in the killing of that woman in St. Paul, I want those persons identified and brought to justice. The very fact that you neglected to mention the brass plate from the *Amador* when you called, alerted me that you have more than the scholar's interest in our affairs."

Tanner admitted his true interest in the papers and thought they both began to sense, at that moment, a lowering of the barriers. They went over what little Tanner could tell him. The only fact not public was where Mary found the plate and Tanner decided that while Harry deVole seemed completely aboveboard, he was, after all, a deVole. But Tanner had the distinct impression deVole was aware that Tanner had left out that small piece of information.

A staff member approached their table. He offered deVole a folded note. When deVole read it, Tanner saw a flicker of distaste flash across the other man's face. "My daughter's husband, Jerome Kald. He insists on seeing me immediately. I'm afraid I shall have to terminate our luncheon."

Interesting, mused Tanner as he left the club. He would not have expected Harry deVole to respond like that. An hour later, Tanner was winging his afternoon way to Chicago with assurances that Harry's brother, Theodore, head of the family and the corporation, would talk to him whenever he arrived at the family home in Evanston. It remained to be seen whether Theodore would be as open and forthcoming as Harry.

CHAPTER 21

Late in the afternoon, Chicago's heat still refused to slacken its grip on the city. Tanner didn't feel as fresh or as alert as he'd have liked for his first meeting with the head of the deVole Corporation. Furthermore, Harry deVole's mention of organized crime had set his teeth on edge.

The sweating, mustached Lebanese cabbie proved to be a fortunate draw. Short on chatter and long on driving skills, he smoothly wound his way through almost unnoticed seams in the fast-clotting traffic. Without exceeding the speed limit more than a couple of times, he shortly drew up before the high, ostentatiously columned, entrance to the deVole Evanston mansion. Tanner was impressed, not by the house, but by the driving, and said so. Not once had the cabbie slammed around a turn and thrown him into one corner of the seat. That kind of driving always gave him a headache.

"Do I drive in?" The man's lightly accented English was perfectly understandable. Tanner checked his watch. He was early.

"Yes."

When they stopped at the broad, curved front steps, the big door was open and a man stood in the dark entrance. A butler? Tanner wondered. The man wore a conventionally cut conservative suit. It was charcoal and it fit him extremely well.

"Mr. Tanner? Mr. and Mrs. deVole will see you in the library. Right this way, if you please." The man may have been an employee, but he was no servant. He led Tanner down a long, high-ceilinged hall, the sounds of their footsteps banging off the hard, white walls. They headed toward the rear of the mansion. It was cool and dim and the air smelled fresh. Passing through an ordinary door, Tanner discovered they were indeed in a library. There were drapes across one end and though they were heavy, he could see windows behind them. The drapes permitted little sun but the indirect, almost shadowless, lighting was a comfortable level for reading. The walls on either side were fitted with floor to ceiling wood shelving crowded with books. There was no one else in the room. Grouped in the center of the space was a small table, a free-standing lectern holding a large dictionary, a comfortable-looking sofa and, beside the sofa a table and lamp. Forming an intimate conversation area facing the short sofa were two reading chairs with a small table between them. Both tables were covered in tan leather.

"The deVoles will join you in a moment," the man said. When he turned to leave, Tanner turned with him and saw that the door was inset into yet another wall of shelving, also nearly filled. He stepped to one wall to examine the books. The collection was varied, with at least two shelves of recent paperbacks to heftier volumes he recognized as textbooks, to more than a few whose bindings were quite old and well worn. Nowhere did he see the long rows of matched leather-bound collections which sometimes graced the shelves of intellectual pretenders. Here was a reflection of varied interests combined with a need for specific as well as general information. Tanner spotted Harvey McKay's *Swim with the Sharks Without being eaten Alive*, on a shelf next to a management text by Peter Drucker and Lee Iacocca's story of the fall and rise of Chrysler. Not far along he also discovered a thick volume, bound in creased leather. It was seriously worn and Tanner could just make out the single word "deVole" on the spine in gold lettering.

The door opened and a tall, slender woman with erect posture entered the room, followed by a stranger. She came directly to him, smiling gently in his eyes. "Good afternoon, I'm Leslie deVole."

Tanner smiled back and pressed her extended hand. You must have been something twenty years ago, he thought, acknowledging her greeting, because just look at you now.

With a graceful, practiced gesture, she turned and introduced her husband Theodore, who crossed to stand beside the sofa. Her voice was high, lilting. She spoke precisely and didn't drop her g's. Leslie deVole evoked several years of careful, private and expensive schooling. DeVole looked at Tanner. The two men shook hands, with firm grips. DeVole's hand was dry, neutral. Tanner thought he looked tired.

Theodore deVole was not quite as tall as his wife, the former Leslie Thomas of the Springfield Thomases. "Let's sit down, shall we?" DeVole's spoke in a deep baritone. His voice fit the husky, heavily muscled man Tanner saw before him. It had faint rhythms as if he'd had elocution lessons. Now in his late sixties, deVole wore his expensive, tailored suit well, but Tanner could easily picture him in overalls and flannel shirt, wearing a hard hat, and working on the Chicago docks or manhandling freight in a deVole warehouse. His short hair was mostly gray, varied by dark patches and streaks.

They sat, Tanner on the sofa, the deVoles in chairs before him.

"Well, Mr. Tanner. I understand you've been talking to my brother Harry today."

"That's right. I wanted to learn a little more about the gift of the deVole papers to the Minnesota Historical Society."

"Yes, he told me. He also persuaded me to talk to you about the *Amador*." DeVole wasn't a man to waste time with trivialities. He glanced briefly at his wife. "I agreed to see you because I understand now that you, or a friend of yours happened on a piece of an engine, apparently from the old *Amador*, is that right?"

Tanner nodded and opened his mouth to say something, but deVole went on with barely a pause.

"It appears the location of your friend's find is at odds with the known facts. Is my information correct?" Again Tanner nodded. For now, he decided, he'd let the other man take the lead.

"All right. I can tell you that we, the deVole family, at least, are interested in that location. We would still like to find the wreckage of that freighter because, if there's anything left of the cargo, locating it might put an end to some of these persistent stories about us. And, of course, it would help emotionally to know where the crew's bodies lie. You've heard the stories, I suppose?"

"I probably know some of them," Tanner smiled courteously.

The man snorted and looked at his wife as if to say, what did

I tell you? "All right, let's not dance around it here. A mysterious cargo was supposed to have been aboard the *Amador*, together with papers that were gonna set Mayhew up forever. By extension, I suppose the people who keep that rumor alive also think that we'd get something out of the deal." His mouth twitched slightly.

"Let me tell you something, Tanner. My grandfather and his father and his grandfather all did things to get along. So did the Mayhews. So did a lot of others. Some of what they did was probably illegal, or is now, anyway. But our family was never part of any criminal organization, and we certainly didn't conspire with the Mayhews to take over northern Minnesota. There is simply no truth at all to those stories."

"Is that why the corporation wanted to stop the donation of the company's papers?" Tanner interjected.

DeVole sighed and rubbed the crease between his eyes. "Mr. Tanner, do you know anything about daily corporate operations?"

"A little. My profession, you see." Tanner gestured in a deprecating manner.

Theodore deVole sighed again and leaned forward, pinning Tanner to the sofa with his steady gaze. "Corporations have lawyers to keep them out of trouble and to deal with trouble from the outside. You try to hire careful, attentive, lawyers who stay on top of things. But they have to be given a certain freedom to act. Nobody knows everything that was in that warehouse Harry has in Champaign. There could have been inside information in some of those files, information that might be damaging, economically. Lawyers tend to want to do nothing until they've thought about it for a year or two. The lawyer who made the first move to block the gift didn't know much about gifts of papers. He didn't realize access could be restricted, or he just didn't think too clearly." DeVole shrugged and waved his hands.

"What you're telling me is that it was all a big mistake?" Tanner carefully kept out of his voice the scorn he felt. Then deVole surprised him.

"Yeah. Oh, not the donation, but the way the thing was handled, especially after the announcement. Wasn't just one mistake, though. Everybody knows we have strong connections to

the University of Illinois, and when it came out that the collection
was going to Minnesota, well. Somebody objected and it happened
in a way that made things look worse. There were other mistakes.
A big corporation looks like a bully when it talks about suing a
historical society, for God's sake. But I take the responsibility for all
that. I'm the CEO. If I'd been paying more attention ..." He
stopped in mid-sentence and shrugged.

"What we need here is a man-to-man understanding. We're
big enough to let bygones be bygones." As Tanner thought about it,
niggling doubt crept in and took up residence in a corner of his
brain. It could be total truth, after all, or a contrived, carefully
planned performance.

"Mr. deVole. I understand what you've said. I'd have little
difficulty accepting your version except for a couple of things. First,
there is the murder of Ethel Jandrice." No reaction from deVole.
His wife blinked hard. "Then the brass piece from the Amador was
stolen and my friend's apartment trashed. It makes me wonder if
something more isn't going on."

"I don't know about any of that. But I'm damn sure this
family had nothing to do with any of it. I'm also damn sure the
corporation wasn't involved. What do you take us for! We're not
a bunch of thugs! You seem to think everybody in Chicago acts like
its still Prohibition! Let me tell you something ..." His voice rose
and then he stopped abruptly and sank back in his chair, a look of
frustration on his face.

"Look, Mr. deVole. I'm not here to accuse you or the family,
or the corporation, of anything. But I am trying to find out what
happened and why." Tanner spoke softly in calm, placating voice.

"Tanner. I'll tell you what. We have money. We're
interested in locating the Amador. Why don't we work together?
I'll bankroll an expedition to try to find that old freighter based on
your new information. We'll hire some divers and go where you say.
Better yet, you be in charge of the whole thing. Just send me the
bills." He paused for a moment, thinking.

"Of course, since you say the brass piece was stolen, the
whole thing becomes a little more chancy. A suspicious man might
want to see some evidence. Still, suppose I agree anyway? Take

your word for it. You'd be there. We'd send somebody, somebody you could really use, or just to be an observer, represent the family interests. There'd be no chance of any hanky panky. Maybe we could get a reporter to go along, write some kind of a story and sell it to the newspapers or whatever they do. What do you say?"

"It's an interesting idea. I'll have to think about it. Meanwhile, can you give me the name of someone at corporate headquarters I can talk to should the need arise?"

"Why? I'm the president. I run the place. You want something, come to me. I'm current on just about everything. It'll be more efficient. If you're talking to someone else they'll just have to clear it with me before you get your answers."

Tanner smiled to himself thinking, and you'll be on top of everything I'm thinking or asking about, as well.

DeVole glanced at his bulky gold wristwatch. But right now, I'm afraid, we'll have to cut this short." If you're staying over, I can make room for another meeting late tomorrow. Would that be satisfactory?"

Tanner declined, realizing he was being expertly shuffled out of the way. Another interview wouldn't help much until he had more to talk about. All three rose and made their smiling good-byes. Both deVoles walked Tanner to the front door and as it was being opened by the same man who had greeted him, he belatedly realized he had no transportation to the airport. He started to turn back to ask for a telephone when he caught sight of the taxicab in which he'd arrived, waiting in the driveway.

Leslie deVole spoke for the first time in several minutes. "We stopped the cabbie before he left. It is sometimes difficult to get a cab out here, and then there's often a lengthy wait. I hope you don't mind."

"Thanks very much." Tanner nodded to the woman, appreciating her thoughtfulness in retaining the cab.

From the open door of his cab the driver watched silently. Tanner went down the steps and then looked up at the couple.

"I'll consider your offer, deVole. Thanks for seeing me on such short notice." Tanner bent his head without waiting for a reply and slid into the back seat of the automobile. The cabbie grinned and put the car in gear. They rolled smoothly away from the mansion steps.

"We going to Midway?" said the cabbie.

"Yes, please. Why are you grinning like that?"

"Mister, I don't know those people except by the newspapers and by seeing their place. Big in Chicago society. DeVole, right?"

Tanner nodded.

"I'm a student of body language. I think you sent a message there. I'm my own man and then you leave, not fast, not running, just confident. That one, he'll pay better attention next time."

"You think there'll be a next time?" Tanner smiled at the face in the rear view mirror.

"Oh yeah, I think so."

CHAPTER 22

Tanner noticed a newspaper on the seat beside the driver. He leaned forward and asked to see it. The driver nodded and handed the paper back. Tanner had missed the morning television newscasts and the *StarTribune* before he left Minneapolis. He scanned the national news. No new wars had broken out; China, Arab states and the U.S. were still warily eyeing each other across the mountains and waters and plains of the world. Tanner noted there'd been a small oil spill in the Galveston ship channel which apparently posed little additional environmental danger to what they already had. Things seemed pretty normal.

In local news, the political scene was taking shape and catching fire. Candidates, potential candidates and party leaders of all stripes were beginning to stake out positions and make their calls to arms, or at least to the campaigns. Even though the elections were not for another fifteen months, in Chicago, politics was fast becoming a game with no season.

NEWCOMER DEVOLE MAKES RUN FOR AG

Tanner had barely settled into his seat as the plane lifted off from Midway Airport for the flight to Minneapolis when the headline below the fold in a Chicago newspaper caught his eye. He beckoned the attendant and asked her for the copy of the *Chicago Sun-Times*.

It was a sidebar to the main story. Robert deVole, an attorney in private practice in Chicago for many years, was putting himself up as a conservative candidate for Attorney General of the State of Illinois. As a first-time candidate for statewide office, he'd impressed the paper with his early organization and energy. The reporter included enough facts about deVole's background to assure

Tanner that this Robert deVole was the son of Harry deVole, son of
Theodore and Leslie. According to the story, deVole's sister, Elaine
Kald, a prominent political activist, would head the campaign.
Tanner dropped the paper onto the empty seat beside him and dozed
the rest of the way to Minneapolis.

****

"It seems to me," Mary said, handing Tanner a cup of hot
tea, "that we've got to make some kind of move to get things going
again. I'd like to know that we're getting closer to the thief who
stole my file and trashed the apartment, to say nothing of Ethel
Jandrice's killer."

"I've been thinking about that. I'll call Detective Teach and
see if he has any news. Then maybe we ought to try shaking the
Mayhew tree again."

"Where we are, is nowhere," responded the detective to
Tanner's call. "We can't even get hold of Sarah Callender to find
out if Tommy ever showed up. Minneapolis isn't actively pursuing
your burglary so there's no progress there, either."

When Mary and Tanner returned from dinner that evening
to their newly refurbished apartment, they hatched a new plan.
Mary proposed that they undertake their own search under the
surface of Lake Superior to perhaps find more evidence of the wreck
of the *Amador*. Mary had found a scuba school based at
Chequamegon Bay. She was unshaken in her belief that a search
north and east of Devils Island might turn up more artifacts, or even
the hull of the missing freighter. Vance told Tanner that in spite of
the chilly water temperature of Superior, divers in full wet suits often
dove on the many known shipwreck locations that speckled the
bottom of the great lake. They just couldn't stay down very long.

"Let's get together an expedition," said Mary
enthusiastically, "but we won't keep it a secret. Maybe when people
learn what we're looking for and see where we're searching, we'll
make someone nervous enough to reveal something."

"You mean, set ourselves up as targets." Tanner was
doubtful. It was a disquieting thought.

"Yes, but carefully."

It made Tanner nervous to think of Mary as a possible target. She'd already survived a direct attempt on her life. She was insistent.

They made a production of preparing for and provisioning themselves for their next foray into Lake Superior. They chose an older, highly respected SCUBA instructor and tour operator based in Pike's Bay, just south of Bayfield. The marina in Pike's Bay was protected from the open lake by a long breakwater, lying parallel to the shore and open at each end. The northern break was the only passage deep enough for the many yachts and motor ships docked in slips that lay along three long finger piers anchored at one end to the land. The dive office was in a small building attached to the back of the large brick building that lay across the landward side of the bay. The structure also housed a second-floor restaurant, Superior Cruises, a charter company, and a real estate and rental office.

Cameron O'Neil was a tall, spare, weathered man, an ex-Navy diver with many years experience. He'd owned Port Superior Dive for over ten years. When Mary and Tanner met him in his small cluttered office, he looked like a man one could easily trust to lead a diving expedition in the lake. He projected an aura of shrewd competence. He scratched his short bristly salt and pepper beard while Mary and Tanner expanded on the tale she had related to O'Neil over the phone the night before.

"So, you think there's a chance the *Amador* is located somewhere on the east side of the islands, instead of off Sisquit Bay." Mary nodded. "An' you b'lieve this piece of brass you say you found is a clue to where she went down." Mary nodded again. Tanner's gaze skipped about the office. There were odd pieces of what he assumed was diving gear, tools and boat parts piled in helter skelter fashion on shelves and tables. A half-open door led into the dark interior of the place. There was a thick layer of dust over everything.

"An' you propose to hire me to take a diving team, consisting mainly of you two, out there and try to locate that old wreck."

"That's about it," said Mary.

"Huh," said O'Neil, moving his whiskered jaws slowly over something in his mouth. "Well, we hire out to take people to dive sites and to other places where they jus' wanna dive. An' we run classes in open lake diving. It would be innaresting to find that old freighter, especially if the stories are true. Hell, even if they're on'y half true, but we gotta make us some arrangements. I don't know what the salvage rights are likely to be, but I'll find out. I got a couple divers in mind who can be trusted if we need 'em, an' there's work boats about for salvage if we get lucky. When you wanna go?"

"As soon as we can make the arrangements. We're here for four days this week, but we can arrange to come back almost anytime."

"I 'spect we could do a preliminary dive or two yet this weekend. Happens I got nothing much on this week." O'Neil paused, even stopped chewing and looked up, first at Mary, then at Tanner. Finally he said, "You'll forgive me, ma'm. I understan' about liberation and equality and all, an' I understan' you found the piece of brass, so by rights, this is your project. But I gotta say something to yer fella here, 'cause in some things, I'm still a leetle old-fashioned, I guess." He stopped and waited, gazing calmly at the two of them. Tanner just looked back.

Mary said, "Oh, that's perfectly all right, Mr. O'Neil. I still like to have doors opened for me, and I even like the man to pay for dinner," she smiled, "sometimes."

O'Neil nodded, apparently satisfied. Then he turned his gaze on Tanner again and said slowly. "You haven't said precisely where she found the brass plate. I noted that."

"No offense meant, Mr. O'Neil."

"And none taken. Matter of fact, I mark it as a certain caution. We could be talking about a significant treasure here, worth some money. It's wise to take some precautions at this stage. I also suspect there's more to this story than you've told me. There's also the question of ownership because of the Federal Island Lakeshore." In the back of his mind, Tanner heard O'Neil's language and grammar improve markedly. His speech became crisper, like a man used to being in charge.

"I take your point," Tanner said. "We may already have

attracted the wrong people." He sketched the background of their quest and his near-fatal car wreck. Tanner was gambling the man was too interested in the challenge to back away now.

"So, things could get a little dicey. You sure you want your lady here exposed to the potential danger? Diving in this lake around these islands isn't as dangerous as in some places, but there are hazards. And then, this is a highly speculative proposition." O'Neil held up a spatulate hand and ticked off his points. "First, you have very little evidence the freighter is really down there where you think it is. Second, even if it is there, we may not find what we're looking for and third, what we're looking for may turn out to be worthless or claimed by someone else."

"You're right, O'Neil. I do worry about Mary, but it's her call, just as you can decide to back out right now."

"Good," O'Neil said with satisfaction. "We understand each other. You two and me, we're going to be a team. I don't expect you want to bring in any more people than necessary and I don't even want to know where you found the piece until I need to. Here's my proposal. We'll make a simple agreement, on paper to be safe, that we'll share any rewards that turn up, assuming we find something to be rewarded for and assuming some authority doesn't get into the act. I'll put up the boat and equipment and my services as an expert diver. You pay our living expenses whenever you're up here and we're working, and we'll share replacement costs if anything gets busted. In the bargain, I'll teach you two scuba diving." He stopped and calmly looked at us.

"I like it," Tanner said after a moment. He stuck out his hand and the two men shook, looking into each other's eyes.

"Ah, male bonding," Mary said softly. Both men turned and looked at her. "Gentlemen, it's a pleasure to be part of this team, but if you think—"

O'Neil held up a hand, grinning, "Share an' share alike, I b'lieve is the way the phrase goes, and that means cookin' 'n' cleanin' 'n' standin' watches and bein' in on the decisions. Yes ma'm. I wouldn't want it any other way." Mary stuck out her hand and O'Neil shook it firmly. "Now you two go check out of your motel and move your gear down here to my boat. There's plenty of room for the three of us. We can go out and stay the night. If I have to come back to the marina, there's always the inflatable."

Mary and Tanner started to leave, then Tanner turned back. "There is one other thing, Cameron. Finding *Amador* is only part of this. We may very well be dealing with a murderer and it may be necessary to go public with our search in order to shake the tree and see what kind of reactions we get."

O'Neil nodded. "Gotcha. No problem on my end, but lessee if'n we kin stir up the muddy bottom a little, first."

Mary and Tanner returned to their motel in Bayfield to check out and have a quick lunch. As they left the motel dining room, Tanner saw a big white Kenilworth semi tractor in a far corner of the parking lot and stopped dead in his tracks.

"Michael?" cried Mary. "What is it?"

"Nothing really, just the sudden sight of that tractor over there. I thought for a minute it was the same one. It's not, though." Mary rubbed Tanner's shoulder in sympathy and they drove back to Port Superior, ready to take on a new adventure.

CHAPTER 23

O'Neil's sixty-five-foot sleek power yacht *Ondine* was moored to the wide wooden wharf on the north side of a recently constructed concrete gas dock. She gleamed white in the afternoon sun and sparkles of gold winked off the bright chrome. Her clean hull line was accented with a wide, deep-green stripe just above the waterline. Tanner looked up at the flying bridge with its large bimini of creamy canvas high above the main deck. Two tall slender antennae attached to either side of the wheelhouse, made little black arcs and circles against the brilliant blue sky as the boat rocked gently in the water. It was hot under the July sun.

Tanner drove to the edge of the wharf opposite the yacht and stopped. The engine ticked, and birds wheeled and called in the sky. It was calm in the bay and the cold water of Lake Superior lapped peacefully against the rocks along the harbor edge. Except for one or two people working on boats farther out in the marina, the place appeared deserted, but there were few empty slips. Tanner left the car and strolled over to *Ondine*'s stern. A large open cockpit with a heavy rail took up most of the back half of the main deck. Tanner glanced at the heavy aluminum brackets that lined *Ondine*'s rail, each cradling a pair of yellow air tanks. Many were scraped and scarred, in sharp contrast to the launch itself, which appeared to be in highly polished, pristine condition. Mary opened the trunk of the car and began to drag out their gear. When the trunk was empty she grabbed a duffel and hoisted it to her shoulder, grunting with the effort.

"Hoy! Michael! Come help with the gear." Tanner turned his head and smiled at Mary, then ambled back to the car and grabbed another bag. When they reached the boarding ladder, a door banged below deck and a tousled, sandy-haired boy appeared in the cabin beside the wheel.

"Afternoon, folks. I'm Greg. Mr. O'Neil told me to expect you. I was just checking the head and stuff. Give you a hand there?" He reached across the coaming and deftly transferred the weight of the duffel from Mary's shoulder to his own. When he turned around, she said,

"Just pile it on the deck, if you please. We'll wait to stow it until Captain O'Neil decides which cabin is ours."

"Oh," responded Greg, "he's done that already. I'll show you." The boy nimbly jumped down the companionway, avoiding putting his feet on any of the five steps while still toting the duffels. Tanner smiled and shrugged, opting to walk normally down the steps into the main cabin and galley.

A large, well-appointed saloon, glowing quietly with oiled teak and mahogany in the reflected sunlight, met their gaze. They could see from the soft sheen off the wood surfaces that the boat was lovingly and meticulously cared for. Mary smiled and nodded at Tanner with approval. On the left was the galley with a deep double sink and gimbaled four-burner gas stove. Just forward of the cabin bulkhead was a short, narrow passage, with a door at the other end.

"There're two nice cabins forward, one on either side of the passage," the boy said, pointing. "Each has a private head—that's the bathroom, with a shower. Mr. O'Neil has a cabin back there, under the aft deck. Yours is the cabin on the left, the port side. Going to do a little diving, I guess."

"Yes."

"Well, it's cold in the water, but there sure are some neat places to dive around here. Going someplace special?"

"Oh, no. This is just a learning expedition. We've never dived before." Tanner wasn't ready to have this boy gossiping about their main purpose just yet. Greg returned to the deck to retrieve the rest of the gear, but he didn't stow it, explaining O'Neil had taught him that guests usually wanted to stow their own equipment and gear so they'd know where it was. He left with a cheerful grin and a wave, leaping off onto the dock. Tanner and Mary set to stowing their personal things in the cabin. They finished just as Cameron O'Neil hopped aboard with a cardboard box of incidental supplies. Smiling widely, he placed the box in a locker against the cabin bulkhead.

"You two have that look that says a couple of cold beers or perhaps a tall gin and tonic would set well, just about now. Am I right?"

"I vote for a g&t," Tanner said quickly.

"In the fridge, just beside the sink, there." He waved at the galley and then sat down in the captain's chair bolted to the deck behind the wheel. "I'll pass for now."

Tanner went into the galley and opened the refrigerator. He glimpsed an adequate supply of beer and tonic and cold gin. It took only a minute to build two drinks and carry them to the aft deck where O'Neil had set up three deck chairs.

"I've a few more things to do and then we can be off, if you'd like to get under way this evenin' yet." O'Neil stretched and then settled his captain's cap more firmly on his head. "We can get out into the islands, find a sheltered spot an' get an early start on your lessons. Course," he shrugged, "*Ondine* is pretty fast and we could leave here at dawn, if you'd prefer to spend the evening in Bayfield and eat out."

Mary and Tanner glanced at each other. Of one mind, and now committed to the adventure, they wanted to get going. "We both cook and like it, so let's get going, if you agree," Tanner said.

"Okay. It's four now. I need a couple hours more. Let's say I'll be back here at six. Meantime you can check the larder. The nearest grocery store is in Bayfield. You can add anything you want you don't see on board. When that's done, relax, get to know *Ondine* a little. We three are the entire crew, remember." With that, he grinned, hustled off the boat and trotted up to his tiny office.

Mary walked around the perimeter, examining carefully stowed sets of diving tanks. On the left side just behind the overhanging roof of the cockpit, she noted an air compressor bolted to the deck.

An open-work metal platform was attached across the stern. She saw that its upper cables ran to a small electric motor in a waterproof housing just outside the rear rail. She figured out the platform could be lowered to rest just at water level, parallel to the surface, making it easier for divers to get on and off the yacht. Two four-inch pipe sections about eight inches long protruded from the deck, one at each rear corner. They might have been mooring stanchions, she thought, except there were no cross tees to secure lines.

Tanner was seated in the captain's chair bolted to the deck behind the bridge, closely examining the controls and gauges.

"*Ondine* is very well equipped," he remarked, when Mary joined him. "Look here, Loran, radar, and even a Satnav system." He tapped the shiny chrome handles of the engine control. "A pair of diesels and twin screws, give you lots of control."

"Think you can handle her?" Mary asked, reaching around his shoulder to snag a sip from his gin and tonic.

"With a little practice, *Ondine* and I will get along just fine."

Mary stretched, working her shoulders back and forth, and looked out across the deck at the sleepy marina. "This is really pleasant, isn't it?"

Tanner nodded, slid off the seat and stepped through a port-side doorway in the wheelhouse and walked along the smooth deck to the bow. There too it was easy to see everything was clean and bright and well maintained. Little rose above the deck surface other than the bright white housing that protected the anchor windlass and several dorades for air circulation below. Two heavy chains ran from either side of the bow to the windlass.

Mary climbed the ladder to the flying bridge above the wheelhouse. When she looked down at *Ondines* prow, Tanner was standing behind the windlass looking at a rectangular line on the deck. It appeared to be a hatch cover that led to the narrow passageway between the two forward cabins. Tanner turned and sauntered down the dock-side deck to the edge of the cabin. Mary looked around, examined the controls and then climbed down the ladder again.

"Pretty view from up there. Just about everything except the Satnav and radar are repeated."

"Very well equipped," he agreed, leading the way down the ladder to the main cabin. They stood together, arms draped loosely around each other's waists and surveyed the cabin again. The navigation station was on the right. It had a marine radio and engine repeater dials mounted on the bulkhead. The slanted chart table hinged and folded up to reveal neatly stacked charts and compartments for dividers, pencils, erasers and other charting tools. Tanner found a parallel rule, a couple of Weems protractors and a roller plotter. In a small mahogany cubby beside the powerful single sideband radio was a pair of yellow marine binoculars. On the other side of the SSB a standard VHF radio, the kind found on most boats on the lakes, was also attached to the bulkhead. Beside that was a GPS unit as well as Loran and a radar screen.

"The man likes his toys," Tanner commented.

A quick glance through the cabinets and cupboards in the galley revealed a well-stocked larder. They'd already examined the reefer and its small attached freezer.

"Well, Mary said, completing a clattering inventory of the cooking utensils, "I can't imagine anything else we could need."

"In that case," Tanner said with a smile. "We still have an hour and a half before Cameron returns, so what say we check out our cabin and that bed?" He smiled back and reached down to give Mary a small soft kiss.

"Sounds like a great idea," she responded.

****

Ondine nosed her sharp bow about and headed slowly along the narrow passage between the piers, past several tethered yachts, toward the end of the protective stone breakwater and the open lake.

Cameron O'Neil stood relaxed at the helm, fingers caressing the polished wood spokes, one foot hooked casually in the bottom rung of the helmsman's chair just behind him. His eyes shifted back and forth and from side to side. Occasionally he looked farther ahead, or aft, ceaselessly checking for boat traffic and other potential dangers in their immediate vicinity. *Ondine* was quick to the wheel, but in the marina's close quarters, only a moment's inattention could result in a serious accident.

In his free hand O'Neil held a tall rum and tonic. Mary stood at the stern, coiling a mooring line. At the bow, Tanner stretched his arms to the sky, having just finished a similar task. People on the dock, recognizing *Ondine* or her skipper, waved as the launch slipped quietly by. After they cleared the breakwater, they turned into the wavelet-rippled waters of Pike's Bay, following the line of red buoys toward the lake. O'Neil nudged the twin throttles up a notch and the engines took on a smoother, deeper sound. There was a brief toot on the horn as O'Neil responded to the happy waves from members of a big party on a ketch just slipping past.

Ondine rapidly picked up speed and arced out of the bay to run north, up across the Madeline-Bayfield ferry track, and then up the North Channel. The low sun sent long wave dappled shadows across the water from the trees along the shore line. Tanner saw what might have been an eagle soaring over the water. Skirting Basswood Island, the trio went swiftly up the channel toward Stockton.

"I figure we'll anchor tonight off Manitou. There's not a lot of shelter there," said O'Neil, "but if the wind holds from the northeast we'll be all right. And with double hooks at the bow, plus another anchor at the stern if we need it, it'd take quite a blow to move us." He paused to take a long swig from his glass.

"Providing, of course, we get the anchors in right," Tanner was smiling when he returned from the bow. The temperature was dropping as it usually did on the open water when the sun went down.

"Well, sure," laughed O'Neil, nudging the speed up another notch. Now he had to raise his voice to be heard over the engines and the rush of wind past the trailing edge of the open wheelhouse. "But those big CQRs with over two hundred feet of chain make it pretty hard to miss."

They swung north between Hermit and Stockton and ran up around the light on Little Manitou. By seven-thirty *Ondine* was safely anchored in fifteen feet of water just off the southwest shore of the island. Three boats in a cluster lay near the rebuilt dock 600 yards away on the south shore of Manitou. The dock was a construction by the park service to provide better access for visitors to the nearby fishing camp, first established over seventy-five years earlier. Otherwise the lake was surprisingly empty. As night fell they finished supper and while the half-moon rose in a clear, star dusted sky, cleaned up the supper dishes and turned in.

"We'll get an early start. Lake is almost always calm at dawn, no matter what comes later," remarked Cameron, disappearing into his cabin. Mary and Tanner smiled at each other, turned out the lights and went to bed.

CHAPTER 24

Dawn came bright, clear and chilly after a quiet night. Tanner awoke to the smell of fresh coffee and hushed sounds from the galley. When he stuck his head into the main cabin there was O'Neil, swathed in an oversized, tattered, terry robe that dragged on the floor, just putting a coffee pot back on the stove. He looked at Tanner and grinned through the steam.

"Morning, Cameron," Tanner said, yawning widely.

"Morning," he returned in a gravelly voice. "Get into swim suits and sweats or a robe so you stay warm before we get into the water. D'you know how to handle the anchor windlass?"

"Think so," Tanner returned. "Let me change and we'll get going." It was apparent that O'Neil didn't intend to waste any time getting his pupils oriented to basic scuba diving.

Not long after leaving their overnight location they were again securely fastened to the bottom of Lake Superior just off the southwestern coast of Rocky Island in eighteen feet of water. A few minutes later, aided by liberal doses of baby powder, they had wriggled into black wet suits, gloves and hoods. When Mary remarked at one point that the close-fitting foam-backed suit made it difficult to breath, Cameron nodded and said, "You'll be glad of that fit when you get into the lake. The small amount of water that seeps into the suit warms up to body temperature and acts as insulation. It helps keep you from getting chilled. It also lubricates the suit so's you can move easier."

O'Neil patiently showed them how to fit the single-lens acrylic mask and to shape the soft plastic mouthpieces of their air-regulator tubes. They looked other-worldly in the suits and the addition of swim fins made walking almost impossible. Tanner felt awkward and ungainly stumbling about the aft deck. O'Neil stood close by until he was sure both had gotten the hang of walking in the suits and fins. Then he lowered the diving platform off the stern until it jutted out parallel to the water just inches over the small wavelets that slopped noisily against the hull. Errant breezes that swirled out of the pine-treed shores of Rocky brought the smell of land and heat.

"I've calculated the weight belts to keep you on the surface," O'Neil said, slipping off the rounded edge of the platform into the water. He hung with just his head above the surface of the lake. "When you get in the water take a minute to adjust to the temperature, then we'll just snorkel around without the air tanks so you get used to the feel of the suits. For the first minute stay close to the platform and if you start to feel any discomfort, just relax your muscles and hang on to the edge."

By this time Tanner was sweating freely and feeling distinctly uncomfortable, but the shock of icy Superior water took his breath away. He knew the water temperature usually hovered around fifty degrees, even late in the summer. Soon both Mary and Tanner, strong swimmers and at home in the water, were stroking about, examining the platform and sections of *Ondine*'s hull that rose blackly above them against the brightening sky.

O'Neil was a patient and careful teacher. After a swiftly passing hour, they clambered back aboard and strapped on air tanks. Then they learned to trust the regulators and the air streaming into their faces from the yellow tanks. Once they got used to neutral buoyancy, maneuvering became easier. Tanner lay face down inches below the surface and peered into the depths of the lake, breathing easily and loudly through his mouthpiece. It was hard work, and tested his fitness.

After another hour in the water, they sprawled on the after deck, regaining energy. The sun was well up now, hot, strong, beating down on the yacht, sending mysterious rays of murky light into the depths of the lake.

The first time Tanner added extra weight and sank slowly under the surface of the water, he felt pressure in his throat. His heart beat more strongly and he realized he was breathing hard. O'Neil swam into Tanner's face, grinning strangely though his mask. He put a calming hand on Tanner's chest and pressed, slowing his pulse. They hung there for a moment face to face. When Tanner consciously relaxed, O'Neil gave him a thumbs up, flipped over and stroked down toward the bottom of the lake.

Mary appeared to have adjusted quickly and when Tanner followed O'Neil's form through the water, he saw her eeling along below him with lazy swishes of her fins. She trailed a rhythmic pulse of bubbles. Tanner realized O'Neil could tell from the rate of the bubble exhaust how fast each of them was breathing.

With growing confidence Tanner swam down and touched Mary's shoulder. She turned her head, reached out and gently squeezed his arm. Together they slowly sank to the bottom, touched and started up again. Everything happened in slow motion. The feeling of weightless suspension was complete. Except for the sounds of breathing, the silent world around them brought a kind of peace neither could remember experiencing. The resistance of the water made strenuous or sudden movement difficult and they learned to choreograph their movements, adapting to the environment.

By midafternoon, they had practiced sitting on convenient rocks at the bottom of the lake, examining nearby boulders, and communicating by sign language and scribbling a kind of shorthand on a slate O'Neil dangled from one wrist. Cameron had them try buddy system breathing. They hung suspended just above the lake bottom, sharing a mouthpiece. Mary seemed reluctant to let go of her mouthpiece at first when Tanner offered his. He finally had to take another lungful of air. Suddenly a hand reached around Mary's head from behind and wrenched the mouthpiece away from her face. It writhed and spewed bubbles into the water for an instant. Mary clutched at Tanner's wrist. Tanner thrust his mouthpiece into her face and saw her take it into her mouth and begin to breathe in. In a moment, her clutching fingers relaxed on his wrist. O'Neil, holding Mary's mouthpiece away from her, turned off the air from her tank and pointed upward, nodding.

Mary swam into Tanner's arms. She offered him the mouthpiece and smiled, blowing a little bubble at him. Together they slowly drifted upward. Quickly they got into the rhythm of it and breathed alternately, one on the regulator, the other slowly exhaling a stream of silvery bubbles into the water, bubbles that raced merrily up and away to the surface. They emerged laughing into the warm sunny air, still closely clasped together.

O'Neil was waiting, sitting on the edge of the dive platform. "You two are apt pupils," he remarked, handing around bottles of cold spring water. "I don't want you to get the idea you're ready for unsupervised dives or to try anything tricky, including deep dives. Normally you should go through more instruction and do several practice dives. But for our purposes, I'd say you're competent. But I want you to do as many shallow dives as you can in the next few hours. The main thing to remember now is planning and careful execution whenever you do any diving. And never alone."

"It was great!" Mary enthused. "Except for my panic down there when you took away my mouthpiece. Even if we never find anything. Scuba diving is fantastic! What a bonus."

"The water close around Devils Island isn't but forty to sixty feet deep but it does drop off pretty quick as you get out into the lake. We're not going deep enough that we'll need gas, just the compressed air we used today," O'Neil said.

"One reason your idea that *Amador* went down close to Devils Island doesn't get much credence is because the shallow water should have released more debris." O'Neil shrugged. "On the other hand, there is always the unexplainable when you deal with ships and big water like this lake."

"The *Flying Dutchman*, and such like," Tanner said, stripping off his gear.

"I was looking at the chart," Mary remarked. "A ship coming into the islands from the northeast would raise the Devils Island light after Michigan, then light buoys at York Island and Sand Island shoals, then the Sand Island lighthouse. They're practically in a straight line going southwest."

"Yep," agreed O'Neil. "I read the newspaper stuff you gave me. Maybe the ship's wireless operator meant to report they were approaching Devils and had the Sand Island light in sight. We'll never know for sure."

"We'll have a better idea if we find the *Amador*," said Mary quietly, her eyes sparkling in the twilight streaming through *Ondine*'s cabin windows.

Tanner laughed and O'Neil smiled. Even cautious and

realistic, they were beginning to feel the insistent tug of treasure-hunting fever. What if Mary was right? What if they found more evidence of the *Amador*? Even more exciting, what if they actually recovered the mysterious crate? It didn't bear too much thinking about. There was serious business to consider first. Dinner for three very healthy appetites.

They turned in immediately afterward, the exercise and fresh air of the day demanding rest. Mary wound her arms around Tanner as they fell into bed. She nuzzled her face into the curve of his jaw and shoulder, murmuring, "I'm too excited. Won't sleep a wink." With that, she fell into the dark, dreamless void. Tanner stayed awake long enough to smile at the realization that Mary was already asleep. It was his last conscious thought until he pried his eyes open in response to a bright light shining in my face.

"What...?" Then he realized it was the sun beaming in the porthole that had awakened him. Morning had come, and it was well past sunrise. Mary and Cameron were already up, and Tanner heard movement in the galley. When he walked into the saloon, Mary smiled.

"Ah, he rises. "Coffee is well under way."

""Hunh," muttered O'Neil, scrabbling around under one of the galley counters. "We all slept later than I expected. Well," he rose with a large frying pan clutched in one fist, "we'll move around to the northeastern side of Devils Island today and do some more diving."

"Why there?" asked Mary.

"We don't want to make it too easy for someone to pinpoint the location we're most interested in," he responded. "We'll be over the Devils Island shoal, which is only eleven feet deep. It's something a loaded freighter could smack into."

"Remember," Tanner interjected, "finding the *Amador* is only part of this. We're also baiting people who may have killed Ethel Jandrice."

There was a pause. Mary and Cameron O'Neil stared at Tanner for a moment. O'Neil carefully put down the big frying pan he clutched.

"Maybe you better tell me the rest of the story."

Tanner nodded and over a sumptuous breakfast of eggs, fried potatoes and ham, along with many cups of coffee, he and Mary told O'Neil everything they knew and most of what they speculated. Cameron asked few questions and when they were through, he thought for a long minute.

"If you want to get out of the deal we made, we'll understand," Tanner said finally, with a glance at Mary. "I feel bad that we weren't completely forthcoming from the beginning. We just didn't want to reveal everything until we were sure of our ground."

O'Neil glanced at them. "Sure of me, you mean. That's all right. I understand your thinking. I woulda done the same thing.

"I was just figuring how we might need to protect ourselves. But I think we're all right. If we get lucky and actually locate the *Amador* and her cargo, it's possible you'll find some new leads to the people you're looking for, especially if they get stupid. It's also possible we won't ever find anything. Either way, the people you're looking for may not bite. Then what?"

"We've been thinking about that," replied Mary. "If it gets out that we're hot on the trail of the *Amador* that may provoke something. But it's possible we're chasing a dead horse here."

O'Neil grinned. "I think that's beating a dead horse, but I take your meaning."

"They certainly seemed to jump on us right away after we talked about finding that piece of brass," said Tanner.

"It is interesting, how quick they came on. Might just be a case of over-reaction," said O'Neil. "There could be somethin' else goin' on we don't know about. Well. I'll play along. Frankly, I didn't think I had the whole story when we started. But my instinct said you'd get to it. An' that you'd be on the side of the angels, so's to say." He smiled. "I jus' couldn't believe a purty gal like you could really be bad." They all laughed and went topside to raise the anchor and move *Ondine* north to Devils Island.

CHAPTER 25

"Now," said O'Neil shutting down the engines. "We're in about twenty feet of water. Over there," he gestured toward the island fifty yards away on the right side of the yacht, "the bottom slopes up toward the island. It's about twenty feet deep where the cliff comes up. On the other side of the shoal it drops quickly to over fifty feet. That's too deep for us without more experience. Of course," he grinned, "nobody else knows that. Right around us is the shoal which varies from about ten to twenty-five feet depth. Tanner, you and I will go down first and find out what that much water overhead feels like. From now on, there'll be just two of us in the water and the other one on deck."

"Paying attention to both divers and to the lovely scene about us," Mary commented. She was just as happy O'Neil had decided to dive with Tanner this time. Behind the men's heads, she watched *Izmir*, a lovely 40 foot C&C sailboat out of Bayfield, cruise slowly by. Her big jib flapped fitfully in the light air. July was always chancy for sailors on Lake Superior. Too often the wind disappeared for days at a time. A woman in an abbreviated bikini, lying on an air mattress near the bow, raised an arm and waved languorously toward *Ondine*. By now both Cameron and Tanner were also looking at *Izmir*, or at the woman. Mary waved back. Then the men bent to final preparations for their dive. Mary lowered the dive platform while Tanner and Cameron strapped on tanks and checked their regulators. As they disappeared under the water, Mary turned to the wheelhouse and checked *Ondine*'s batteries. Then she flipped on the marine radio, adjusting the volume so she could easily hear traffic on the hailing channel. When she glanced again at *Izmir*, the yacht had made a large curve northwest, picking up a bit more wind. Three people stood at the rail gazing over the water toward *Ondine*. One held a pair of binoculars. At that distance, Mary couldn't tell for sure what they were looking at. It might have been something on shore that had attracted them. On the other hand... With a fresh cup of coffee, Mary set her wristwatch alarm to remind her to check the weather channel in twenty minutes, just before Cameron and Tanner were supposed to return to the surface.

The weather report was favorable so she relaxed and just glanced over the side occasionally at the bubbles marking the location of her divers. By now, she figured, they must be on their way back up. They were taking lots of time coming up to allow the slight pressure changes to equalize in their bodies. O'Neil believed in establishing careful safety routines from the very beginning, routines which would soon become so ingrained that it would take reasoned thought to alter basic precautions. That way, he told his pupils, even in a crisis, they'd have to make a conscious decision to risk a faster ascent from deep water.

The men broke the surface and Tanner spit out his mouthpiece and whooped. The sound bounce off the low cliffs of the island. At almost the same moment, Mary heard a hail from shore.

"Everything okay?" Mary called to the men in the water.

"Great!" Tanner responded. "It's cold, but I'm really getting into this diving stuff."

Mary raised her head and waved at the figure standing on shore. "Hi. Problems?"

"Not here," responded the figure. "Just wanted to say hello."

"Sorry, I can't talk right now," Mary called back. "Got a couple of divers to retrieve."

"Treasure hunting?" called the man in a casual tone.

Mary laughed and shook her head, at the same time reaching over to give Cameron a hand up. Tanner had already clambered over the platform and onto the deck. When Mary looked up again, the man on the island had disappeared.

****

On Monday, *Ondine* returned to the dock at Port Superior. They had left practically unnoticed, now there seemed to be quite a few people about. Willing hands, watched closely by O'Neil, grabbed mooring lines and pulled the yacht to the cushioned pilings in her regular berth. Tanner and Mary parried the mostly idle questions from bystanders with near-breathless descriptions of the wonders of the world they'd found beneath the surface of the lake. They set to work cleaning up and getting *Ondine* ship-shape once again.

Finished, they went to O'Neil's office. They could just as easily have completed their talks prior to landing in Port Superior, but they wanted to be seen conferring in private if anyone happened to be paying attention.

"Now," said O'Neil, settling into his beat-up old swivel chair and hooking one deck shoe up on the edge of the scarred desk. "I figger we'll gauge the interest, or lack of it, by the traffic around here after you two have gone back to the cities. You give me a call, beginning of next week and we'll see where we are."

"All right," said Tanner slowly. "And if no one seems to take our bait, so to speak, we'll figure out something else before we come back up. In any case, we'll see you again Saturday morning in two weeks, just as we planned."

"Yep. I got it in my book. You two have a safe trip home now, an' watch your rearview mirror." They shook hands and Tanner and Mary Whitney cranked up the new station wagon and headed west toward Duluth.

****

Three days went by and everything seemed normal, except for Mary's stomach. She noted an occasional tenseness in her partner's demeanor, as well. On Friday, Tanner called Cameron, who reported several significant events. His office had been searched. Somebody now knew he was booked for another dive charter with Tanner and Mary Whitney at the end of the month.

O'Neil also said several people called requesting charters. But they all somehow wanted the same weekend. Tanner wondered what they would have said if he'd agreed to book them.

"Probably called back later and cancelled if they weren't legitimate," said O'Neil, chuckling.

Tanner related the call to Mary, saying, "he told me he had a call from some kid who claimed to work for the county newspaper. The boy told O'Neil there were stories going around that he was diving on some sunken treasure ship."

"Really? What was Cameron's response?" Mary asked.

"He said he laughed a lot and tole' 'im it was purty ridiculous and so on without comin' right out and flat denying the rumor." Tanner's imitation of O'Neil's voice made the conversation seem funnier than it was.

"Cameron said the paper comes out on Friday so he'll see then if the kid gets anything in print. I told him we planned to get an early start and that we hoped we could be out at the island by midafternoon and get in at least one dive."

"Good," Mary responded. It sounds like there's at least local curiosity now. Maybe the word will spread."

"Oh, I think you can count on that, especially if I'm right about that trucker deliberately trying to wreck me."

****

Mary slid into the driver's seat and hooked her seat belt, brushing doughnut crumbs from her chest. "C'mon, tiger, let's get going."

"Yeah," Tanner responded, coming around the car. "I'm kind of surprised we've had no overtures of any kind from either Mayhews or the deVoles. Maybe we're completely off the track."

"What d'you mean?" Mary drove back onto 35W heading north.

"Maybe I'm seeing conspiracy where there isn't any. Maybe Jandrice's death and my accident and the *Amador* are all just coincidence, unconnected."

"How d'you explain the trashing of our apartment and somebody stealing my brass plate from the Park Service?"

He nodded. "Yeah, there is that."

They reached Port Superior at ten. It was already a hot, cloudless morning. The marina was busy. The parking lot was crowded and many slips were empty. There seemed to be people on every boat still in the harbor. Others strolled up and down the docks, looking at the boats, the marina and the buildings. Most of the tables in the second-floor restaurant that overlooked the marina and the lake beyond were filled too.

Mary parked at the back of the lot and sat for a moment looking at the scene. "Gosh, I don't remember this many people the last time we were here, do you?" she said.

"Watch," Tanner pointed out, "several people are staying where they can see O'Neil's office door."

They unloaded their gear and locked the station wagon, then strolled toward the water. They were ignored until they turned left down the long wharf toward *Ondine*'s berth. Murmurs arose and there was a sudden surge in their direction. A figure appeared at *Ondine*'s bow, black against the hard light coming off the water. Mary hesitated, then recognized Greg, the youngster they'd met the last time. He waved and jumped to the dock.

"Cameron asked me to hang around *Ondine* in case folks got too curious," he remarked, easily swinging back aboard with a box on one shoulder.

"The story in the paper yesterday brought you folks some kind of attention."

"I'm anxious to read it. Have you had any trouble?" asked Tanner.

"Nope, just lots of calls and these folks." He wagged his head at the people strolling by and standing on the docks.

Twenty minutes later Cameron O'Neil appeared and smiled a welcome at Tanner and Mary.

"You folks all settled?"

"Yessir," Mary smiled back. "Loaded, settled and ready to go."

"Greg, we'll stand radio watch every hour on the half. You do the same so we can reach you pronto if we need to. But don't hang around after regular quittin' time. Oh yeah. I've checked the *Rum Runner*. She's full of gas and working fine. That misfire was just dirt in the fuel filter. I cleaned it and she runs fine. Use 'er whenever you want."

Mary stepped aboard, hearing the faint whine of the bilge

fan. O'Neil ran the fan for several minutes to clear any lingering fumes before starting the big engines, even though they ran on diesel fuel instead of more volatile gasoline. The chances of diesel fumes creating a flash fire were remote, but both Tanner and Mary were pleased at this further evidence that O'Neil took seriously everything about boating and diving safety.

"Okay, Cameron," Greg replied. "Good trip, you guys." He turned, trotted to the bow and loosed the mooring line, tossing the free end to Tanner and leaving a single loop around the bollard. Mary leaned over the stern mooring bollard and untied that line, carrying it aboard also leaving a single loop over the post. The deck trembled underfoot when the engines turned over and caught. Mary heard the exhaust burbling out of the water at the stern. O'Neil looked all around and then at each deckhand in turn to see all was ready. The vibration underfoot changed when he engaged the twin props in reverse and signaled Tanner who slacked his line. *Ondine* slid out of her berth. O'Neil waved at Mary and she turned, dropped the free end of her line and quickly pulled it around the bollard and back aboard. O'Neil countered the backward thrust of the engines so *Ondine* paused in the water. From behind the building a car, engine racing, screeched around the last corner and into the parking lot. A man jumped out.

Tanner's stomach tightened. They were about to start another chapter in their adventure under the scrutiny of a lot of people whose motives they could not assess. Who knew where it would end? He coiled the line and looked aft to see Mary looking at him. Instinctively he knew they were sharing similar feelings. This was different from the previous voyage. Now they were about to make a serious attempt to find a ship that disappeared over a hundred years ago. And they would be searching in an environment that was, if not hostile, not entirely friendly.

Cameron took another quick look around and engaged forward gear, spinning the wheel to port. He increased his engine speed slightly and *Ondine* turned gracefully toward the entrance to the breakwater. People ashore waved. Tanner noted that several had cameras raised to their eyes. Once more they left the protection of the breakwater and ran smoothly out into Pike's Bay.

CHAPTER 26

Ondine's powerful engines sent her swiftly north up the channel to the eastern side of Devils Island. Enroute they crossed paths with several pleasure boats, as well as the usual commercial fishing vessels. None came close and none appeared to give them special notice. Of course, as O'Neil pointed out, *Ondine* was big enough and well-enough known to be readily identified, even at a distance. A small plane droned overhead, heading northwest across the lake.

The water was smooth again, with long gentle rollers crossing *Ondine*'s course at a slight angle from the west. Mary pointed out the three ferries when they crossed the Bayfield-Madeline Island ferry track. Tanner watched her return from the bow, wind blowing her dark curls around her ears, and thought again how lucky he was to have the companionship and love of such a woman.

"You seem to have a lot of extra line aboard," she commented when she entered the wheelhouse. "The chain locker is crammed full. What should I do with the mooring line?"

O'Neil nodded. "Yep. Had Greg load it last night. We'll be getting into deeper water this trip and I don't want to have to run the engines to keep us on station. Just make a coil of that line on the foredeck and lash it to the rail. Tanner, in that locker under the bench you're sittin' on are some short lengths of light line. Use a couple to tie off the mooring line."

They continued in a northwest direction and cleared Stockton on the port side, then made a long sweeping curve to head straight north between Outer and Cat islands. Later, they would turn west and approach Devils Island from the northeast.

Two hours later, *Ondine* slid smoothly over the mirror-like surface of the quiet lake, headed directly toward the Devils Island lighthouse. Tanner was at the helm on the flying bridge while O'Neil stood beside him, peering steadily ahead through a pair of binoculars. With the sun high overhead and still behind them, they searched the water for any indication of something below the surface that might be man-made. They didn't expect to see anything, but O'Neil had shrugged when Mary suggested that surely someone would have sighted a sunken wreck before this if it had gone down so close to the island.

"Maybe, but far as the records go, there aren't any wrecks out here. It's likely no one's ever really looked hereabouts." He smiled briefly. "Anyway, it won't hurt to keep our eyes open."

"Hundred fifty feet," Tanner called. They were six miles northeast of the island. The engines patiently drove them forward at a placid rate, their wake the only disturbance on the surface. Gulls wheeled and squawked overhead. They cruised alone within the circle of their horizon.

"Depth is now one-thirty. Bottom's rising," Tanner said quietly. "Wow, now it's only sixty feet. That was fast."

"Hold it here," said O'Neil. "There's a sort of ridge that runs out from Devils Island Shoals right along here. Seems a likely place to start." Tanner reversed the props and stopped Ondine dead in the water. Mary sent eighty feet of chain following the heavy anchor to the bottom. When she signaled, Tanner reversed the yacht at dead slow until the chain stretched taut between Ondine's bow and her heavy anchor, clawed securely into the bottom of Lake Superior. They were just over three miles from Devils Island and from the flying bridge the lighthouse and volunteer attendant's house were clearly visible.

By one o'clock the temperature on the aft deck had risen into the nineties and everything made of metal was too hot to touch with unprotected hands. The trio worked in the shaded portion of the deck behind the open wheelhouse, readying tanks, laying out weight belts and flippers, dripping sweat on everything.

"Phew," said Mary. "The lake is going to feel good after this."

O'Neil nodded once and said, "I hooked up a hose with a shower head on the port side." Use that if you get too hot. The little pump takes water directly from the lake. Switch is on the pump body." When all was ready and they'd checked the gear twice, O'Neil nodded with satisfaction. "Okay, I guess we're ready. Mary? We can stay down about twenty minutes before the cold gets us. I have this waterproof chart we'll mark as we search. Tanner you're our keeper. Keep your eyes peeled. Sooner or later we'll get some visitors and I wanna know about it. You haul the signal line up to the mark I showed you just as soon as you see anyone headed anywhere near us. It'll raise the weight and I'll notice it.

"We shouldn't expect real trouble, but we oughta look like we're alert." The radio squawked and he cocked his head. "That's us they're calling. Will you get that?" Mary stepped to the bridge as the radio came to life again.

"*Ondine, Ondine, Ondine.* This is Coast Guard, Bayfield station calling motor vessel *Ondine.* Over."

"Coast Guard, this is *Ondine* on 16. Respond on channel 78, over." Mary glanced over her shoulder at the two men. Cameron nodded. The radioman confirmed the change to a different channel to vacate the hailing channel for other radio traffic.

"Coast Guard, Bayfield, this is *Ondine* on seven eight. What can I do for you? Over."

"We have a query indicating you may be having difficulties. Do you require assistance?"

Mary glanced again at Cameron who shook his head. "Nope. Tell 'em, but don't be specific about anything unless he insists." He and Tanner continued final preparations for the dive.

"*Ondine,* what is your location? Over," came the hard masculine voice of the Coast Guard radioman after Mary had assured him they were in no difficulty.

Mary pressed the transmit switch again. "We're north and east of Devils Island, just catching a few rays. Over."

"Thank you, *Ondine.* Out."

"*Ondine* returning to channel 16. Clear." Mary replaced the little mike in its bracket and looked at Tanner, a question on her face. "Apparently someone was checking on us. DeVole? Mayhew? The trio walked to the rail. Mary walked, Cameron waddled.

Tanner helped Mary with her fins and tank, kissed her cheek and watched her disappear into the lake.

While they were dropping slowly through the blue-green waters toward the bottom of the lake more than fifty feet down, Mary envisioned Tanner with a cold drink resting on the warm padded seat of the flying bridge. From there he'd have a panoramic view of the surrounding lake and the Apostles, somnolent in the hot sun.

Thirty minutes later, Cameron and Mary rested shivering on Ondine's rear deck, grateful for the sun warming their cold skin.

"It's really great, Michael," she said enthusiastically, "but really cold!"

"What did you see? Did you find anything?"

"Lotta green water, rocks, silt, a little gravel and sand, old logs, some tree roots, stuff like that. Nothing unexpected," responded Cameron. "Anything happening up here?"

"Nope. I got a few rays, almost fell asleep, the radio squawked but nobody came near." Tanner stretched and yawned.

O'Neil stood up to peel out of his wet suit and pointed. A cruiser was coming across the water from the direction of North Twin Island.

"Here's company." The cruiser, a sport fishing boat considerably smaller than Ondine, cruised by at a sedate speed and a respectful distance. Three men could be seen in the open cockpit under a small canvas bimini looking across the water at them. Mary impulsively gave them a friendly wave which was not returned.

The afternoon went on. Tanner and Cameron made a dive to the bottom that brought smiles to Mary's face when he agreed with her assessment of the underwater environment and then Mary went down again briefly with O'Neil. They left a marker on the floor of the lake beside a large boulder. It would be a reminder of where they'd already searched, the next time they visited the bottom. They were marking a chart with a grid to identify the area covered. So far, they had found nothing that might have come from a ship or boat. Twice more, motor boats cruised by.

"We'll have to call it quits now and move to a safer anchorage," said Cameron.

"I've heard the latest weather," replied Mary, "and Rocky looks like a good bet." Cameron nodded agreement.

"Let's take our time so we leave here just before sundown. If anyone is planning to dive on this location, we want to make it as difficult as possible for them."

"Of course, the deVoles could very easily hire a big diving firm to come up here and work day and night," Tanner said. He was standing at the controls raising the dive platform to its traveling position.

"Sure they could," responded Cameron. His teeth were startlingly white against his dark skin. "But that would make a big splash, wouldn't it?"

"True. They may prefer to let someone else find whatever there is to find—"

"If there is anything," interjected Mary.

"—and try to take it later," Tanner finished.

"A thought just occurred to me. Cameron, who owns what we find?"

"Wisconsin owns the lake bottom here, but there are some gray areas in the law. Generally, salvage in these islands isn't legal anymore. But I suspect if we found some serious valuables, such as a quantity of old silver or heirlooms of some kind, the deVole Corporation could make a legal claim."

"Unless it would be embarrassing for them to do so," said Mary.

When the sun just touched the western horizon, Mary went forward to the anchor windlass while Tanner started Ondine's engines and Cameron finished tidying up. A few minutes later they were moving swiftly southeast toward the end of Rocky Island. There was a nice anchorage across a narrow channel from South Twin that would shelter them from the projected westerly winds that night. Tanner was tired from the dives, but he knew he might have a restless night. The apparent lack of concern over their activities was wearing on his nerves.

****

The next morning, the dull red sun had barely struggled into view and hadn't yet burned off the mists that swirled in clouds across the still quiet surface of the lake when *Ondine* got under way.

"Look at that," exclaimed Mary. She was standing on the flying bridge with Tanner, peering through binoculars toward our destination.

"What?"

"It's a mob scene. We may not be able to anchor where we were." Where yesterday had been empty water off Devils Island, now there appeared to be a dozen boats clustered near the place *Ondine* had anchored. There were small open fishing boats with one or two occupants, bouncing in the chop. There were sport fishing boats and even a couple of larger launches. They all seemed to have a fishing line or two hanging over the side. Other boats trolled across *Ondine*'s path, downriggers and fishing lines set.

"Somebody must have put the word out about our location," remarked Cameron from the deck below. "Either that or there's an uncommon big salmon run out here."

They all laughed, but there was a nervous tension underlying their chuckles.

"Could they really be fishing?"

O'Neil chuckled again. "Not'n a million years. The closest to real are those guys with downriggers and trolling gear. Remember it's almost sixty feet deep out here. Try to get us as close to our original spot as possible. Can you see the marker on the fish finder yet?"

The odd shaped reflector they'd left anchored to the bottom the night before presented a distinctive signature on the scanner, but this morning it was gone.

"Nothing so far," Tanner responded.

"GPS puts us close to the spot. It looks like that launch just ahead is right over yesterday's location. Let's anchor here and see what happens," said Cameron from the cabin wheelhouse. "Tanner, stand by the anchor windlass. Mary, in that starboard locker are several more fenders. Hang 'em out between the stanchions on both sides."

They finished their allotted tasks while O'Neil adroitly

nudged *Ondine* into the wind and backed away from her anchor with a little more line than necessary. They still couldn't detect the shape of their marker on the fish finder. There'd been no storm last night and the marker had been securely fastened. It looked as though someone had picked it up.

CHAPTER 27

When *Ondine*'s engines died and she rocked easily at the end of her anchor line, Cameron and Mary once more laid out the scuba equipment while Tanner brought the ungainly wet suits up from the cabin. Under the scrutiny of the surrounding boats, they tried to act casual, but it was difficult. Mary was about to get into her wet suit and handed Cameron the big can of baby powder to dust her back when Tanner shook his head slightly. O'Neil paused, arm outstretched for the can and looked back.

"Let's not be too hasty, Tanner said. "We're putting on a performance, as well as really looking, so we have to consider the effect of everything we do." He paused and scratched his ear. "And it's all live and unrehearsed, as they say."

O'Neil chuckled, releasing a little tension. "Gottcha. Sorta like advertising, right?"

"How about a quick look at the charts?" Tanner said.

"Well, sure, I got them right—"

"Not those," Tanner interposed quickly. "The special charts. "I'll just get them from our cabin," and he disappeared below.

Mary's voice floated after him. "I can see occasional flashes of light reflecting off binocs from that big launch over there. Do you recognize it, Cameron?"

"Nope, can't say I do, but things do appear to be gettin' interestin'. Y'know, it occurs to me we might start practicing a little concealment when we talk. Nothin' too obvious, but people have some pretty tricky ways of reading lips or recording conversations at long distances." Tanner returned to the deck in time to see Mary staring at O'Neil, amazement on her face.

"Did you get that idea from watching television, or from your military experience?" Tanner grinned. He was holding a long cardboard tube.

O'Neil turned his head and fixed Tanner with a stare. "I take it you have been doing some research?"

"Yes sir. I have a few contacts in the services. You have quite a distinguished record in military intelligence. Korea, wasn't it?"

For a moment there was utter silence aboard *Ondine*, then Cameron O'Neil laughed, shrugged and scratched his ear again. "You do get around, Mr. Tanner, you do get around. Well, let's take a look here."

Tanner opened the end of the tube and began to extract a roll of chart paper. Then he coughed, put a hand over his mouth and said, "In view of the faint possibility of electronic eavesdropping, you might follow my lead." O'Neil just nodded.

He dropped his hand and continued to extract the roll of paper from the tube, "We have to be careful with these charts. Some of them are getting brittle. When he began to spread them out, Cameron and Mary could see there were some blank sheets, together with a modern large-scale chart of Lake Superior; the standard NOAA chart readily available from any map or ship's store. There was one chart that looked different.

"Hey," said O'Neil. "What's the date on this one? Isn't this a 1900 navigation chart for the lake?"

"Right. And I have an idea these notations and plotted courses may be helpful. This was probably used to plan or keep track of ships from a shipping line's traffic office."

"Where'd you get this, Mary?"

"A friend at the Society found it among the deVole papers."

"What?" O'Neil said. "Well, that's a pretty exciting find."

"We could be--"

Cameron O'Neil hunched his shoulders and cleared his throat loudly. "Gottcha. Let's have some coffee and look at this." Without waiting for a reply, he turned and walked down the ladder into the saloon. Mary and Tanner followed him. Once out of sight he turned and said, "It's a fake, right? You want someone to assume we might have a chart of the *Amador*'s last voyage, or something like that?"

"That's right," Mary responded. "We had the chart already. Michael found a place in the Twin Cities where they copied and sort of aged it. Of course, I added a few things to give it a certain authenticity and then had it copied again."

O'Neil grinned widely. "Oh, duplicitous woman. That's very good! Okay. We don't want to be acting like we're trying to feed this to somebody. We were starting to sound like this was the time to plant a particular piece of disinformation. Let 'em make some guesses. Always assuming someone is paying attention. Long distance eavesdropping gear is pretty expensive. Maybe we gave a party here and nobody came."

"Oh? Look at this traffic and remember, deVole's got piles of money," Mary pointed out, pouring fresh coffee all around. "And so do the Mayhews."

"I think it's safe to assume one of our little flotilla here has people on it being paid by one of those. And my bet is on deVole," said Tanner.

"What now?" asked Mary, settling down on one end of the bench seat in the cabin.

"Let's try this. We've examined this fake chart and decided that we're in the right place. Next let's do a dive and a small search," offered O'Neil. "Main thing I'd like to know is if we've just lost our marker or it was moved, although I'm pretty sure of the answer."

"How 'bout Mary and I dive and you stand watch," Tanner said. "We have a pretty good feel for this stuff by now."

"All right, but this is deeper an' you'll have a lot less light than yesterday."

"Since we don't really expect to find *Amador* down there, why don't we make it a short dive and just look around for the marker and then come right back up?" said Mary.

Mary and Tanner soon slipped backwards off the dive platform into the water. O'Neil grinned at Mary's startled reaction to the temperature as the cold water closed over her head. He'd dropped a long line on a weight off each side of the yacht so the divers could stay in touch with the surface. Tanner looked up to see Mary following the trail of bubbles from his mask as they slowly, steadily sank deeper into the lake. The color of the water changed gradually from bright silver blue to deeper blue and then became greenish. The light grew dim. All the while they were descending Tanner felt the increasing pressure of confinement, even stronger than yesterday.

Along with the cold and the pressure, detritus suspended in the water restricted their visibility. There'd been little apparent change in the water during earlier, shallow dives, but this was different. The sound of his breathing through the regulator was loud in Tanner's ears. After what seemed to be an hour of slow steady swimming, down into increasing darkness, Tanner checked his wrist fathometer and slowed until Mary swam closer. The dial read fifty feet. They had reached the bottom. He turned around and perched on the edge of a large rounded boulder. Mary tapped him on the face mask, pointed to herself and made a thumb and finger okay sign.

It wasn't cold enough to be uncomfortable yet, but there was a tiny sense of disorientation. Just enough light filtered down from the surface so they could see shapes around them. In this unfamiliar, alien environment, he found a certain pleasure, different stimulation to his senses, bordering on euphoria. He could tell Mary was having similar feelings, as she hung there in the water, her face mask close to his.

Tanner made a large, slow circular motion with one arm. Mary nodded and swam a few strokes away. She switched on her underwater lamp and began to make a slow circle around his position. At one point she slipped behind a large boulder, and was completely lost to sight. Then she reappeared a little farther on, peering at the bottom, looking for the missing marker. A little farther and she was gone entirely. He could only tell her position from the light she carried.

For several minutes they continued this search pattern, alternating being searcher and watcher. Tanner felt his strength ebbing and chill settling in. Mary swam to him and jabbed a finger up, toward the surface. Tanner nodded okay and exhaled a big cloud of bubbles at her. They began their slow ascent to the surface. At twenty feet they stopped and rested. The signal line hanging from the yacht and the shadow of the hull overhead were clearly visible now. *Ondine*'s dark shape was a protective umbrella. Tanner looked up and watched his bubbles float to the surface. Once more they swam upward, toward the light, feeling the water temperature increase. They surfaced about five yards off the stern. The water was still calm, but now tiny wavelets splashed in their faces as puffy breezes swept across the lake. Mary raised her mask and saw O'Neil grinning at her from the platform.

"So?" he queried when both divers were back aboard.

"No marker," Tanner said, "but I'm sure we were in the right spot. I saw fresh scars from an anchor chain that must have been ours. I think we found the boulder where we secured the marker."

"It may have been removed or carried off some other way. We'll probably never know."

"We'll know when we find *Amador* and figure out what's going on," said Mary tartly as she skipped below to dry off and change to shorts and shirt.

"Let's just sit here on the deck a minute. Now look out there," gestured Cameron.

The wavelets had increased slightly under stronger puffs of wind. The sky was still brilliant blue, but the afternoon haze had thickened. Another fishing yacht cruised by the knot of loosely clustered boats.

"What?"

"It's gettin' a mite crowded and things could get dicey. I don't think some of our neighbors are all that secure in this water and their anchors may not hold 'em. What's more, a few of them fellers appear to be gettin' impatient with us."

A newcomer showed up, moving too rapidly through the other boats, before Tanner could reply. There were a few shouts and one yacht sounded its electric air horn in a sharp piercing blat that carried over the mutter of idling engines. The windlass on a lean forty-footer chattered and the anchor line rose dripping from the water. A blast of cool wind swept over the boats, sent smaller ones dancing nervously on the disturbed water. There were more shouts of warning. Then came the crunch of two fiberglass hulls smacking together. Several engines started and soon a low level of pandemonium stole over the scene as some decided to leave and others to lay out more anchor line.

Two more boats came together off *Ondine*'s port side and Tanner saw a stanchion on one of them bend inward amid imprecations flung back and forth. Suddenly two burly men began to swing at each other across the bent rail. It looked like a few blows were scored, but the bobbing hulls made it difficult to land solid hits, or even to maintain solid footing. The real danger was someone falling into the water and being hit by a boat or not being missed until later.

"Raise the dive platform," snapped O'Neil, grabbing a long boat hook from a rack beside the rail. He ran to the other side of the deck to fend off an approaching boat that had maneuvered too close. He was too late. Tanner felt the jar of the collision through the soles of his feet just as he reached the controls.

"What's happening?" called Mary reappearing through the hatch.

"Mary," called O'Neil, "raise the Coast Guard on the radio. We've got a mini-riot on our hands." Her face blanched. She grabbed the mike, called the Bayfield Coast Guard Station, and twisted the volume up in one hurried motion. The response boomed from the bridge speaker and echoed across the water.

"Coast Guard, Bayfield Station, to *Ondine*, over."

"We have a small riot here, Bayfield," responded Mary, a little out of breath.

"Roger, *Ondine*, we're already in your area. Stand by."

She signed off and hung up the mike and everyone heard it. A loud siren whooped across the water and the Coast Guard cutter out of Bayfield charged across the roiled water. At almost the same instant the raucous horn of the National Park Service's smaller Boston Whaler sounded as a pair of park rangers arrived from the opposite direction.

Tanner looked at O'Neil, who stood scowling in the direction of the motor yacht that had smacked *Ondine*. Fortunately, the fenders along *Ondine*'s side had prevented any damage.

"A major storm is moving in from the northeast," boomed the Coast Guard officer through the ship's loud hailer. "You should all seek shelter forthwith."

Boats began to disperse in several directions, only the three largest, including Ondine, still remained tethered to the bottom. A voice muttered across the water from an unseen mouth. "This don't end it, O'Neil." Tanner and O'Neil were too busy to locate the source of the implied threat. Mary glanced up at a wall of black clouds that was bearing down on them.

The air temperature dropped, and it wasn't just from the rising wind which now gave itself voice in the rigging. The temperature behind the front was colder. Mary ran to the foredeck and engaged the anchor windlass. The foredeck was pitching much more than the bridge and when she looked down for the few moments it took to organize the windlass, she lost sight of the horizon. Tanner saw her backward glance and guessed she was getting nauseous. She gasped, stood up and held tight to the clutch handle and the rail. She took a few deep breaths to clear her head.

O'Neil had the controls so Tanner grabbed a life vest and a safety harness and ran forward.

"Is that a green tinge about your eyes?" he said, helping her don the apparatus.

"Certainly is, sir," she responded flatly. "But I got everything here under control, sir."

Tanner laughed, nodded and moved quickly and carefully back down the deck to the wheelhouse. He felt the vibrations of Ondine's big diesels through the deck plates, ready to take them away from there. When he glanced around, the smaller boats, including the Park Service boat, had already departed, running for shelter among the islands. In the middle distance, the Coast Guard cutter was just turning to starboard, heading away from Devils Island. Ondine couldn't go until the anchor was safely up and secured. It takes a long time to raise nearly two hundred feet of anchor chain and while Mary watched the footage markers, O'Neil and Tanner watched the line of racing clouds looming over them. A sudden crack announced a jagged streak of lightning that flashed between lake and cloud bank. Moments later came a rolling boom of thunder. The clouds grew fuzzier. Higher swells and white-capped gray waves rolled toward them. A thick fog bank was rolling along beneath the clouds.

The wind began to moan in Tanner's ears. It flailed at Mary's hair. The windlass clanked and snapped as the automatic clutch released the line to avoid seizing the windlass motor. The anchor was up. Tanner saw her set the securing pins in anchor and chain and cover the windlass. *Ondine*'s bow rose, dipped and rose again toward the gray sky. Mary got up off her knees to signal them just as the bow dipped again, and this time it didn't rise fast enough. A big wall of cold gray water smashed over the bow, nearly upsetting her where she crouched, clinging to the railing. Lake water cascaded over her. Then it was gone, the water sluicing out through the scuppers along the toe rail. Tanner started out of the wheelhouse, but Mary waved him back, then scampered along to the bridge.

"Whooey! Was that a rogue wave or what?" Tanner grinned. Mary unhooked her tether, glared at Tanner, and without a word dropped below deck to dry off and make yet another change of clothes. When she returned to the main cabin, Tanner had hot coffee ready in the galley, *Ondine* was buttoned up and they were running swiftly south, heading for Port Superior. Mary took the mug without a word and climbed to the wheelhouse to stand beside O'Neil. Things were getting rugged aboard the yacht and it wasn't just the weather.

CHAPTER 28

"Hello? Yes, this is Michael Tanner. To whom am I speaking? Mr. Caine? Oh, sorry, Professor Caine. Yes, well, we seem to have a poor connection. What can I do for you, professor?" Who, he wondered is Professor Caine? Tanner was sitting in their apartment living room Monday morning, a day after he and Mary had returned from the Apostle Islands.

The drive home had been anything but pleasant. Tanner and Mary had argued most of the way back. They didn't fight very often, but occasionally found themselves operating on different planes. Tanner realized he should have been more aware of her feelings when the big wave hit her. He'd tried to apologize, but he'd done it with a smart crack. The ensuing squabble had covered a number of other topics, including the business of the *Amador*.

"You are being pretty flip about all this. Somebody could get hurt out there," Mary snapped at one point. "Somebody has already been hurt, in case you don't recall!"

"Sure. But remember there wouldn't be any incidents, rogue wave and all, if you hadn't been so insistent on this watery wild goose chase."

Then Mary called Tanner an insensitive clod. He'd put a hand on her thigh, and she'd slapped it off.

After that, conversation deteriorated to grumpy silence for the rest of the drive back to Minneapolis.

Professor Caine whispered and hawked in Tanner's ear. He was calling from Duluth, he said, and was desperately afraid of being overheard. Tanner listened to muttered imprecations against the Mayhew family and repeated urgings to get a copy of the recent Sunday edition of the *Duluth Herald*. Professor Caine hung up the phone in mid-sentence. Tanner stared at the phone for a moment. In addition to other problems, now he had unknown nuts calling.

Tanner walked up the street in the morning sun to a corner vendor who was a good source of most out-of-town newspapers. How, he wondered, had Caine gotten the right telephone number? The newsstand had several copies of the *Herald* in an untidy pile beside the door. It was the Sunday edition and like most Sunday newspapers was thick with extra ad sections. Back in the apartment Tanner faced the task of going through the entire issue since he didn't know what he was looking for. It took less time to find the item than he'd expected.

On the first page of the local metropolitan news section, just below the fold, was a short story. Tommy Callender was dead. His battered body had been discovered by a Duluth policeman late Saturday night, behind a bar near the waterfront. That kind of violence was unusual for that northern city.

Tanner knew that Duluth, though an international port, didn't have the kind of seedy, run-down area near the docks that one found in Chicago or Seattle or New York. Along some waterfronts, brawls, cuttings, even death, was a frequent visitor. Not Duluth. Tanner wondered about the impact of Tommy's death on their inquiries. This was more than slightly troubling. What the hell were they into, Tanner wondered? Jandrice killed, an attempt on him, now Callender beaten to death. These couldn't all be random coincidences.

"Mary?" Tanner called. "I just had a strange call from some Professor Caine up at UMD. He sent me to the Sunday Duluth paper."

"What's a Professor Caine?"

"Dunno. Anyway, Tommy Callender's dead," Tanner said.

"What!" She came into the living room, brow furrowed.

"There's not a lot of information in the article. It seems he was a victim of a barroom brawl near the docks. I don't know what to do now. Jesus, I hope we're not responsible in some way."

"Are you going back up there?"

"I don't know, Mary. What do you think?"

"I'll try to reach his mother, Sarah."

"Good idea. I'll call that cop, Teach, and see if he can open a door or two with the Duluth police."

"Well, okay." She sighed. "God, this is turning into such a mess. Maybe you're right, we should stop. Just go home and forget about the *Amador*. But I find it difficult to believe these murders are all because of some ancient cargo that might throw a little dirt on a couple of prominent families."

"Agreed," said Tanner. "Something more current has to be involved. Which is why I'm anxious to figure it out."

****

Detective Teach was surprised to learn of Callender's death. He promised to contact a department acquaintance in Duluth.

An hour later he called back. "I just got off the phone with Captain Mackay. He isn't in homicide any more but he asked around and here's what they know." Teach paused and Tanner heard paper rustling. "Callender got into some kind of argument with two bums at something called Seaman's Inn. It's just an ordinary bar, a little rougher than some, I guess. The bartender ordered them out and all three left. It appears Callender cracked his head in the fight that must have resumed outside the bar. He was killed by a blow on the head that appears to have come from the edge of a trash bin right where he was found."

"Could it have been deliberate?"

"I guess so. Somebody could have slammed his head against the trash bin hard enough to kill him. He was beaten pretty good, but nothing unusual for having been in a brawl with two other guys."

"Drunk?"

"Yes, but you know the rate the body metabolizes alcohol changes when the heart stops. Or maybe you didn't know. Anyway, the ME made some calculations and reported his blood alcohol level was high. The guy was legally intoxicated."

"Charges?"

"Yep. They located the two guys from the bar and charged them with involuntary manslaughter."

"If I fly up, could you get me into Tommy's room?"

Teach laughed. "You don't want much. What're you after?"

"Callender was chasing information about the Mayhews and

the *Amador*, just as we are. Even if that didn't get him killed, he may have found something that'll help us."

Teach sighed. "Call Mackay when you get there. I already told him you might show up."

"Thanks, Detective."

Tanner made a reservation on an early morning Northwest flight to Duluth. That night, after consuming a slightly burned quiche and an indifferent salad, Mary and Tanner sat in the living room in facing chairs.

"Mary." Tanner tried a tentative smile. "I've been thinking about our...discussion on the way home."

"You mean our squabble?"

"Well, yes, and..."

She sighed and put down her magazine. "So have I. Why do you think it happened?"

"Tension, worry, fear."

She nodded, and Tanner's heart turned over. "I agree exactly, sweetie. Ever since that asshole tried to kill you on the highway, I've been worried sick. And then after that near riot on the lake..." she was getting out of her chair.

"...and I was so flip over that wave that damn near drowned you," Tanner finished her sentence, starting to get out of his own chair. He was too late. Mary was across the space and in his arms. Tanner responded and they made it only as far as the floor on the other side of the coffee table before their passion was raised to mutual peaks. The second time, still on the living room carpet, was slower, sweeter, more fulfilling. It was after two in the morning before they finally turned out the lights and made it into bed.

The next morning after a smooth pleasant flight, Tanner was introduced to Captain Peter Mackay, a beefy cop who had been one for too many years. His office was on the second floor of the old brick fort-like building that housed the city jail and the police department. He moved with slow economy, a sour expression of distaste hanging perpetually on his face. He'd seen too much evil perpetrated by humans on one another.

Mackay rose slowly from behind his big metal desk and stuck out a hand. "I dunno why we gotta get civilians messing in this, but

Teach says you're okay. I just hope you aren't planning to stir things up and make this complicated. What we got here is a nice simple involuntary homicide. The two guys in the tank admit fighting with Callender and leaving him by the trash bin."

"I'd like to talk to the two men, if I may."

"That's up to their lawyer, public defender," muttered Mackay.

"I'd also like to see Callender's room and the stuff he's collected since he got here. I've no interest in complicating your life, Captain," Tanner said quietly.

The public defender, a young lawyer recently admitted to the Minnesota Bar, was amenable to an interview with his clients. Tanner talked with them in one of the small interview rooms in the basement of the station.

The older man, "Tom," he said his name was, "Tom Watt," was surly, truculent and still very hung over. He said very little and volunteered nothing. The other man who said his name was Amos Wellby, was voluble and forthcoming. He was willing to talk at length about almost anything, whether Tanner asked about it or not. Both men seemed to have trouble keeping their attention focused on the questions.

It was a difficult interview. Even though the men had been required to bathe and were wearing clean city-issued clothes, their sour breath was like the inexorable waves of Lake Superior, rolling continually across the table into Tanner's face. He learned little. The men were too drunk to remember much except that it was dark and hard to see. No they couldn't remember passersby or traffic on the street. It wasn't clear what the argument with Callender was about. Finally Tanner thanked the young attorney who'd been silent throughout and returned to Mackay's office.

"Bailey!" bellowed Mackay, when he saw Tanner standing there again. "Run this gentleman over to Callender's room and let him poke around. Notes he can take, even pitchures, but he don't remove nothing from the premises, got it?"

Ted Bailey proved to be a younger homicide detective, with a slightly better attitude. His grammar was also better.

"You must have some juice with City Hall if you've got

Mackay opening doors for you," he remarked, gunning the unmarked squad out of the parking lot behind Police Headquarters. It was a hot day and the air conditioner in the car refused to work.

"I know a friend of Mackay in St. Paul. The name Caine mean anything to you?" The detective thought a moment then shook his head. "He's a professor at UMD."

"Wait. You must mean Professor Jonathan Caine. Old coot. Calls us sometimes. He seems to think the moon has some influence on campus happenings. He also seems to have it in for almost everyone of any prominence in the city." Bailey laughed shortly and muttered something about higher education that Tanner didn't catch.

They pulled up in front of a rooming house that seemed from the outside to be aging rather well. The big, brick four-story box had a cracked concrete sidewalk and weathered wooden window frames, but the building looked sturdy and didn't have that about-to-collapse feeling. The ornately carved, massive door needed to be stripped to the bare wood and varnished, but it opened easily on well-oiled hinges. Looking at it more closely as they passed into the cramped lobby, Tanner supposed it would be a tedious job to clean out the cracked and crazed varnish from all the carvings, but it would be worth it. There was no elevator and Bailey led the way up the uncarpeted stairway. Intermingled cooking odors assailed their nostrils as they climbed to the second and then the third floor. There were six small apartments on each floor, Tanner counted. Lots of people to interview, perhaps. Too many, probably.

Tommy Callender had rented a small apartment at the rear of the fourth floor. There was no police seal on the door. Detective Bailey took out a key and unlocked it. It was a two-room affair with ugly, faded, flowered wallpaper on the walls, holding up what had once been a white painted ceiling. It had been many years since that ceiling felt a paint brush. The larger room had two windows that looked out on the alley and the back of the building across the way. The furniture was late-attic and looked as if it had grown tired of life. In a small curtained alcove there was a sink, a two-burner gas cooking unit and a small refrigerator that hummed and vibrated.

Opposite the kitchen alcove a door led to a small bedroom

and beyond, a bath crowded with a claw-foot tub, sink and stool. Cracked yellowing tile surrounded everything and clung precariously partway up the walls. The stool had a white porcelain tank overhead with a rusty chain ending in a loop of dirty twine that dangled over the side. It was a depressing place, not altogether the end of the line, Tanner thought, but a place he suspected Tommy Callender would have preferred to be gone from as soon as he could.

Tanner returned to the front room. The detective stood in the center of the room grimly surveying the place. "Something?"

The man shrugged. "No. I've never been here before. Depressing, isn't it? You know this Callender?"

"Only second hand."

"Yeah? We haven't reached his mother. Nobody seems to know where she's gone."

"Who identified Tommy's body?" he asked.

"He had ID and I think they got a cousin to come in. I'm not on the case, you understand."

"Is there a case?"

"Well, not really, but we like to be sure. Tie up loose ends. Especially since there's still that open inquiry from St. Paul. About the Jandrice killing? And of course, his relatives here are important people." He gestured vaguely. "You know."

Tanner nodded. He poked through papers on the table by one of the windows. There were scribbled notes and several books from the local library, histories of the county, of the city and of the Mayhews. Tanner would have liked to take the material, but knew it wouldn't be allowed. He made a note of the titles of the four books on the table. When he examined the titles he began to see a pattern. Callender had been tracing Mayhew business dealings over many decades. It appeared he was trying to build a framework into which he could fit the mysterious shipment aboard the *Amador*. Tanner made a few more notes, some names, a date or two. It was discouraging, the lack of coherent information.

"Okay, Mr. Bailey. I guess I've seen everything for now. What happens to all this stuff?"

"His mother gets it when the court is through with the case."

"I'm not trying to tell you your business, but I hope someone is looking for a possible connection between the two men Callender fought with and the Mayhews."

Bailey looked sideways at Tanner, locked the apartment door and headed down the hall to the stairs.

"Another thing. Has anyone asked the medical examiner if it was possible someone came along, found Tommy Callender senseless on the ground and slammed his head into that trash bin?"

Bailey stopped on the stairs and looked around. "Mackay said you were gonna be a pain in the ass. Are you suggesting that someone deliberately murdered the guy after our two bums knocked him down?"

"Isn't it a possibility?"

"Anything's possible, Mr. Tanner. Anything's possible." They started down the steps again.

Even after the close atmosphere of the rooming house, the sun was a physical weight, pushing down on their shoulders, slowing the men's movements. Heat from the cracked sidewalk penetrated Tanner's shoes. He saw a line of sweat break out on Bailey's forehead and he felt trickles of perspiration starting to run down his sides.

The squad car was stifling and the men stood on the sidewalk with the windows open for a few minutes. Then they drove off, turning at the end of the first block to take the most direct route back to the station. As they turned the corner, Tanner heard nearby the wracking cough of a big diesel engine winding up. It startled him into immobility, his mind rushing back to the similar sound of an idling diesel engine after he'd struggled to the crest of the grassy hill outside Cornucopia. There must have been an odd expression on his face, because Bailey was looking at Tanner instead of the road. "You okay? You look pale. Heat gettin' to you?"

Tanner shook his head to dislodge his ghosts. "So, Detective Bailey, how do you like living in Duluth?"

CHAPTER 29

Tanner and Detective Ted Bailey parted company at the police station and Tanner took his rental car to a nearby restaurant for coffee and reflection. The coffee was hot and fresh-brewed. It chased away his lingering depression after seeing Callender's last known residence. After two cups, Tanner took out a quarter and went to the public phone in a corner of the restaurant.

"Mayhew residence."

Tanner identified himself and asked for an opportunity to meet with J. J. Mayhew. After a few minutes of being bounced around among servants and two family members, it was agreed that he could see the old man for a short time if he could get there within the hour. Tanner was surprised. His call had been pure impulse. Why had Mayhew agreed to see a stranger? Or maybe he wasn't unknown. Did they have some reports on his inquiries? Was he upsetting some unknown apple cart?

This time the gate was open and Tanner drove up the graveled drive, stopped by the front door. He was met by a small blonde woman with very fine very long hair. It was gathered at the top, then flowed like a river of honey down her very straight back. The device she wore at the back of her head allowed shorter strands of hair to hover like a misty cloud about her face. Her name, she said, was Carole Ann Myer. J.J. Mayhew was her grandfather. She smiled gently when she said it and Tanner received a message of love and concern for the old pirate. She showed Tanner to a small sitting room off the main entryway. The Mayhew mansion was large. He tried to estimate the number of rooms behind the imposing and ornate brick walls and gave up. In a cool central foyer, a large terrazzo floor in gray and white anchored the long curved stairway leading to a second-floor balcony which joined two wings of the house. The walls of the foyer and the balcony were white and hung with carefully placed, well-framed oil paintings that were certainly originals. The paintings were all landscapes.

The sitting room was close and warm, though not uncomfortably so. It might not be used very much, Tanner considered, following the woman's gesture and sitting on a hard chair. The afternoon Duluth sunlight reflected off the tiled walk outside the south-facing windows and lighted the room with a sterile fire.

"We decided to let you see my grandfather because we now know what you are. Naturally, we think your quest for the mythical silver aboard *Amador* is a waste of time. But we do understand that you are not some tabloid reporter or fortune hunter." She sighed with well-disguised impatience. "Perhaps if you talk with grandfather, you'll understand the futility of your search." Carole Ann's voice was cool, detached. She paused a moment, looked down and then said. "We hope by letting you in, some of the stories...some of the lies...may finally go away. I suppose that's a forlorn hope. But, we've tried everything else."

"Miss Myer, I'm not sure you and your family do understand. I'm not seeking the mythical silver cargo as you characterize it, except in a very peripheral way. This is the first time I've heard the cargo specifically referred to as silver, by the way. I'm here for entirely different reasons.

"Some weeks ago, a cataloguer for the Minnesota Historical Society lost her life. At the time of her death she was beginning to catalogue papers donated by the deVole family and corporation from Chicago." Tanner stopped, watching. The woman had flinched, just slightly when he mentioned Ethel Jandrice.

"I see you are aware of the circumstances of Ms. Jandrice's death."

"We do read the newspapers, Mr. Tanner, and the deVole name is a familiar one. If you will wait here, I'll fetch my grandfather." The way she said grandfather, the word should have been capitalized, Tanner thought, watching her leave the room.

Once again, Tanner mused, I wait, in a room inside the mansion of another lead character in this drama, in another city. This time there were no books to examine. Except for the windows and thin curtains, the walls were bare. The door opened again and Carole Ann wheeled in the legendary J.J. Mayhew. Tanner stood up immediately but the woman waved him down and pushed the wheelchair up to the chair so the two men faced each other at eye level. Mayhew's granddaughter spoke over his thick thatch of white hair.

"You may find that he drifts in and out. Sometimes we aren't sure just how much he understands. At other times, he'll carry on a lengthy conversation. He's had at least two strokes and he's partially aphasic."

Tanner nodded, keeping his eyes on the lined face of the old man. He made no effort to raise a hand from his lap robe, and Tanner wasn't sure if the old man knew he was there. J.J. Mayhew was gaunt, he appeared emaciated. The wheelchair seemed too small for his length. The man's knees, in loose summer-weight tan slacks, rose almost as high as his chin. Long, tapering fingers with clean, neatly trimmed nails lay quiet. Except for his thick brushy eyebrows, which were coal black, Tanner saw a pale, monochromatic gray man. But Mayhew held his head erect and when Tanner looked into those deep-set eyes, they gleamed with alertness and curiosity.

"My grandfather rarely speaks, Mr. Tanner. We use a system of signals. He taps once for yes, twice for no and when he refuses to answer or ignores us, as is common, he'll just sit silently or he'll look away."

Tanner nodded. The woman withdrew to a chair across the room. "Mr. Mayhew, I appreciate your willingness to see me..."

The old man raised one finger as if to say, "Get on with it."

"I want to ask you about a ship called the *Amador*."

Tanner told his tale of a ship lost in the lake and of recent murder without wasting words. He could see the old man was closely following, but at the same time was puzzled. Tanner began to understand that Mayhew had some of the same questions he had; why had Ethel Jandrice been murdered and why was the brass inspection plate stolen from the Park Service? Tanner also came to understand that though the questions were similar, their motivations were different. The man in the wheelchair appeared interested in the dead woman only as her death might provide answers. His concern was focused on his family. Was his great grandson Tommy murdered? Where was his granddaughter, Sarah, and what did all this have to do with Mayhew Enterprises?

The loss of the brass plate and what Tanner had learned in Tommy Callender's apartment was of interest. The old pirate was assessing the new information in the light of what he already knew. Tanner began to wonder if this visit had been a mistake, if he wasn't giving more than he was getting. He began to have an uncanny feeling the old man could read his thoughts.

He changed direction. "Mr. Mayhew, I want to ask you about your greatgrandson, Tommy Callender." Mayhew raised one bony hand. The sleeve of his white dress shirt slid down his arm, revealing a knobby wrist covered with mottled, dry skin. Tanner noticed a dark band just above the wrist that looked like a circle of bruises. Had he been in restraints?

In a sudden burst of energy Mayhew spun his wheelchair around and spoke for the first time in Tanner's hearing. "Carole Ann!" Startled, she rose with alacrity and stepped toward him. "Leave us!" The command, in a whispery, sand-filled voice was nevertheless as commanding as a bellow.

"But granddad..."

"Now, please."

It was apparent that even as infirm as the man appeared to be, J.J. Mayhew commanded instant obedience from those around him. Back straight, shoulders squared, Carole Ann Myer marched out of the room, her fine hair bouncing about her head and shoulders. Mayhew watched her go. When the door latch clicked shut, he spun his chair back and said in the same harsh tone, "You are here under false pretenses. My great grandson has nothing to do with the *Amador*, whatever may be the truth of that matter."

Tanner stared back. He could feel the immense power that seemed to emanate from the man. What, if anything, had he to do with the dark events of the past weeks?

"I am sorry to disagree, but everything we've talked about thus far is connected in some way. Remember, there has been at least one murder, and an attempted murder, since the story of the

Amador entered my life."

The two eyed each other. Tanner expected to be thrown out at any moment, but then Mayhew apparently changed his mind. He knew, he said, of his great grandson's death, hadn't seen his granddaughter Sarah in several weeks and refused to say whether he knew where she was. He vigorously denied knowing anything about the death of Ethel Jandrice or what Tommy had been doing in Duluth. So far as he was aware, he told Tanner, he didn't think Tommy had tried to see him or had even come to the house. He denied any previous knowledge of Tanner's accident on the highway outside of Cornucopia.

"You think Tommy was murdered, don't you." It was not a question.

"I think it's a distinct possibility," Tanner replied. "When my wife, Mary Whitney, talked with his mother, she said Tommy had never expressed much interest in the family until—"

"You people have talked with Sarah?" Mayhew interrupted.

Tanner nodded. "I think Tommy felt ill-used and thought his mother was unfairly treated by the family. His mother seemed more mellow."

Mayhew snorted and indicated Tanner should continue.

"Tommy showed up at his mother's, claiming he had a way to force the family to treat her better, to pay him large sums of money. It had to do with a letter he somehow turned up about a cargo on the *Amador*. He—" Of course! Why hadn't he seen it sooner? Tommy Callender must have gotten information about the *Amador* from Ethel Jandrice. She found something among the deVole Corporation papers. That's where the letter Tommy showed his mother had come from. Whoever killed her must have been looking for the letter, which wasn't found among Jandrice's things.

When Tanner again focused on the old man in the wheelchair, only seconds had gone by, but electricity seemed to crackle in the room and he again felt the force of the old man's intellect.

"Mr. Tanner." Mayhew's tone was harsher still. "Have you talked to Tommy's mother in the past few days? Do you know where she is now?" His voice carried an urgency Tanner hadn't heard before. Tanner shook his head and watched an astonishing change come over the old man.

His eyes began to fade, as if a light behind them was dimming. His hands started to flutter randomly. Mayhew's spine curled forward until his head almost touched his upraised knees. He straightened a little, then slumped to the right, head lolling. Drool began to run from the corner of his mouth. A low, keening sound filled the room, coming, Tanner realized, from J.J. Mayhew himself. Was he having a stroke?

The door was flung open and a short, stocky woman with auburn hair stalked into the room. She had apparently just arrived at the mansion. She tore a hat from her head which did little to disturb her layered razor cut. Carole Ann was with her.

"What's going on here? Who is this man and why is he talking to father?"

"The younger woman flinched at the harsh tone. "Aunt Mary, we couldn't find you and everyone here agreed it would be better to have Mr. Tanner in to see granddad now." Tanner tracked the older woman with his eyes, mentally reviewing his notes on the family. This obviously was Mayhew's daughter.

"Tanner? Michael Tanner?"

Tanner rose and took a chance. "Mrs. Watt?" The woman snapped her head up and fixed him with an angry glare. He'd guessed right. Mary Watt, Sarah Callender's older sister.

The keening sound became louder, making continued discourse impossible. Mary Watt made an imperious gesture. "Take father away, Carole Ann. Mr. Tanner, I'll have to ask you to leave. Now." Mrs. Watt pointed toward the wheelchair disappearing down the marble floored hall. "He was doing so well and now you've upset him. This is exactly what I was afraid of." She turned on one expensive heel and stalked rapidly toward the front door, almost physically dragging Tanner along in her wake. Their goodbyes were perfunctory and Tanner found himself alone on the sun-blasted front portico of the Mayhew mansion.

CHAPTER 30

A sudden harsh yowl gave him a start. A police car, lights flashing, pulled alongside. The patrolman pointed Tanner to the curb.

"Sorry officer," he said when the man approached his window. "I guess I was thinking too hard about other things."

The officer nodded. "Mr. Tanner? You're wanted at headquarters; Captain Mackay wants to talk with you immediately."

"How did you find me?"

"Avis gave us the license and description," said the patrolman, heading back for the air conditioned comfort of his patrol car. Tanner checked his watch, turned left at the next intersection and drove to the police station.

In Mackay's office, he found a sour, irritable police captain on the telephone. Mackay waved him to a seat.

"All right, Detective Teach, he's here now. Thanks for the update. Well, Mr. Tanner," he growled, hanging up the phone, "there's been a new development. Have you mentioned to anyone, anyone at all, since you've been here today, anything about the Callender investigation or anything you saw at his apartment?"

Tanner frowned and thought. "No sir, with the exception of you and that detective, Bailey? Hardly anyone even knows I'm here. There's been no reason to and I haven't talked with anyone except police and those at the Mayhew mansion. My conversation with J.J. Mayhew only touched on Tommy's death as a fact. I certainly didn't reveal that I'd been to his apartment. Why?"

Mackay stared at Tanner for a moment. "You must have some kinda clout, getting in to see old man Mayhew just like that." Mackay snapped his fingers and blew out his breath. "After you and Bailey left Callender's apartment building, someone broke in and went through it. Whoever it was, was careful, thorough and quiet. What do you suppose they were looking for? Nobody in the building admits to hearing anything and it's the wrong part of town for professional burglars. It's barely possible somebody was after a quick score for drug money." He poked a finger in his ear. "It's also possible they were looking for something connected to you or the Mayhews. We're pretty sure from the way the apartment was trashed they tried to conceal their true purpose." Mackay stabbed a meaty finger at Tanner's chest from across his cluttered desk. "What was a simple case of assault has turned into something complicated and I don't like it."

"Something connected with my research into his family," Tanner mused. "It could indicate that Tommy was murdered."

"Now the D.A. may have to take the case to a grand jury. Damn, this started out plain and simple."

"Captain Mackay, I appreciate your telling me about the break-in and being so cooperative. I'll return the favor when we turn up something that might help your investigation."

Tanner left the sour-faced Mackay slouched at his desk and went on his way. In the lobby, he found a phone booth and called Professor Caine, the man who had pointed him to the article about Tommy Callender's death. There was no answer so Tanner drove to the airport.

****

When he entered their apartment, Mary was at the dining room table, a table littered with books, pamphlets and scraps of paper. When she rose to greet him, there was a satisfied smile on her face.

"Well, traveler, welcome home." He was across the room in two strides and swept her into a close embrace. "Mmm. Missed you too. How'd things go?" Mary murmured in his ear.

"It was not a landmark trip, although I did get a brief interview with John Jeffry Mayhew."

"Old 'Black Jack' himself?" She leaned back to look Tanner in the face.

"None other. My, you smell good. He still has those bristly black eyebrows that apparently gave him the moniker." Tanner set down his briefcase and looked at the table. "What's all this?"

"I have been busy, doing more research and organizing our information. And running up long distance phone bills to Utah."

"Utah? Who do we know in Utah?"

"Salt Lake City, to be specific." She smiled. "Did you know the Mormons have a huge genealogy repository in Salt Lake City?"

Tanner frowned. "No, I don't believe I did. Have you suddenly become interested in tracing your murky ancestry? Be careful, you may discover someone or something that's disagreeable. I recall my dad used to do a little ancestor research until he discovered some very questionable types in the family closet." Tanner laughed. "That called a sudden halt to the whole project."

"Not my family, a certain prominent Duluth family."

"Mayhew? Great! We could diagram them just like the police task forces on TV do for the organized crime families." Tanner grinned.

"And the Chicago deVoles. I decided we need a little more background in this investigation. I also set up a series of files on the laptop for the people we've already interviewed."

"Excellent idea," Tanner responded. "Chronology too?"

"Yep. But here, look at this chart of the Mayhew family. I just finished it. I'll make us a couple of drinks. G&T or do you want rum instead?"

"Umm," he responded, already absorbed by six generations of Mayhews spread out and carefully interconnected with Mary's neat black lines. Under her prodding Tanner looked up and smiled, "Gin, I think. Helga Po-what? That's a real tongue-twister."

"The carry-over of names to later generations is interesting. There are some first or second name commonalities between the two families as well," Mary said, bringing in two tall Collins glasses. She placed the drink near Tanner's hand where he sat on the new couch. Mary joined him.

"You found a Jeffry deVole and we have John Jeffry Mayhew, known in some circles as 'Black Jack'. Odd, isn't it?" Tanner murmured.

"Between us, we've met several of the living Mayhews listed on my chart. There are some gaps and some dates we'll have to fill in."

Tanner smiled at her. "Maybe you can sell the chart to the family when this is all over. Wait a minute," he exclaimed. The sheet filled with names of the deVole clan slid to the floor, unnoticed. "I met this woman, Mary Watt, at the mansion. I assume she's related to Robert Watt, the exec I met at the Mayhew offices, probably his mother. She practically threw me out. I see here she has three kids, one named Anthony."

"Clever of you to notice," quipped Mary.

"Especially because just this morning I was talking with a man in jail named Tony Watt."

"Same man?"

"I don't know. The Watt I talked with is one step from being classed as a derelict and a chronic drunk. If Mary Watt is his mother, she must be upset about him. He's being held in connection with the death of Tommy Callender, who, as we now see, might be a nephew."

"Quite a stretch, isn't it?" Mary responded.

"Or, an indication of greater family involvement? We'll have to follow up on that, and I better inform Captain Mackay, if he doesn't know already."

Mary said, "I think we should find out what all these people do. The deVoles as well."

Tanner nodded assent and found the deVole chart on the floor. He studied it while Mary took a healthy swig of her gin and tonic.

"The whole thing is still murky," she remarked. "I find it hard to believe these two powerful and prominent families could be so concerned about what's probably a nonexistent crate of who knows what, that sank in Lake Superior a hundred years ago."

"I know. I feel the same way, except for this persistent feeling that there was a cargo and more importantly that there's some kind of document floating around that could create problems for somebody. Or perhaps somebody just thinks the document is troublesome. I'm beginning to believe the document is more important than the missing cargo. Well, what about dinner?"

Mary smiled. "How 'bout I thaw something from the freezer?

First I'll whip up a snack while you rest your bones." She went to the kitchen and moved a package of frozen prawns from the freezer to the microwave. "Another drink?" Tanner shook his head.

There was a sudden loud bang from the kitchen. They jumped and ran to the other room. "What a mess!" Mary exclaimed. The frozen prawns had exploded in the microwave, spraying food scraps and plastic all over the inside of the oven. When Mary pulled the door open, pieces of prawn and plastic fell to the kitchen counter.

Mary managed a rueful smile. "I guess I forgot set the power lower and vent the package before I thawed it."

"How many times has this happened?" Tanner laughed, handing her a wad of paper towels.

"Too many," she said. "What say we forget the whole thing and go out for dinner?"

"Great. I'll shower and you make a reservation." Tanner turned, still laughing, and left the kitchen. "Nothing too elegant, though. I don't feel like dressing up tonight."

Later at dinner the conversation returned to the deVoles and the Mayhews.

"I think the key is with the deVoles. Maybe we ought to go to Chicago for a few days, do a little local research," Mary suggested.

Tanner smiled, reaching across the table and touched his partner's slim hand where it rested on the tablecloth. "I'm amazed yet again. How do you do that—anticipate me so often? I was just thinking the same thing."

Tanner scanned the surrounding area as they exited the restaurant. On the return trip to the apartment he checked the rear view mirror and once made a deliberate wrong turn. Mary glanced his way but said nothing.

The following morning while they packed, the telephone buzzed.

"Detective Teach," Tanner said, "anything new?"

Edward Teach sighed through the connection. "What am I gonna do about you? Ever since you showed up in town, you seem to be upsetting my contacts and my friends. You're building some kind of reputation."

"You've been talking to Mackay in Duluth?"

Teach's dry chuckle whispered over the line. "He knows you aren't directly responsible, but he figures that if you hadn't gone poking around, whoever burgled Callender's apartment might not have bothered. Can't you poke around without making such a fuss?"

Tanner laughed. "We have a hundred-year-old mysterious cargo possibly carried on a sunken freighter that can't be located, a dead woman in St. Paul, a dead man and a missing woman in Duluth and two prominent families, one in Minnesota, the other in Chicago. Sounds like a tabloid scandal to me."

"Why don't you push a few Chicago buttons?" Teach suggested.

"You mean get out of Minnesota?"

A chuckle. "Yeah, preferably before sunset."

Tanner smiled and said, "You'll be happy to know Mary and I are flying to Chicago tomorrow morning. I don't expect any problems, but I'd like you to know where we are, so while we're there, I'll call your office, say every twenty-four hours. Have you any contacts among authorities down there?"

"Every twenty-four hours, huh? Sounds serious. Are you positive you aren't following some lead I oughta know about? Sure, I got contacts in Chicago."

"Just being careful, Detective. I still flinch when a big semi rolls up behind me on the freeway."

"Yeah," said the detective. "I can relate to that."

CHAPTER 31

The Boeing 737 bucked and bounced through the uncertain air above Des Plaines. The aircraft was making a straight-in approach to O'Hare field, northwest of Chicago, and as their descent began, the weather closed in until the wing tips were only occasionally visible. Tanner looked over at Mary, gazing pensively out the small oval window. Tanner hoped the air controllers were up to full complement and alert. Mary reached over and took his hand, applying gentle pressure. Tanner returned it. The plane bucked and dropped.

"You okay, honey?" he murmured.

"Sure," she smiled back. "It's just this airport is so busy and I'd rather sail in a fog than fly in it. Plus my left ear isn't clearing."

Tanner nodded. With a crunch of compressing metal, the airplane settled heavily onto the concrete runway and began its runout. It wasn't raining at the moment, but the ground was wet and heavy mist bloomed around the lights marking taxiways. They were received promptly at the assigned gate and restless passengers immediately clogged the aisles, struggling to remove carry-on luggage from overhead. Mary and Tanner waited patiently until most of the other passengers had begun to stream out into the terminal. Mary had decided that a car would be more nuisance than useful and opted for a limo that took them on the twenty-mile ride to the near north side of Chicago's loop, where they checked into the Bismarck Hotel. Clouds, occasional showers and damp fog continued to hang over the city, obscuring the upper floors of taller buildings.

"How 'bout Greek for supper?" Tanner suggested as they unpacked.

"I beg your pardon?"

"Greek, Greek. You know, head cheese, boiled goat, ouzo, circle dancing, plates breaking."

"Sounds delicious."

"I'll see if the Parthenon is still open."

Later, after a delicious dinner of broiled lamb, a crisp green salad with kalamata olives and that special white cheese, even the happy throngs ceaselessly passing by on the street outside could not tempt them away from a prompt return to their hotel. In the lobby, Mary speculatively eyed the dark intimate bar of the hotel, so Tanner left her and went upstairs. He fell asleep almost before he made it between the sheets and he didn't hear Mary return three hours later.

In the morning the sun filtered through the curtains when a slightly red-eyed Mary joined Tanner at the breakfast table in the hotel dining room.

"Nightowling seems to agree with you. There's hardly any blood at all in your cheeks."

"Hunh," she muttered, downing a tall glass of fresh orange juice in a long draught. "It was worth it. Met an old geezer in the bar. According to the bartender, he's a fixture there and something of an amateur historian."

Tanner's mouth was full of succulent eggs and ham so he only raised a questioning eyebrow.

"He told me some interesting things, which if true, could point us to some answers."

"Yes? And this veritable fountain of information about the deVoles just happened to be waiting for you at the bar last night? The bar in our hotel?"

"Not at all. Don't be so suspicious. We talked about a lot of things before the deVole name came up and then I raised it, not Meyers."

"His name is Meyers?"

"Yep. Chet Meyers. Nice guy."

"So, Mata Hari, while he was plying you with drinks and hitting on you every few minutes, what did you find out?"

"Actually, we plied each other with drinks. And there was no hitting. It came out even, I think, and was mostly white wine and coffee later"

"Ah, coffee later," Tanner responded.

"As for hitting, the gentleman is probably eighty years old. I think he was just looking for conversation."

She took a big swig of hot coffee and smiled benignly at her companion. His jibes hadn't touched her in the least. "Did you know there are deVoles involved in the history of this town from 'way back?"

"Some. We know the old man, Theodore, was here before the Civil War and had some property and business along the South Branch of the Chicago River.

"That's right," Mary confirmed. "And he was instrumental in forming something called the South Branch Merchant's Society."

"What's that?

"Some kind of neighborhood mutual support club. Exclusive and apparently very protectionist."

"Ah."

"Yes, ah. He had help at the beginning from his great and close friend, Elgar Mayhew."

"Uh huh," Tanner said, "and so those two established themselves here in the mid 1800's. Do you seriously think the answers are in the ancient history of this family?"

"I can't say for sure, but the deVole histories may give us some clues. I think I will go off to the Chicago Historical Society and do a little research."

"You have the address?"

"Yes, LaSalle and North Avenue. I'll get a cab."

"Okay. I'll come with you as far as the Hancock building. I have an appointment with an attorney named John Taylor. It's a name I got from Harry deVole."

A short time later Tanner stood on busy Michigan Avenue before the John Hancock tower, watching Mary's cab disappear north up the street. Behind him, the crenellated shape of the old Chicago Water Tower stood out starkly against the blue sky.

After meeting with the attorney, Tanner had a solitary lunch in a little deli just off Rush Street. Next door in a small dark bar, he spent a few minutes in a telephone booth and then nursed a mug of dark beer while he waited.

The man who finally slid into the booth across from him was

taller, heavier and looked a few years younger than Tanner. His
sparse sandy hair was brushed back from a high, shiny forehead. His
pale amber eyes were watchful. He said nothing until he had taken
a long swallow of the frosty mug of beer a waiter delivered to his
elbow.

"You're Tanner, correct?"

Tanner nodded. He could play the silent game when
necessary.

"I understand you want a few hours work running down
some information about members of one of our prominent families,
the deVoles? I also take it you don't want to do it yourself, even
though most of my sources are going to be public records. Unless
you want some serious digging, which will take a lot more time."

"No, Mr. Fellowes. Your occasional employer, John Taylor,
tells me you're thorough and fast and reliable. I don't want word
filtering back to the deVoles or anybody else that I'm looking into
their family. You can restrict your inquiries to the ten people on this
list." He slid a small piece of paper across the table. "They represent
the present and immediate past generations of the family. I want
employment, key associates, police records, although I doubt you'll
find much of that. I figure forty-eight hours should give you enough
time to do a general search. If you find something startling that you
think I should know, call me at this hotel." Tanner added a business
card with the name of the hotel scribbled on it.

"Just what do you mean by 'startling'?"

"Frankly, I have no idea. Maybe you better call me with a
preliminary report tomorrow about this time and I can decide then
if you've turned up something that requires a follow-up."

"Good enough. Taylor explained my rates?"

"Yes, your daily rate plus expenses. I want a copy of
anything you think I ought to see."

Fellowes finished his beer, wiped the foam off his upper lip
and rose from his seat. "You want to watch your back, Mr. Tanner.
These people come out of the Gold Coast, Astor Street. Before
that—" he shrugged.

"Before that," Tanner finished, "something called the South
Branch Merchants Society." He watched Fellowes carefully but he

saw no reaction.

Later Tanner met Mary at the Chalet, a midtown restaurant and watering hole, and reviewed the day's accomplishments. Through the big windows they watched Chicagoans hurrying past in the shimmering heat waves steaming off the pavement in the heavy humidity.

"I trust you were circumspect in your inquiries," Tanner said.

"Oh, you bet. As a result, I wasted some time. The people at the Historical Society were helpful and showed me all the materials they have on the deVoles. But speaking of circumspect, that's the way I'd describe some of the material I looked at. Maybe not laundered, exactly, but close. I got the sense that there is another story, between the lines, as it were, or certain events were deliberately left out."

Tanner nodded. He knew Mary's instincts about such things were usually accurate. "I know what you mean. I've had the same feeling sometimes when I've been looking at a potential client. It's not that somebody has lied or distorted things exactly, they just slid by some information better left unsaid."

"I couldn't find any mention of the South Branch Merchants Society, for example, yet Mr. Meyers was very explicit."

"Well, maybe he got the name wrong or perhaps it didn't involve the deVoles at all."

"No, no. Not only doesn't the name appear in any of the deVole references, it doesn't appear in the Historical Society index files at all."

"Really? I casually mentioned the name to the private investigator I hired, Fellowes? He didn't bat an eye."

"That either means he never heard of it or he knew exactly what you were talking about."

"I'll ask him tomorrow when he calls. For tonight, I made reservations at Gambino's for lasagna and/or spaghetti."

****

They finished dinner and Tanner leaned, laughing, away from the colorful table that was littered with the remains of their meal. In the background they could hear the gabble of several languages. A pert Chinese waitress hurried across the room, slim hips switching from side to side as she avoided tables, chairs and late diners. She carried a steaming coffee server and refilled the heavy white pottery mugs.

"Super supper," Mary smirked at Tanner. "I'm gonna have to double my running for the next several weeks to work it off. That sauce was marvelous."

"Of course," Tanner responded, "you could have just opted for the salad."

"Where'd you get the name? I couldn't find it in my guidebook."

"The lawyer I saw this morning."

"That's right, John Taylor, isn't it?"

Tanner nodded. "He also gave me Matt Fellowes name, the private investigator I talked to? Happens the man, has some acquaintances in the deVole family."

"Is that a good idea?"

"Taylor assured me the man is reliable and his previous knowledge will save us time and money. Investigators don't come cheap, you know."

Mary smiled. "I know. This whole business is getting both expensive and complicated, isn't it?"

"Yeah, but we're in it for the long haul now. I really want some answers."

Mary yawned, "I'm bushed. Let's go back to the hotel. Hopefully your Mr. Fellowes will have lots of answers tomorrow."

"Right. That hotel bed sounds pretty attractive, right now."

When they returned to the hotel, Matt Fellowes was waiting in the lobby. "I've turned up something I think you'll want to hear—and see, but you'll have to come with me right now."

Tanner looked at Mary and then shrugged an affirmative.

Mary stared at Fellowes. "Excuse me?" she said.

"I just want to take—"

"I don't think this is such a great idea, but I'm coming with you."

Fellowes started a protest but swallowed it when he looked

at Mary's face.

"Just hang on a second while I give the desk a note," she said, turning away.

They got into Fellowes's big Ford Crown Victoria. He drove west into the blue-collar neighborhood across the Dan Ryan Expressway.

Down a dark street with few streetlights, he pulled to the curb in front of a small unassuming bungalow and said, "We're picking up an old friend of mine here. I'd like you two to get in the back seat and just watch and listen. Otherwise, the guy may get angry and leave. okay?"

"This is very strange, Michael," murmured Mary watching Fellowes stand at the door. "DeVole could be setting us up."

"I really doubt it. I think we go along for now."

The man who answered the door was short and heavy. His face was shadowed under the overhead porch light. His legs looked bowed as he and Fellowes came slowly down the steps. Fellowes called him Stan and he sat in the front seat. Fellowes drove off. He didn't introduce Stan and Stan ignored the back seat.

Miles away on a dirty, trash-littered block of South Wabash, Fellowes eased the car to the curb and killed the lights. He left the motor running. The occupants of the car looked at an empty lot across the street.

Matt Fellowes opened his window a few inches to let the stinking odor of the cigar stuck in Stan's teeth dissipate into the summer night.

"There it is, Stan. The former home of the South Branch Merchants Society."

Tanner felt Mary's fingers tense and tattoo his palm.

Fellowes nodded. "Just an empty lot now, but those old walls on either side could tell some stories, I bet."

The other man grunted and worked the wet cigar stub carefully to the other side of his thin, pale lips. In the wan glow of a dirty street light, Tanner could see moisture on his chin. The cigar smelled at least two days old and when Stan exhaled, his sour stomach combined with the tobacco in an almost lethal mix of foul odors. He peered across Fellowes's big shoulder and shook his head.

"He grunted. "Where isis? Isis Wabash? Oh yeah. That's where Big Jim's used to be, right?"

"Right, Big Jim Omerra's. Look, Stan. Like I said, we're not trying to stir up anything. Our families are too close. But I know your aunt married Georgie deVole and once I heard his dad, "Big Tony," was the one who shut down the society, or maybe turned it over to Omerra. Isn't that right?"

The older man wheezed and blinked. "I ain't sayin' it was or it wasn't. That all happened 'fore I came along. But I'll tell ya this. I recollect th' same thing. I heard me ma and one of my aunts yellin' about it once after somebody got kilt. But geez, Teddy, that was all over a long time ago. Why you pickin' at it now?"

"Man payin' me to find out some things, Stan."

"Things 'bout the deVoles?"

"That's right. Most of it about the present folks , but just at the end, man says to me, What's the South Branch Chicago Merchant's Society?"

"You tell 'im?"

"Not exactly, Stan, not yet. Maybe never."

The old man shrugged and muttered under his breath something Tanner didn't catch. Then he passed a hand over his face and said, "I'm tired, Teddy, take me home, willya?"

Fellowes drove back through the edge of the loop and at a brightly lit intersection, Mary and Tanner got out saying, "Thanks, guys. We'll catch a cab from here."

"What do you think about that?" Mary asked. They were back in the hotel room getting ready for bed. At least Mary was. Tanner was watching Mary.

"Hmm? What I think is we may have touched a sensitive spot here, the connection between the Merchant's Society and deVole."

"An organized connection, don't you mean?"

"Yeah, possibly an organized connection."

CHAPTER 32

The call came at eleven the next morning. "Mr. Tanner? This is Matt Fellowes. I've completed some research on your list of people. I think we should go over it now. Then you can decide if you want me to continue."

"Fine, Mr. Fellowes. Tell me when you'll arrive. I'll arrange for some food to be brought in so we can have lunch in private and talk at the same time."

"I can be there in about an hour and a half, if that's satisfactory."

Room service and the investigator arrived at almost the same moment. The trio sat at a small table beside the window. Through the window they had a nice view of a portion of the junction of the South and North Branches of the Chicago River, water gleaming in hot noon sunlight. Lunch was cracked crab cocktail and a crisp green salad. They shared a magnum of dry white wine.

"Well, Mr. Fellowes, what have you learned?" Tanner poured more of the pale yellow wine into Mary's glass.

"All of the ten people you asked about are direct descendants of George deVole. He was the third son of Anthony deVole."

"Big Tony," interjected Mary.

Fellowes glanced at her. He was speaking without notes. "Right. I assume you know there were a bunch of other descendants from George's brother and sister and from his cousins."

"Yes," Tanner said, "but for the time being we're going to ignore them. My theory is that because George's son Theodore—"

"Little Tony," again interjected Mary quietly. This time both men looked at her. She shrugged and smiled slightly. "I've been doing some research too, remember?" Fellowes frowned and nodded.

"I see. Well, George married a woman named Shannon Matloch in 1917 and they had three children, Elissa was the oldest. She married James Miller in 1936 and they moved to Minnesota, specifically, Minneapolis.

Tanner nodded.

Fellowes continued. "Harry deVole, George's oldest son was born in 1918. He married Susan Peters and they had two children, Robert, born in thirty-four and a girl, Elaine, born in thirty-two. Robert is married and is an attorney here in Chicago. In fact, he's—"

"Running for office this year," said Mary. She rummaged on the bed and found the section of the *Chicago Tribune* she was looking for. She held it up for the others to see. DeVole's name was in the headline of a story about candidates moving to the forefront in various Illinois political campaigns.

Fellowes grinned at Mary. "Right. His sister is his campaign manager."

"Really?"

"Right. Elaine. I've never met her but I understand she's some piece of work. Active in politics since her student days. She's married to a Jerry Kald who does something in transportation.

"Anyway, their father, Harry, was in the family businesses for a long time. He's an attorney, Harvard Law School. He's retired now and lives in Champaign."

"That's right," Tanner said. "I met him too. He's the one who gave the corporate papers to the Minnesota Historical Society."

For a moment there was silence. Matt Fellowes sipped from his water glass, ignoring the wine. Then he reached into his brief case and extracted a large brown envelope. From the envelope he took several pages of typing which he shuffled through. He looked at Mary and Tanner.

"George and Shannon had two other children. First there was Anthony. He was born in 1919 and died of measles a year or so later. Then there's another Ted-Theodore, or "Little Tony" as you called him a moment ago. He married Leslie Thomas in 1942 and they have two kids. One is Melvin. He's a Teamster and works for the family trucking business as a driver. He has a brother, James deVole. James holds an upper management position in the company here in Chicago. That's about it." He took another sip of water.

"You have a written report for me?" Tanner asked.

"Yes. Here it is," responded Fellowes, handing over the sheaf of papers with the envelope. "My bill is in the small envelope."

Tanner opened the small envelope and glanced at the paper, nodding. "Will a check be all right?"

"Certainly. I know where to find you if it bounces." Fellowes smiled and winked to take the slight sting out of the words. Tanner turned and wrote a check at the table by his elbow. He tore it out and handed it across, saying, "Anything to add about the South Branch Merchants Society?"

Fellowes sighed. "That society died a long time ago."

"I'm not surprised to hear it. What you don't know is that most of what we're interested in happened a long time ago, around the turn of the century."

Fellowes nodded again. "Well, I talked to Stan some more and made some additional inquiries. There was some kind of loose group of merchants who banded together to offer each other private protection against certain kinds of encroachments. They hired private security people. They tried to keep the unions out, and the Bolsheviks, they claimed. Pullman was probably involved, McCormack, possibly. Others. It was all carefully and informally handled. Nobody has ever located any records, just a lot of suppositions based on speculations."

"What about deVole?"

Fellowes shrugged. "That name keeps cropping up. Many stories start with the deVole brothers, led by 'Big Tony,' who was a founding member and who controlled the society for many years."

"What about the name Mayhew? Any talk about a Mayhew having anything to do with the association?"

Fellowes frowned and thought for a moment. "Mayhew? No, I don't think so, and I didn't find the name in any documents."

"What happened? Many organizations like that, in other cities, evolved into legitimate civic organizations," said Mary.

"That's right. But here in Chicago, there were other forces at work. In the late 1880's we had the Haymarket riot and some other really bad labor fights. Some say that's when the society started.

"The Everleigh Club opened in 1900 and that's one of the places the society probably met, in their private meeting rooms. It wasn't a very big group, after all, just a few powerful men who controlled a lot of Chicago's wealth. Later they moved to those rooms on South Wabash where we were the other night, a club called Omerra's." Fellowes sighed and continued the history lesson.

"Then came Mayor Bill Thompson and big time gambling and prostitution and bootlegging and we had the circulation wars between the newspapers. That's how Capone got here, you know."

"How did it end?" Mary asked.

"When Omerra was murdered, the society just sort of faded away. Of course, the people who started the group were getting richer and more powerful."

"And more respectable," Tanner commented.

""Right," Fellowes agreed with a small grin. "And that's about all I know about the South Branch Merchants Society."

He took his leave and Mary and Tanner smiled at each other. "Well, Michael. That was a pretty good investment. I still wonder why I didn't run across any mention of that society in the books about the deVoles I looked at yesterday."

"Oh, I expect if you dig deeper it would turn up, but I guess some of the people who wrote those books did a little sanitizing along the way, just as you suspected."

"Sure. I didn't start with primary sources. I wanted to get a feel for what was there first. Should I go back, do you think?"

"Before we decide that, let's go over Matt's notes and the rest of our information."

"Okay. I'll run through it, you take some notes. More notes." Mary stood up and, pacing around the room, began to tick off what they knew or suspected.

"First, deVole and Mayhew come to Chicago before the Civil War. They're in business together. Mayhew goes to Duluth and later one son marries Leah deVole and takes his bride back to

Duluth."

"Right." Tanner ticked off notes he had already made and arranged papers on the table.

"DeVole forms that merchant's society with some others and begins to get bigger in lake shipping and trucking, banking, and probably real estate. It sounds like, from the way the society went, that they all may have had links to gangsters here."

"There was certainly a lot of corruption in political life then and it would be pretty surprising if deVole and the others didn't make the most of the possibilities. It might have been so common everybody did it."

Mary nodded agreement and went on. "Around 1900, prosperous and expanding, they decided to help out their northern friends, the Mayhews, which, owing to a depression, weren't doing quite that well."

"Probably through Leah," Tanner said, shuffling papers.

"Enter a deVole ship named *Amador*. Tony deVole, now head of the family business, offers a proven method of corrupting officials to gain advantage as well as the wherewithal to finance the operation, thus hoping to give Mayhew a leg up on the competition."

"Sheer speculation," reminded Tanner.

"Yes, but those persistent rumors give a certain amount of heft to the speculation. Anyway, *Amador* sinks, the cargo is lost and is never found. Life goes on."

Tanner poured a cup of coffee for each of them and said, "And then, ninety-plus years later, Harry deVole gives the corporate papers, until then just moldering in some Champaign warehouse, to the Minnesota Historical Society, apparently because of the Mayhew connection."

"And I find a piece of brass from the *Amador* right around the time Ethel Jandrice finds something which may have imprudently mentioned the *Amador* and the Plan." The way she said it the word was capitalized. "Boy, I wish we had a copy of that letter from Tony, or whatever it was."

"Then Ethel is murdered and her boyfriend who happens to be a shirttail relative of the Mayhews, disappears. We decide to look into the murder as part of our search for the *Amador*."

"Then I get run off the road by a truck."

Suddenly they were staring at each other, across the small table.

"What was it Fellowes said?" Tanner frowned, trying to remember the exact words.

"Here!" cried Mary, snatching a sheet of paper from the table. "Melvin deVole is a truck driver. A Teamster. Could there be a connection?"

"That's a little too neat to be a coincidence," Tanner said sourly. "That points at something I've felt all along. I told you I can't shake the feeling that the whole thing is being directed out of Chicago. Now here we have this trucker, Melvin."

"This is all so tenuous, we have to find some solid proof," said Mary.

"Sure, but proof of what?"

"I don't know, but I think more answers are up north," said Mary.

"Let's pack up and go back to Minneapolis," responded Tanner.

CHAPTER 33

Gravel rattled under the wheels as Mary brought the new station wagon around the last curve and onto the black-topped parking lot behind the main building at Port Superior marina.

In front of them, the placid blue of Lake Superior stretched to the horizon.

Tanner and Mary Whitney had flown back to Minneapolis from Chicago and spent a day in idle circulation, attempting with no success to determine if they were under surveillance. On Thursday, they made a date with Cameron O'Neil and *Ondine*.

Mary found a parking spot in the middle of the lot and they got out, surveying people and the boats, in particular *Ondine*, gleaming in the afternoon sun. It was a pleasure to look at the sleek vessel once again. The door to the dive shack was open.

O'Neil stepped from his office and waved, grinning as they walked across the lot to where he stood.

"Good to see the two of you again," said O'Neil quietly. "How you been keeping?"

Mary smiled up at him and nodded. "Good, Cameron, how 'bout you?" They laughed quietly together and went into the office, out of the sun.

"What I want to tell you is that I made a couple of quick dives last week while you was off in Chicago, and I think I may have found something that'll help." Tanner's pulse speeded up just a little. O'Neil leaned forward, resting his arms on the desk. He was enjoying himself.

"I went in a little northeast of where we last worked. There's something down there, sort of buried in the rock and sand. Old timbers an' something that looks like it could have been some ballast, maybe some metal pieces." He shrugged.

"The *Amador*?" Mary's eyes opened wider and she sat straight in her chair. "Is it really possible? You've found the *Amador*?"

O'Neil looked at her. He grinned again. "Don't know for sure, doubt it, actually. We'll take another look, but it could just be trash tossed overboard, or from another wreck altogether."

"How soon can we get out there?" Mary asked, glancing at her watch and calculating the amount of daylight still available.

"Soon as you two get your gear aboard," responded O'Neil, rising to his feet. Mary and Tanner hurried to the station wagon and Tanner drove it to the end of the parking lot, nearest where *Ondine* was moored. Mary flipped open the rear door and they quickly transferred duffel bags and other gear. Within minutes, *Ondine*'s engines rumbled to life, and while Mary and Tanner tended the mooring lines, Cameron expertly slid the yacht away from the dock and into the narrow channel. Once more they headed north, toward Devils Island.

They quickly returned to the routine established on earlier trips. Mary in shorts and a loose cotton blouse stood in the wheelhouse, guiding the big vessel up the channel. Tanner had also changed into light jeans and a tee shirt. He and O'Neil squatted at the rear of the deck carefully checking each piece of diving gear. By six that afternoon *Ondine* was anchored over the dive site. Wavelets sparkled blue in the sun. Two sailboats were anchored at the north end of the island, just below the lighthouse. Except for a lone freighter on the horizon, inbound from the Atlantic Ocean to Duluth, *Ondine* and her passengers were alone, riding peacefully atop 10 percent of the world's fresh water supply.

"Okay," said O'Neil at last, "we're ready. I'm gonna drop a grapple hook and this wire cage to the bottom. You and I will make a quick dive to see what we can find to put in the cage or hang on the hook."

Mary looked askance at him and started to say something. The benign look on Cameron's face stopped her. "You can expect a boat or two to come by, sort of casual like, look you over a wee bit. Just ignore 'em unless they try to get pushy, particularly if someone tries to come aboard. Here. Take this thing." He handed her a small orange pistol-shaped device.

"A signal gun?" Mary questioned.

"Yep. If anyone tries to come aboard, just lean over the side and shoot this shell right into the water. I've rigged a small explosive charge in this one. It'll go off about five feet down and we'll feel it. That'll be the signal for us to come a runnin' After that—"

"After that," Mary interrupted, "I'll play it by ear." She reached into the small locker beside the wheel and pulled out a box of flare shells. They could be dangerous and even lethal if they were fired at someone and they had been known to set boats afire. Tanner grinned at the look on O'Neil's face, squeezed Mary's shoulder and donned his wetsuit and flippers. A few moments later O'Neil and Tanner were sinking toward the lake bottom. The sun was also sinking toward the watery horizon and the light would soon fail. None of them wanted to work at night using underwater torches, so they wasted no time on the bottom.

The debris O'Neil had located could very well have been from a ship. In the dim light Tanner easily imagined he was looking at remains of the *Amador*. In Superior's cold waters there are few forces to rot water-logged timbers. Other wrecks have been located in remarkably well-preserved condition, even after decades underwater.

On closer examination, what O'Neil had found looked mostly like junk. Tanner was discouraged but bent willingly to the task of gathering up what they could find and break loose from the rocks in which the stuff was wedged. They loaded the wire cage with smaller scraps. O'Neil swam out around a huge boulder and came slowly back, carefully maneuvering a long piece of something that might have once been a deck plank. It was too large for the wire basket so he had Tanner wire it to the grapnel and they began a slow rise to the surface.

Halfway up, a narrow, dark, shadow passed overhead and Tanner saw the turbulence at one end which identified a propeller. The intruding boat came to a stop beside *Ondine*. With more urgency O'Neil and Tanner kicked their way upward, spiraling around and around the cable leading to the cage still resting on the bottom of the lake.

Tanner broke the surface only a few feet off the dive platform. Two quick strokes and he was able to crawl aboard, pulling off his mask and hood. The long cigar-shaped boat was on *Ondine*'s port side. Behind him he heard O'Neil's soft grunt as he clambered onto the platform. Tanner cautiously raised his head and peered forward toward the wheelhouse. Then he motioned to O'Neil and stood up.

Mary was relaxed beside the wheelhouse door, talking with a man who stood at the side of a racy runabout, holding onto *Ondine*'s scupper to keep the two boats from rubbing. Mary felt the movement of Tanner and O'Neil and turned her head to give them a brief wave.

"Everything okay below?" she said obliquely.

"Yes. We untangled the anchor," Tanner improvised. "A piece of old cable. It'll come up now with no more trouble." Tanner could see Mary's right hand inside the wheelhouse door, resting on the flare pistol in the cubby hole beside *Ondine*'s bright wheel.

O'Neil grunted softly as he and Tanner waddled to the rail, not bothering to remove their fins, and gazed calmly down into the cigarette boat. Three cylindrical bumpers hung in the space between the two craft, further protecting them.

"Meet Roger Watt," said Mary.

"We've met," said Tanner. "Evening, Mr. Watt. I'm surprised to see you out here."

Watt shrugged and smiled easily. "Ahh. Well. We were just going by, just going by. Back to ahh Washburn, and I recognized this, the yacht. How are you Cameron?" He bobbed his head.

"Mr. Watt. What brings you out here this evening?" O'Neil's voice was flat, almost bored sounding, but Tanner sensed tension in him.

Watt gave a dismissive wave of his free hand. His thin smile flickered on and off. "As I said, ahhh, just, just passing by, just checking." His eyes flickered to Mary's bare legs and back to the two men.

"Watt, you must know we have permission to be here, diving in these waters. Park Service and Coast Guard both are aware that we're out here this evening." Cameron's voice was calm, matter-of-fact.

"Well. Well, O'Neil, it's an open secret that you, that you are searching for some evidence of the *Amador*, our old freighter that went down, went down out here somewhere. We have a stake in that vessel, you know. Ahhh, and the deVole Corporation has also, regardless of current law. I guess you have some special reason for anchoring in this location."

"You've changed your story," Tanner remarked.

Watt shrugged. "Well, why not? You've stirred it all up, creating another *Manistee*. My grandfather is upset, you know." He licked his lips nervously. "The rest of the family is angry. We start to hear from, from our cousins in Chicago. You seem to, you seem to have a talent for rubbing people the wrong way."

A large beefy man in jeans and a stained tee-shirt appeared in the cockpit from the small forward cabin. A well-chewed, stubby cigar, stuck out of one side of his mouth. The tee-shirt strained over his biceps and protruding belly, which hung over his belt.

"Let's go," he said, looking up at *Ondine* from pale eyes. Without another word, Watt gave a shove which separated the two boats. Expertly with an unexpected economy of motion, he twisted the small rudder wheel and started the engine. With the drive engaged, he eased the throttle forward and the launch idled just a little faster until they were ten yards away. Then Watt pushed the throttle lever to the max and the boat sprang to its step and raced away into the twilight.

Mary watched them go and then turned, smiling. "Did you guys see the tattoo on the second man's arm? To me it looked like a heart with mom and MD in it."

"I didn't notice. Did they try to come aboard?"

"I've seen that big guy before," said O'Neil, staring after the other boat. He shook his head briefly and unzipped his diving tunic.

"They didn't have a chance," said Mary. "I saw them first coming from the direction of Devils. They could have come up the west side. Then they turned and headed east, made a sudden turn and came over here."

"Sort of like they just happened to see us, recognized *Ondine* and dropped by?" Tanner said.

Mary nodded. "I warned them off when they got close.

Told them there were divers below. They didn't exactly ignore me, but they didn't shear off, either."

"Sounds like an impulse move," interjected O'Neil. "Oh, I'm sure they were out here to check on us, but I bet they were playing it by ear. I've seen that boat before, when we've been out here. It's one boat I'm pretty sure has been keeping track of us since this little game got started."

"I expect they just wanted a closer look at the three of us," Tanner said, yanking off his flippers.

"Well. Heck with those guys for now," said Mary. "Let's see what you've found." There was rising excitement in her voice.

"First, we have to get it off the bottom." Tanner grinned at Mary's excitement and went to the stern where O'Neil was checking the cable that ran through a large shackle now attached to one of the two standpipes welded to the transom.

"Well, in that case," Mary said. I would really like to dive to see the place where you found the stuff."

O'Neil hesitated but the look on Mary's face decided him. "That's fair. Get your wet suit on." He glanced skyward. "We haven't much time before dark. Tanner, drag out the power pack. We'll go down with the big work light. After we get to the bottom I'll signal you and you can raise the cage. We'll just make a short dive and then come up and help." But it didn't work out quite that way.

****

The cold water took her breath away. She glanced up at Michael smiling down through the wavery vision in her mask, then Cameron and Mary sank into the lake. It was very cold. She was excited, her heart banging in her chest. Had they really stumbled across the remains of the *Amador*? Mary tried to slow her breathing, even though she knew they were only going to be down for a few minutes, but her excitement grew as she and O'Neil dropped. Cameron was leading and his bubbles were clearly visible rising past her mask. The bottom came up surprisingly fast. It was all rock, mostly flat with a heavy layer of silt. A jumble of boulders loomed up to one side. They swam side by side like two strange bottom-living creatures toward the wire basket. Mary couldn't see the basket and wondered how Cameron knew where it was. They undulated over a few larger boulders. O'Neil made a signal and Mary switched on the powerful underwater spotlight they'd brought along. It helped, but not a lot. They'd only been down a few minutes, but already Mary could feel the cold gripping her ankles.

Something caught her eye. She curled around on herself to see if the flash of light came again. There. There was something. Mary Whitney was vaguely conscious of O'Neil beckoning her to come on but she ignored him and dropped the few inches further to touch the bottom. Beside a small clutter of rounded stones, lay a small bright object. She picked it up clumsily in her gloved fingers and held it to her mask. It was a fork! A silver-colored dinner fork. How odd. Her breath was loud, roaring and pulsing in her ears. On the back of the handle were tiny marks she couldn't make out. When Mary turned it over she recognized the raised dV. Her lips loosened their grip on the mouthpiece and water leaked in. She started to choke and dropped the fork. She blew out the water in her mouth with a huge breath and sent large bubbles screaming to the surface. Her mouthpiece floated in front of her. She grabbed it and resealed her mouth against the lake.

Scrabbling about to find the fork again, Mary was raising silt and making the water murkier. Cameron realized something was up. He swam over and gripped Mary's shoulder. He made calming motions to settle her down. She found the fork again and showed it to him. He gave a high sign and the divers began to search more diligently in ever widening circles, around the place where the fork had lain. Time flew by and suddenly, O'Neil was holding Mary by the arm and tugging her upward. He held his wristwatch in front of her mask and tapped it several times. A piece of plank on the grapnel and other bits in the wire cage were the only foreign objects to be seen. Except for the fork.

Cameron yanked hard on the cable and they started for the surface. Mary held the fork clutched tightly in her hand, unwilling to trust it to the wire basket.

****

Tanner was starting to worry. Mary and O'Neil had stayed down much longer than he expected. Just when he started to consider going after them, a great burst of bubbles exploded on the quiet surface beside the swim platform. Mary rose out of the water and practically leaped onto the platform, spitting out her mouthpiece.

"Michael! Michael, honey, I found something!"

"What?"

"She shore did. The lady has sharp eyes." Cameron had surfaced right behind Mary. Quickly aboard, Mary displayed her find. The fork was scratched and slightly bent, as if it had seen hard use. The surface was lightly tarnished. On the handle in an ornate circle of carved relief petals were the letters dV. "These look just like the letters on the brass plate you found," said Tanner smiling at her excitement.

"We're right! The *Amador* must have sunk somewhere close by!" Mary said. "Hot damn!"

Tanner laughed and hugged her. He turned the fork over. At the base of the handle was the small mark of the silversmith and the letters SS.

O'Neil grunted. "Let's get the rest of the stuff aboard."

The cable to the wire basket ran from the small winch drum through a shackle to a second pulley fixed to a short piece of pipe welded to the side of the boat. From there it led over the side and straight down into the water. O'Neil checked the clamp, then reached over and switched on the electric winch. The motor whined and the cable slowly wound up, cold lake water running off and down the scuppers. O'Neil intently watched the cable, one hand on the switch. There was little possibility of a jam, but O'Neil knew the unexpected could destroy costly equipment. There was no hurry.

"Mary, switch on the anchor and afterdeck work lights," he said. A moment later, two lights brightened the aft end where the treasure hunters watched the wet cable coming in. The light glanced off the water, triggering silvery sparkles. Tanner shivered.

A long swell rode under *Ondine*, lifting her in a quiet surging motion.

"Northeaster coming," muttered O'Neil. A bright yellow swatch of paint appeared on the line and he cut the power to the winch.

Tanner was ready, O'Neil having earlier explained the procedure. He swung the small detachable crane boom around and positioned it over the cable. He paid out another cable attached to a large pulley with one open side, a snatch block. When the cable from the wire cage, now hanging just five feet below the surface, was secure in the second cable, the two men pivoted the arm out away from the hull. Then O'Neil resumed bringing in the cage. With a loud gurgle it broke the surface and O'Neil raised it above the deck where it hung gleaming in the light, water running from the objects crowding the cage. He let it drain a few moments and then using the temporary boom, swung the cage aboard and lowered it gently to the deck.

Reconnecting the winch to the grapnel cable, they repeated the procedure. As they worked, *Ondine* rocked more frequently underfoot, responding to the building swells rolling in from the open lake. Night was fully upon them by the time everything was properly stored and the anchor rising. By now, the swells were larger and Mary, standing on the plunging bow deck, wore a harness tethered to the safety line that ran from bow to wheelhouse while she worked the anchor windlass.

When the anchor appeared in the hawse hole, she bent, pushed the safety pins through the chain to hold the big anchor securely in its cradle, then rose and waved. In the distance multiple lightning flashes illuminated the approaching squall line. Mary made her way quickly back to the wheelhouse and Cameron brought *Ondine* around and nudged the throttles up.

"Seems like every time we're out here, a storm comes up."

"An omen?" responded O'Neil. They laughed together, relaxed, secure in the still-warm wheelhouse. Then O'Neil fed more fuel to the engines and headed back down the lake with a load of old timbers and metal scraps and a single fork from the bottom of Lake Superior.

CHAPTER 34

On the return trip, O'Neil and Tanner examined the detritus from the lake bottom.

"I dunno, we could get some of this stuff analyzed for age, I suppose, but I have me doubts."

"You don't think any of it came from the *Amador?*" asked Mary. "But what about my fork?" She was standing at the wheel guiding *Ondine* through the water, holding the fork in one hand.

"The *Amador* made several trips through these waters, right? And even if those letters are deVole, the company had other ships, right?" Mary nodded, reluctantly, Tanner thought.

"The fork could be from another ship, another voyage. It could have been thrown out with the garbage," O'Neil said.

"Or, it could be part of the old silver deVole was sending to Mayhew to help him through hard times," Tanner said, patting Mary's shoulder.

She shrugged out from under his touch. "Well, of course I know that! Just let me have this fantasy for a while, will you?"

"What now?" said O'Neil after a brief pause.

"We have to continue our ruse," Tanner said. "It doesn't really matter whether we've struck it rich, but whether people believe we have." O'Neil nodded and winked at Tanner.

Word spread rapidly that *Ondine* had returned with something new from the lake bottom but the coming storm thinned the welcoming crowd on the docks.

Mary had wrapped the fork in a soft cloth and stowed it in her duffel bag. The rest of the salvage was piled on the aft deck under a carefully secured blue plastic tarp.

When the sun was well up, Mary stepped off the yacht, walked to the marina office and bought a *Duluth Tribune*. She glanced at the front page as she strolled back to *Ondine*, ignoring onlookers, several of whom tried to question her. Back aboard, she dropped the front section and began to scan the rest of the news. Watching through the open hatch, Tanner observed her read part of the paper and then return to something that had caught her attention.

"Michael," she called down, "Bill McTaggert just got another grant."

"Good for him. Is it significant?"

O'Neil peered out a cabin window at the people on the docks. "I had an idea while shaving this morning. Let's take *Ondine* to Duluth. Seems to me you need to ask some questions there. We'll avoid this crowd and we can deal with our booty," he smirked sourly, "on the way." To the evident surprise of those waiting on shore for some word of what had been found, *Ondine* picked up her mooring lines and headed back out onto the lake.

Ondine went west, threading through the islands and then straight down Superior toward Duluth's harbor. Late in the afternoon, watched by scores of vacationers, O'Neil expertly brought *Ondine* under the famous Lift Bridge and turned toward the public marina. Once docked and hooked up to power and communications, Tanner sat down in the comfortable main cabin and spread his notes on the table. He examined once more the information they had amassed about the Mayhews, deVoles and the freighter *Amador*. O'Neil brought Tanner a fresh cup of coffee, then he and Mary withdrew to the steps of the companionway and talked in low tones.

"I guess you were a little disappointed when you saw the junk we brought up from the bottom."

"I was, Cameron. I took what you said the day before to mean you had found something from *Amador*."

"Wishful thinking. I said it was interesting and it is. I didn't say I was sure it came from the *Amador*."

"True."

"Still, those planks and other stuff might have."

"No way to prove it, though."

Cameron scratched his ear. "People watching will wonder for a long time what was under that tarp and what happened to it."

"Do you think there are people here who'll come looking for us?" Mary frowned. "We don't seem to generate much interest."

"We may be creating more interest than we know," said Tanner. "Hey, you two," he said, stretching to ease his back. "We've been assuming this all started with the murder of Ethel Jandrice for no known reason, except she was cataloguing the deVole papers and may have found something valuable, or maybe embarrassing. To someone. Then we had the appearance and later disappearance of that piece of brass from the *Amador*. I still think they're connected in some way, but I'm damned if I know how."

Mary nodded agreement.

"Rumors say the *Amador* may have carried some cargo someone doesn't want to see the light of day, even a hundred years later. If that's true, it must be linked to the killing of Ethel.

"Then I get run off the road by some trucker. Then we find out about Melvin deVole, the Chicago trucker."

"Yeah?" said O'Neil. "What's this fellow deVole look like?"

"No idea," said Tanner. "Why?"

"Jus' wondered. 'Member the big beefy guy on the launch the other night with Watt?"

Both Mary and Tanner nodded. "Could he have been this deVole?" Mary and Tanner shrugged.

Tanner shook his head in mild frustration and gathered up his papers into the expandable file.

"I'm going to change and go ashore for a while. Maybe I can get in to see old Mayhew again, or talk to someone in the family. I know I'm just grasping at straws, but..."

Tanner was surprised when his call to the Mayhew residence resulted in an immediate invitation to return to the mansion. "I wonder what's changed?" he thought as a cab took him through the city and on to the North Shore Drive. When he reached the Mayhew mansion gates, they were standing open and a man beside the pillar waved the taxi through.

At the top of the steps beside the massive door, stood a woman Tanner didn't know. "Won't you come this way?" Her well-modulated voice was softly husky, reminiscent, he decided, of Lauren Bacall at a much younger age.

Together they walked swiftly down the echoing hall to a sunroom where a slender woman in a white nurse's uniform waited. Tanner's escort approached the door and stopped. She gestured that he was to continue. The nurse had her hand on the doorknob, as if to bar his way. Beyond, he could see the figure of "Black Jack" Mayhew, hunched over in his wheelchair with his back to the door.

"Mr. Tanner," whispered the woman. "I beg you not to upset him. His health and his mental state are very fragile right now. His hold on rationality is tenuous at best. I..." her voice broke slightly. "He's just had some extremely bad news." Tanner detected the harmonics of intense devotion in her voice and her stance. He wondered if she was this protective with other members of the family. "Come," she said.

Together they entered the warm sunroom and walked across the tiled central stage to the man in the wheelchair. Tanner saw that a white plastic chair had been placed in front of the wheelchair. The nurse indicated he should sit and she stepped beside the figure to touch his blanket-covered shoulder. It was almost a caress. Mayhew raised his head and gazed at Tanner. Immediately, Tanner realized that this was the same man, but a much different man than he had been the last time Tanner talked with him. This time, his deep eyes carried a penetrating gaze that seemed so strong as to be like a physical touch, almost a blow, when his gaze touched Tanner's eyes.

"Ah," his husky, papery voice wafted up and floated about the room, "young Mr. Tanner."

He made a sharp gesture with one hand that came into view from beneath the blanket draped over his lower body. The nurse reacted instantly and moved away to sit out of earshot, on a white stone bench beside a large banana tree.

Tanner started to speak, but the bony hand rose again, imperiously signaling him to silence. "I know you have questions. Perhaps I will even answer them, but our time is short. I have no way of telling when I may slip back."

His fierce gaze studied Tanner, searching, he guessed, for a reaction. Tanner waited.

"Oh, yes, I know I am sometimes gone from mortal sense.

But there are two of us who know I can bring it on if I need protection." He nodded once. "Now there are three." I'm going to tell you some things you want to know," he said after a pause. "But I won't elaborate. You'll be able to ask me questions when I'm through. Maybe you'll get answers, maybe not. Time is short. Others are coming soon and they will separate us. I cannot allow you to take notes. So now, you listen."

Tanner nodded. Mayhew took a deep uncertain breath, paused and began to speak. He talked fast in his odd monotone, showing little emotion. But gradually Tanner came to realize that the old pirate was enjoying the telling of family secrets, that he was relieving himself of a burden he had carried almost his entire life. Mayhew confirmed that the stories about a mysterious cargo aboard the Amador were true, that his cousin in Chicago had been planning to assist the Mayhews in corrupting local officials. A list had been developed, he said, based on a variety of contacts by deVole and his people in Chicago. Mayhew named names and places and dates. Tanner concentrated. He wanted to retain as much as possible so he could verify Mayhew's story. But it was difficult. The flow continued almost without pause for many minutes.

Then Mayhew smiled a brief rapacious smile and said, "Now to the present. The woman, Jandrice, found part of the original letter of transmission. The details, on other pages, were missing, but that's not known to many. I don't know how the letter came to be among corporate papers. I know the letter because years ago a cousin sent me a free-hand copy as a keepsake." His mouth twitched. "The woman, Jandrice, was killed. It was an accident," he paused and struggled for breath. "She returned home at the wrong time.

"My great grandson, Tommy Callender, died because he talked freely to the wrong people about blackmailing us. Yes, your suspicions are correct; my great grandson, was murdered outside that bar," he continued.

"I learned about that. He was trying to find out more about the old relationships between the deVoles and our family. I wish he'd come to me. I might have saved him." The old man's voice was becoming weaker. Tanner bent toward him. From the corner of one eye, Tanner saw the nurse frown and lean forward as if about to intervene.

"I understand you have had some...troubles." Mayhew raised a feeble hand. "Be careful, Mr. Tanner. There are powerful men in the families who will block you if they can. They are overzealous. This attempt to besmirch our two families, with this old tale, especially since it never happened, is stupid. You must be careful. I have concluded there is more going on than we presently know. Something related to present day."

Finally Tanner had an opportunity. Mayhew paused and the nurse was there instantly with a glass of water and a straw. Mayhew turned his head and sucked the water.

"Why are you telling me this now?"

There was a longer pause. Mayhew slowly turned his head and his black gaze seemed to again impale Tanner. Improbably, tears began to well up and run down his seamed face. The man appeared to shrink before Tanner's eyes. It was as if all the power, the life force, was running out of him in those tears.

"Sarah." he whispered. His voice broke. "My Sarah." He gasped.

"Yes," Tanner said.

"Where is she? You must know! Tell me!"

The door crashed open and Roger Watt accompanied by two men Tanner had never seen stalked into the room. Mayhew jerked, gaped and began to drool. As Tanner watched, stunned, the man in the wheelchair transformed himself into a mewling, demented creature.

"Ah, you see," said the nurse softly, "he's gone again." Louder, she went on. "I'm afraid he's been like that for days," an obvious lie. She didn't meet Tanner's eye. She reached in to wipe Mayhew's slack lips with a soft white cloth.

"What's been going on here?" Watt demanded in a loud voice. I thought I gave strict orders not to disturb grandfather. Ahhh...What's, what's he been saying?"

The nurse raised her head and looked blandly at Watt. "Mr. Tanner just dropped by to pay his respects. Mr. Mayhew had a nice chat with the gentleman earlier, you remember." Her voice was calm, professional, uninvolved.

"Yes," Tanner said starting to rise. Mayhew's head, now sunk against one shoulder and turned partially away, jerked almost imperceptibly. The lid on the one eye Tanner could see drooped, then flicked down and up again, the pupil darkening. Tanner stared. Mayhew was winking at him.

Tanner looked at Watt. "I'm afraid I may have pressed him too hard," he said in an apologetic tone. "I had hoped he might be lucid enough to answer some questions but..." Tanner shook his head.

"Roger!" Carole Ann Mayhew appeared at the door. "I thought it would be all right. Granddad seemed comfortable and the company might have done him some good. You have no reason to be so sharp with Mr. Tanner."

"Ahh. You're a fool, Carole, just a fool." Watt looked at his grandfather, then spun on his heel and stalked out, brushing the woman out of his way. The other two men went with him.

Tanner left a few minutes later, studiously avoiding eye contact with Mayhew. He was afraid he might betray something of Mayhew's deception. The main questions still remained. Who? Who was responsible for at least two deaths and the attempt on Tanner? And why was it happening? The still missing Sarah Callender was likewise perplexing. Tanner realized now that he had been assuming all along that she had gone to be with her father, apparently an erroneous conclusion. He walked toward the front door hardly aware of who was beside him.

"Mr. Tanner?" With a start he realized Carole Ann was addressing him.

"What? Oh, I'm sorry, Miss Mayhew. I didn't hear you."

"Oh, it's all right. I'm used to going unheard." Her lips twisted briefly in a bitter smile, then her face smoothed out again. "I just wondered if it was your associate, the man who was here yesterday?"

"No, I'm sorry." Tanner shook his head. "My associate is a woman and we were in Wisconsin yesterday."

"How odd. A man came to see granddad yesterday afternoon and I was quite sure both Nurse James and my grandfather appeared to expect him."

"What did he look like?

She shrugged. He was average. Light brown hair, a little shorter than you, I think. Nothing particularly distinguishing."

"He was a stranger, I take it."

"Yes."

"I have no idea who he was. Thank you for allowing me to see Mr. Mayhew. Goodbye."

Mary took the news that Sarah Callender was still missing hard. O'Neil and Tanner sat at the table in *Ondine*'s cabin while he related everything he could remember that Mayhew had told him, a small tape recorder running silently on the table. Mary, tears in her eyes, went for a walk along the waterfront.

Darkness fell and Mary returned. She and Tanner sat together on *Ondine*'s foredeck while O'Neil rattled about in the galley, preparing supper.

"This is so sad. I liked Sarah Callender. Do you think she's dead?"

"I just don't know. It's likely. I'm pretty sure the old man thinks so. That's why he let me in to his family secrets. He's more than a little upset with what's been happening. I think he hired someone to look for her, an investigator who went up there yesterday to report what he learned." Tanner paused. "If she's in the lake, her body may never be found. Remember what we read about some of the wrecks in the Apostle Islands?"

"Like the *Edmund Fitzgerald*," Mary murmured.

"Or the *Manistee*."

"Or the *Amador*." She sighed. "Did you know there's another *Ondine* here?"

"What?"

"Yes," said Mary. "It's a big old cabin cruiser on the other dock."

CHAPTER 35

At two o'clock on that warm night in Duluth, a huge explosion roused the waterfront. Tanner fell out of bed after Mary scrambled over him. By the time he sorted himself out and slipped on shorts and shoes, Mary and Cameron were already racing down the dock.

When he caught them at the end of the pier, they stopped, stunned, watching big balls of orange flame soar into the sky closely following muffled whumps of small explosions as gas bottles or fuel tanks overheated and exploded in the body of the cruiser. A swirling column of thick smoke betrayed the presence of petroleum in the flaming wreckage.

"Oh God," said Mary quietly. "I was walking along that dock earlier. That's where I saw—" she stopped suddenly. She clutched Tanner's arm. "That's where I saw the other *Ondine*. Right there! It's that boat!" Tanner stared down at her, watching her eyes darken as the full realization flashed over them that if that was *Ondine*, there was a strong possibility they were the real target.

Sirens wailed closer and the night filled with flashing red, blue and white lights, and the sounds of emergency crews rushing to the scene.

"I think," said O'Neil quietly, "that we're outta here. We're not waiting to find out if that was an accident, just in case it wasn't and there was a bomb meant for us." Mary and Tanner looked at each other for a moment longer and then without a word, turned to the task of getting *Ondine* under way.

"Where will we go, Cameron?" asked Mary, hauling in a spring line and coiling it on the deck at her feet.

"I'll call a friend of mine. He has a boatyard across the bay. He'll have room and someone usually monitors their radio all night." He reached for the radio and then stopped, hand in the air. "On second thought, a telephone will be just as good and a lot more private."

While O'Neil made the call from a booth near the dock, Mary and Tanner warmed up the engine and prepared fore and aft mooring lines so they could slip away without having to go back onto the dock. O'Neil jumped aboard and went to the wheelhouse, his dark form etched sharply against the still billowing fire. With a quiet word, he eased *Ondine* away from the dock. The engines barely ticked over and the running lights remained off. It was dangerous but there were no moving ships close by. *Ondine* idled unnoticed across the water toward a different mooring.

"Fortunately we don't need to have the Lift Bridge raised," Tanner remarked.

O'Neil nodded and said, "Mary, keep your eyes peeled astern. I want to leave the running lights off as long as possible, but we don't want to get run down. That would be too much attention, right about now." O'Neil glanced at Tanner and the men concentrated their gaze forward, alert for any boat traffic.

In a few minutes they crossed the main harbor and turned southeast down a channel toward the Wisconsin boatyard of O'Neil's friend. With running lights now ablaze, *Ondine* slid through the smooth water toward a new haven. The radio in the wheelhouse squawked and muttered. Then a voice came clearly from the speaker, louder than the others.

"Trumpet, this is Zodiac. Come in Trumpet."

"O'Neil grabbed the microphone. Trumpet here, Zodiac. Over."

"Blink twice, Trumpet," said the quiet voice. O'Neil switched *Ondine*'s running lights quickly off and on as directed.

"Gotcha, Trumpet. I'm dead ahead, twenty yards. Follow me. Out."

O'Neil pointed ahead over the bow. A moment later, from a dark gray inflatable runabout, a flashlight flickered twice from its position ahead of the motor launch. O'Neil reduced speed and followed the little boat along the length of the small yard, past rotting hulks, ships on cradles, boats pulled up on the hard ground. There was no one about. Apparently the explosion across the harbor had roused no curiosity here.

They approached a high dark shape that lay against the land at the end of the yard, screened by a small point that stuck out on the landward side of Minnesota Point. The voice on the radio spoke. "Fenders to port. Bow and stern lines."

Mary and Tanner scrambled quickly across the night-shrouded deck to secure four fenders against Ondine's gleaming hull and O'Neil laid her quietly against the high rusting side of an old dredging scow resting on the lake bottom at the edge of the channel, her stern in water just deep enough to comfortably hold Ondine. When Tanner went to the bow, he saw a shadow against the stars standing on the old hulk. The figure waved and Tanner threw the mooring line at him. Quickly the shadow drew the line taut and then trotted down the hull to Ondine's stern where the action was repeated with the other line. A moment later the shadow landed aboard with a soft thump and materialized into a smiling, grizzled Barry Kanton.

After introductions Kanton explained where they were. "There's very little water under us, as I'm sure you know, but its soft bottom, so you'll be all right. You might want to cover your transom before dawn, and I guess I'd try to alter Ondine's lines a little."

"Any word about the explosion?" asked Mary.

"Not much. No bodies yet. Boat's a total loss of course. The fire's about out."

"I'm exhausted," said Mary suddenly. "I'll see you in the morning."

Kanton soon left and Tanner helped Cameron tie an old tarp over the stern, obscuring the name. Then they laid some gear on the foredeck and covered it with another tarp.

"I'm afraid this won't do much to hide us except to a very casual look," grunted O'Neil.

"True, but we only need a little time. I'll call the police captain I met in Duluth and have a chat with him after sunup."

Around ten the next morning, still a bit bleary-eyed, Mary and Tanner stood together in the wheelhouse finishing their coffee.

"If you look carefully, you can just see a faint smudge of smoke rising over the harbor," Tanner commented. "I'm going to walk to the yard office and call a cab."

"Don't you think we ought to get Cameron and *Ondine* out of here pretty soon?"

"You're right. I'll get us a hotel room after I see Captain Mackay and Cameron can take the boat back home."

"I'll pack up while you're gone." Mary started down the companionway.

A half-hour later, Tanner sat in an interrogation room talking with Detective Bailey again. Mackay had turned him over to the detective handling the Tommy Callender murder case, and he'd found an empty interrogation room where they could talk undisturbed.

"So, you think that explosion and fire early this morning was really meant for you and your friends? Any hard evidence?"

"None, just circumstance and gut feelings."

"Well, we all learn to trust that sometimes. I'll make inquiries. Where can I reach you?"

"I don't know yet. I'm going to a hotel or motel room. The yacht we came on is returning to Bayfield right away."

Bailey nodded. "Make it a hotel." He looked at Tanner. "Safer than a motel. Fewer entrances and exits."

"Good point."

"You got anything else for us?"

"No, 'fraid not."

"Right. Oh, we checked out Professor Caine. He's been a dull thorn pricking at the Mayhews for years. Conspiracy nut. He learned about your interest in them and when Tommy was offed, he figured to stir things up by calling you."

"Does he know anything?" Tanner asked.

"Doubt it."

When Tanner returned to Kanton's yard, he found Mary in the office, gear piled on a four-wheel dolly at the door. O'Neil stood beside her.

"I'm heading back to Port Superior as soon as you two shove off," he said. "You thought about my story?"

"Yes, try this. We found nothing significant, you ferried us to Duluth for a part or something for *Ondine* and we decided to stay here for a while. You don't know why or where we are. We'll figure out how to get the car later."

Mary hugged O'Neil and he and Tanner shook hands. The taxi arrived and picked up the gear. O'Neil turned and sauntered down the walk toward the big ugly barge where *Ondine* was moored. He was already under way and moving smartly up the narrow channel toward the harbor entrance while the taxi worked its way through traffic and across the freeway bridge into Duluth. By the time Tanner and Mary Whitney reached a downtown hotel, *Ondine* had cleared the Lift Bridge and was powering through the waves east toward the Apostle Islands.

"Well, what now?"

"I'm going to call Chicago and Minneapolis. Then let's sit down and talk about our next move."

"Okay. I'll run down to the lobby and buy some toothpaste and see if I can find out anything about the fire." Mary slipped out the door and Tanner sat down at the desk with his file.

He made three calls to Illinois. The first was to Matt Fellowes, who was able to tell him that the South Branch Merchants Society was rumored to have links to Capone and others in the Chicago gangs even after its public demise. Tanner asked Fellowes to check on the present whereabouts of Melvin deVole.

His second call was to Champaign. He located Harry deVole, the donor of the deVole papers, at home watching baseball on television.

"I'm sorry to disturb you, sir."

"Well, the Cubs are losing again, so I don't mind at all, really. How may I be of assistance?" deVole asked.

Quickly Tanner sketched the events which had occurred after their one meeting. When he finished, there was a long pause. Tanner could hear deVole breathing.

"Dammit. I was afraid of something like this."

"Like what?"

"Mr. Tanner, I learned something just yesterday. I've been debating with myself whether to call you with the information."

"Sir?"

"A member of the family called me to discuss this infamous

letter. From what she said, and the way she said it, I got the impression that she may have seen the letter, and rather recently, I think. I'm also quite convinced she could not have had anything directly to do with its apparent theft from the Historical Society."

"Have you ever run across something called the South Branch Merchants Society?"

"Why, yes, I have. Goodness," deVole said, "that goes back a long way. When our family moved away from that organization, it apparently became entangled in local gangland activities, and, though it is unprovable under the law, it is common knowledge in certain circles that some members of the society participated directly in illegal activities. I mention it because it now seems likely that connection to the wrong side of the law had some bearing on these recent events of which you and I are speaking. In any case, I've learned more details about the letter from Tony deVole to John Mayhew. It was several pages long. It contained names of Duluth area officials and citizens of importance whose influence apparently could be purchased. At least, Tony deVole thought so. Some of them already had been corrupted, in other, earlier deals. There was an incomplete draft copy of the letter, without the names, created for the company files. I am sure that's what was found in St. Paul. The irony is that while that letter might be mildly embarrassing, it isn't enough, by itself, to accuse anyone. Without names and other evidence, it's useless." He sighed again.

"Yes, but everyone in the family didn't know that, did they?" Tanner said quietly.

"Quite right." There was another pause. Tanner scribbled a note.

"I think I have told you everything I know about this wretched affair. As I said, I believe that information in that letter, when put together with other facts, may present a very unseemly picture, something that could be damaging to someone connected with the family."

"Mr. deVole, at least two, maybe more murders are linked to this affair. Hurt is not the right word."

There was another pause and deVole sighed. "You're correct, of course. It is only right that the facts come out now, although I doubt the entire story will ever be known. But whoever is responsible for the murder of that poor woman at the historical society should be punished, if he can be apprehended. I am assuming that it is not the same man who killed John Mayhew's grandson. Still..." his voice trailed off.

"Thank you for talking to me, Mr. deVole. I know it could not have been easy." Tanner broke the connection.

CHAPTER 36

Tanner made another call and reached the head of the corporation, Theodore deVole, in his office in downtown Chicago. The conversation lasted several minutes. Tanner made more notes and hung up. Then he wrote some more, paced the room and waited.

Twenty minutes went by. Just as Mary entered the room the telephone rang. Tanner answered Mary's smile of greeting and scooped up the telephone.

"Tanner."

"It's Fellowes. I need a little more time. Where can I reach you tomorrow?"

"That depends on a number of factors. I'll have to call you. Two, tomorrow at your office?" Fellowes agreed.

"You look very satisfied all of a sudden," Mary said. "What have you learned?"

"There are still a few questions, but I think we have most of it. I've been bothered all along by the coincidental randomness of this thing. Obviously, Ethel finding that letter and you finding the brass plate from the *Amador* could not have been anticipated."

"I think the murders are directly connected to people in Chicago, people who grew more and more desperate to keep the *Amador* and it's cargo out of the news. I suspect there was money in the crate, probably negotiable securities of some kind, and after hearing from that lawyer in Champaign, Harry deVole, we know there was also a letter listing the names of people here in Duluth. But I think there had to be other names, names of Chicago people linked both to the Duluth contacts, and to the South Branch Merchants Society. My conversation with Jack Mayhew confirms part of this. I also think none of this will ever be proven. The money in the crate is of secondary importance. Chicago must believe that the list of people was in the crate and that's what they're really worried about."

"What about my fork?"

"It's probable that it came from the *Amador* when she broke up and sank."

"Of course," Mary pointed out, "whoever is behind all this didn't know how much of the original letter Ethel Jandrice found. They didn't know the names weren't included."

"Until somebody burgled Jandrice to steal back the letter. Somebody found out she had the letter after Tommy Callender began waving a partial copy around Duluth."

Mary said, "You're saying the deVoles in Chicago tried to protect their reputation by stealing the letter and my brass piece, by running you off the road and by stealing my file? Seems a little far-fetched.   And an awful lot of trouble just to protect a few reputations."

"Yes, but Ethel's murder must have been a mistake. Whoever hit her was probably surprised during the burglary and hit her too hard.   I think the original motive for the burglaries is something else other than protecting reputations from a hundred years ago."

"Who killed Tommy Callender?"

"The same man. A big man, remember the description?"

"Who ran you off the road?"

"Same guy. A—"

"Truck driver," interrupted Mary. "Sure, Melvin deVole? That Chicago truck driver?"

"Remember the big man on the launch with Roger Watt at Devils Island? I agree with O'Neil. That man was Melvin deVole."

"You think he's behind all this? But why?"

"Not on his own. He's being directed by someone in Chicago, someone who thought he had an opportunity to make a name for himself.

"Fellowes gave me some of this and Tony deVole part of it as well. In 1980, a man named Jerry Kald who appears to have some minor connections with the unsavory side of Chicago society, married Harry deVoles daughter, Elaine. Kald is a real estate deal maker who seems to frequently have inside information. He has a reputation as a kind of wheeler-dealer who's willing to push the envelope. Kald met Elaine through her brother Bob's wife, Cheryl Ames. Robert deVole is now a candidate for Attorney General in Illinois and Elaine Kald, Robert's sister, is managing his election campaign.

"I think when Jerry Kald learned that his brother-in-law was going to run for Attorney General of Illinois, he decided to help. No problem with that. But, when the business of the *Amador* came up, he saw a potential scandal that could hurt his candidate."

"I could understand that," Mary said, "if it was here in Minnesota. But Illinois?"

"Ordinarily I'd agree, but remember, deVole is new to politics and running on a clean government campaign. Kald probably wanted to keep any hint of scandal from touching the new fast-rising politician. The newspapers were predicting big things for that guy, if he won the election."

Mary nodded. "So by helping suppress a possible scandal ancient and small though it might be, Kald hoped to get an inside track with a new AG, or at least with the staff. People on the fringes, like Kald, sometimes have an exaggerated sense of the danger of scandal. Actually, you know, the sort of swashbuckling story of the *Amador* lends a kind of attraction to the family, especially since there's no hard evidence of any other corruption."

"No hard evidence we know of. Ambitious wheeler-dealers like this Kald are always looking for inside connections. Helping a candidate, even an unknowing one, especially a brother-in-law, could be beneficial to Kald, both financially and to his wise-guy associates.

"I think Kald is telling Melvin what to do, and Melvin has been handling the dirty work.

"Well, it hangs together for me but where's the proof?"

"Proof? Proof, my dear?"

"Yes, proof. Somebody has to pay for these murders."

"I'm afraid real proof may be impossible. Maybe the cops in Chicago will agree to pick up Melvin. He could always confess and implicate the others, but that's pretty unlikely."

Mary frowned. "A confession is about as likely as the harbor freezing over tomorrow. Damn! This is really frustrating. Let's get something to eat. I have incontrovertible proof that my body needs food."

They left the room and turned toward the elevator and the hotel dining room.

****

The next morning was clear and hot. Right after breakfast Tanner talked with Detective Bailey, telling him everything he knew and supposed. Tanner suggested that Roger Watt be picked up and questioned.

"It's pretty thin, Mr. Tanner. I don't think Captain Mackay will buy it. I'm not sure I buy it."

"I understand. I haven't any proof, but will you run it by Mackay anyway? Maybe he'll go for it."

"Okay. Will you be in town for a while?"

"Yes, we're still waiting for Chicago to call with more information. If that turns out to be useful to you in making a case, I'll get back to you again. We'll be here at this hotel."

By eleven, Mary and Tanner had decided to get some lunch out of the hotel when the telephone rang. It was Chicago.

"Matt? What have you learned?"

"Well, Tanner, I'll tell you, there's a bit of a flap down here. I've checked out Mel deVole and things fit pretty good right down the line. He was on a run to Northern Minnesota through Minneapolis at the time of Ethel Jandrice's murder. He could easily have been in Duluth when Thomas Callender was killed, and he was apparently not in Chicago when you were run off the road. DeVole usually drives a big customized blue and white Kenilworth diesel tractor."

A chill ran down Tanner's back and he shivered.

"Yeah," Fellowes continued, "It fell into place when you told me what to look for. There's no trace of him in his usual Chicago haunts. Melvin, never what you'd call a clean livin' type, looks good for it, all right."

"Well, it's all circumstantial," Tanner remarked. "There may be an innocent explanation."

"He seems to have gone missing, by the way."

"What? Who? DeVole?"

"Police in Des Plaines towed Mel's truck off a freeway. No evidence of violence. The blue tractor was just sitting there. According to his friends, he drove it somewhere up north last week."

"Well, deVole didn't set this thing up by himself. I'm sure he's working for someone."

"That makes sense," Fellowes responded. "Here's something else you may find interesting. The paper's just come. A potential major political light has just gone out."

"I don't follow you."

"It'll be on the news in your area soon, I'm sure. The front runner in the Democratic primary for Attorney General of Illinois, Robert deVole, has just quit the campaign. They had a press conference a couple hours ago and he announced he's quitting. No explanation, refused to answer any questions. For personal and family reasons, he said. According to this reporter I'm reading here, his campaign manager Elaine, who is also his sister, was not in the room when he read his statement."

"So, you think there's a connection?"

"Yeah. I have— I have a source here who told me about Jerry Kald and more about the South Branch Merchants Society."

"That wouldn't be your evil-smelling friend Stan, would it?"

"No comment. Anyway, Kald apparently gave Elaine a look at a possible political and personal disaster when the business about the *Amador* and that letter surfaced. She's a very ambitious woman. Kald could have hatched this little scheme and sold it to his wife. Then one thing led to another and the plan got outta control."

"Matt, I've come to the same conclusions. The sad part is, they would have done themselves less damage by ignoring the sunken freighter."

"Yeah," responded Fellowes. "Funny, the way things break sometimes. Incidentally I ran into some evidence that another party has been looking into this affair. Frankly, when I called you this morning, I hadn't decided how much to tell you. After I ran across this other guy's tracks, I was going to do some independent research. Didn't want to get caught looking the wrong way. Then I got this call from a woman who filled in some gaps. Helped me connect Kald and the political stuff."

"Really? Who was it?"

"Well, she never said, but she had a whole lot of factual stuff. She confirmed some of your speculations about Melvin deVole." Fellowes sighed. "She told me that some guy in Duluth was involved, too. Guy named Watt."

"Roger Watt! Anything else you can tell me about her?" Tanner looked blankly at Mary.

"Well, I figured out she must have called from up there, Duluth."

An earlier conversation with the nurse at the Mayhew residence, a conversation about a visitor who had upset the old man jumped into Tanner's mind. "Yes, I think someone from Duluth was looking into this business," he told Fellowes.

After thanking Fellowes for his help Tanner severed the connection and related the news to Mary. Then he called the Mayhew company offices. In a short, abrupt conversation, Tanner told Watt what he knew and most of what he suspected. He learned that Watt had already been contacted by the Duluth police. Watt sounded upset.

"I don't understand. Who called Fellowes?" said Mary after Tanner completed that call.

"I think we'll know pretty soon. I wonder if she called anyone else."

"Michael, do you think the old man, Mayhew, is involved in this mess?"

"I don't know for sure, but I think so. Let's try to see him again."

It was not immediately possible, Tanner was informed, but if he showed up the next day at three, it was likely he would be admitted.

CHAPTER 37

While Tanner was on the phone to the Mayhew mansion, Mary went over their information yet again. There were still too many loose ends. She was angry about the murders of Ethel Jandrice and Tommy Callender and about the attempt on her husband outside Cornucopia. In spite of his protestations to the contrary, Mary saw him flinch sometimes when big trucks roared by. The attempt on his life outside Cornucopia was having a more lasting effect than he was letting on.

And where was Sarah? In the short time Mary had talked with her, she had felt a personal connection. Sarah Callender's continued absence worried her.

"I have an idea," Mary interrupted Tanner. "I think we ought to try to do something more aggressive."

"Such as?"

"Let's go public with the fork. If Melvin deVole is around, maybe we can trap him."

"You want to set us up as a target?"

Mary nodded. "The diving business didn't do the job, did it. Let's call a press conference. If we hurry, we'll make the afternoon newscasts here."

"I'm calling the cops."

"Michael, honey, don't you want to catch this guy?"

"Of course! But I don't want either of us hurt in the process. We don't even know if deVole is in Duluth."

"What if it isn't only deVole? What if Watt or some other Mayhews are involved? Maybe stories about finding the fork will force them out too."

Tanner sighed and got that resigned look he occasionally produced when Mary set her mind to something that worried him. She smiled inwardly, thinking, Michael is a good person, and I love him a lot, but sometimes he could be a little less cautious.

They were surprised how little time it took to set it up. The newspaper and the radio and TV stations all responded immediately to the mention of the Mayhew name. Then when it was linked to the deVoles of Chicago, the *Amador* and the explosion on the waterfront the previous night, an instant press conference was the result. They decided to stage it in the hotel. Management was reluctant at first, but again the magic of the Mayhew name opened a meeting room for later that day.

"I talked to Captain Mackay, Mary. He's unhappy with the idea, but he'll cooperate if we will."

"Meaning?"

"Meaning we agree not to go wandering around town the rest of the day. He wants us to stay in the hotel where he can have us watched."

"Okay, let's do it."

The press conference was quiet, at first. The reporters seemed polite and not quite ready to believe Mary's recitation. Mary and Tanner agreed to concentrate on the *Amador* and Mary's finding of the fork. She talked a little about finding and losing the brass plate and her research, and the stories Sarah Callender had told her. Then she said, "We decided that if the brass plate was part of the *Amador* when she sank, we might find other pieces in the same place.

"We went diving and this is what I found."

Tanner had located a box at the hotel gift shop that was just the right shape for a piece of tableware, and Mary brought it out and opened it on the table in front of the reporters. Her hands shook just the tiniest bit as she opened the box.

"This is a piece of sterling silver I found on the bottom of Lake Superior, northeast of the Apostle Islands. It's a fork with the initials dV on the handle." A hubbub rose and questions flew through the air. The fork looked quite nice displayed on a bed of white cotton in the brown box, but the TV camera people wanted it out on the table for better shots.

Tanner fielded questions about the wireless aboard the *Amador* and why they thought the operator might have become confused or sent the wrong signal. Mary refused to be specific about exactly where she'd found the brass plate or the fork. "We aren't sure if the fork was inside the park boundaries, so we don't know who will get custody."

Tanner deflected questions about who might be responsible for the explosion in the harbor except to say that he was convinced it had been meant for the other *Ondine*. The question reporters kept coming back to over and over again was why. Why were people trying to keep them from finding the *Amador*? What were the mysterious adversaries afraid of? Did it mean the old stories of crime and corruption that still swirled around the Mayhews and the deVoles were true? That was such a long time ago.

"I'll try to be plain," Mary said. "We think we know who killed Ethel Jandrice and Tommy Callender. But we aren't going to accuse anyone until the rest of our proof arrives."

That did it. The shouts rose in volume. Reporters surged forward. Had they really said they knew who killed Tommy Callender and Ethel Jandrice? Mary grabbed the fork and they fled to their room, escorted by plain-clothes detectives.

Watching the evening news on WDIO, Mary thought she looked nervous. "I'm embarrassed. My voice squeaked."

Tanner assured her she did the job. "From a public relations perspective, it was everything we could have hoped for. Everybody in town now knows," he said.

The police put several men in the hotel and requested Mary and Tanner use room service, rather than eat in the restaurant. At first Tanner declined. Late in the day he went to the lobby to get a *New York Times* and was approached by several people, including a stringer for the *Fargo Forum*. After that, they decided to have a quiet dinner in their room.

Cameron called. "Well, friends, I see you on the tube here."

Mary switched on the speaker phone and said, "Did we do all right?"

"If I was one of those fellas, I'd be gettin' out of town about now."

"You don't think he'll try to get to us?"

"Me, I'd figure on a guard. Course, I wouldn't get into that sort of fix in the first place."

"You're right, Cameron, but sometimes those types think they're smarter than the rest of us. That's what we're counting on," Mary said.

"I'm counting on Melvin and the others getting out of town," said Tanner. "Being a target isn't my idea of a good time."

Exhausted from the stress of the day, Tanner and Mary turned in early.

Suddenly, Mary was awake and sitting up in the dark bedroom.

They'd left the heavy drapes partway open and the lights of Duluth filtered in, providing a little light. What had disturbed her? She rolled over, away from Tanner in the big king-sized bed to turn on the lamp. A dark shape flew by and something heavy crashed into the pillow where her face had been.

"Michael!" she yelled and grabbed for the lamp. It fell to the floor. The dark shape rose and slammed again at the pillow. There was another crash and Tanner hollered something unintelligible from the other side of the bed.

He rolled onto the floor, dragging bedclothes with him

A light came on. Naked, Mary stumbled to her feet. Instinctively she reached for her robe. A light came on overhead. Melvin deVole swung the heavy piece of pipe he was holding, missing Mary again. He twisted around to confront Tanner. Mary saw he had flung himself across the room to the table by the window.

"Help! Police!" Mary screamed at the top of her lungs.

She grabbed for the telephone on the bedside table and swept it to the floor.

DeVole swung the length of pipe at Tanner. He ducked away and the table disappeared in splinters of broken wood and crushed aluminum.

There was another crash across the room. Two policemen who'd been waiting next door stormed through the unlocked connecting door, guns drawn. DeVole spun toward them and Tanner threw himself across the remains of the table. He slammed into deVole, knocking him to the carpet. The pipe slipped out of deVole's grip.

Two detectives rushed in, shouting. They fell onto deVole, hammered him back to the floor and quickly handcuffed him. After that, things quieted down. Mary struggled into her robe and the police hustled the intruder out the door.

Captain Mackay arrived with another detective whom Tanner introduced to Mary as Ted Bailey.

Reporters, alerted by police radio calls, surged through the halls, held at bay by uniformed patrolmen. The next morning, in response to a call, Tanner and Mary were brought to Police Headquarters where Captain Mackay ushered them to an interrogation room.

"Melvin deVole is singing like a bird. In fact, it's getting hard to sort everything out. So far, he's admitted killing Jandrice and Tommy Callender and trashing your apartment. He was after the file on the *Amador*. Apparently he tried to conceal his real purpose by destroying the place."

"Did he tell you who put him up to all that?"

"No, ma'm, not exactly. Somebody named Kald, in Chicago, apparently has a lot to do with it, but he accuses Roger Watt here in Duluth, and maybe a Tony Watt as well. The guy rambles a lot and getting direct answers is difficult. Eventually we'll sort it out."

"Did he say anything about trying to run me off the road?" Tanner asked.

Mackay sighed and rubbed his face. "Yeah, he did. He gave us the name of the guy who was with him, but he's not in the system. No record. There is one other thing. Bad news, I'm afraid. Sarah Callender is dead too."

Tears came to Mary's eyes. Tanner reached over and took her hand.

"I'm sorry. DeVole told us where to find the body, in a landfill out northwest of town. I got a call just before you got here. Deputies found her in a plastic trash bag. Broken neck."

Mary put her face in her hands and cried.

CHAPTER 38

Mary and Tanner caught a cab to the Mayhew mansion and were taken immediately to see the old man. It was obvious that the entire household had seen the news or it had been reported to them. There was palpable tension in the air.

Carole Ann met them at the door. "We haven't said anything to grandfather," she murmured. "About Sarah."

Black Jack Mayhew was in the same sunroom, sitting in the same wheelchair where Tanner had last seen him.

"He looks," Mary murmured in Tanner's ear as they crossed the tiled floor to the nurse and the old man, "almost completely wasted away."

Silently Tanner agreed. "Mr. Mayhew, I'm sorry to intrude again, but I want to bring you up to date on a few things." Mayhew's eyes brightened momentarily and his hand twitched.

The nurse looked up at them and said softly. "He has something to tell you, as well."

Tanner introduced Mary and then quickly sketched the sequence of events of the past two days. Finally Tanner told Mayhew about the arrest of Melvin deVole. The old man had no visible reaction. He stared at the floor, and his breathing seemed to slow. Mary frowned and Tanner was beginning to think the news was crushing the old man. The nurse leaned in and took Mayhew's pulse. She glanced at Tanner and shook her head ever so slightly.

Then Tanner had a flash of insight. "But you know most of this already, don't you?"

The old man nodded slowly. Once.

"You hired an investigator, didn't you?"

The old man nodded again.

"I wonder just how much of this was your doing?" Tanner knelt down and stared at the old man's faded eyes. Mayhew seemed to have gone off again to some other place, perhaps a more peaceful place. Tanner glanced at the nurse and realized that she must be the woman who called Fellowes. Tanner started to rise when Mayhew turned his head and said in his weak, papery voice,

"Who's the woman?"

Surprised, Tanner introduced Mary again. Then he saw that wasn't what Mayhew had meant. He said, "Mary found the brass plate from the *Amador*, in the water near Devils Island. The plate that was stolen from the Park Service in Bayfield." Frustration and anger made his voice harsh. "Why did you hire the investigator? Why are you involved and why did you have your nurse call Chicago?"

Mayhew only nodded. Drool ran in a thin stream from one corner of his mouth. His eyes remained half-closed. The nurse leaned forward and gently wiped his chin. Mary stepped around Tanner and knelt in front of Mayhew. The nurse touched Mayhew's shoulder and looked at Mary. Mayhew had fastened his eyes on Mary. The nurse stepped away and so did Tanner.

"I met Sarah," Mary said softly. Mayhew blinked. Mary leaned closer. "I knew her a little and I liked her. I felt an immediate connection. She was a strong woman, a good woman. She told me about you and about Piers and about Tommy. Your grandson. She told me about the *Amador*. I think she loved the lake and I know she still loved you." Mary stopped as tears came. "She's dead, you know. Sarah."

Mayhew seemed to nod. The nurse flinched.

"I brought you something to help remember her. From the lake." Mary reached in her purse and took out the cloth-wrapped fork. She placed it gently in his hand. Tanner stared. He hadn't known she was going to do that. But then he thought how right it was that a piece of the *Amador*, whether it was part of a treasure or not, should finally reach the hand of a Mayhew. Of this Mayhew. Mayhew looked at the fork. Then his hand moved and he took the fork onto his lap. He fumbled under the blanket over his bony knees. He reached for Mary with his other hand. With great care he withdrew a shining brass plate from under the blanket and placed it in Mary's hand. The plate had a hole in it. He wrapped her fingers around its smooth edges. The word *Amador* in raised letters was clearly visible on its surface. Still holding her hand, Mayhew turned his head and stared up at Tanner. Suddenly the dull, vacant, eyes cleared and blazed great fury at him. Tanner felt again as if he had been struck a physical blow. In his dry, cracked voice Mayhew answered all the remaining questions with a single word.

"Sarah!"

****

Tanner stood, hands on hips, surveying their Minneapolis apartment for the final time. Vance Jordan had just helped him bring the last of their luggage to the front door.

"Mary?" said Ella.

"Yes."

"I get most of it but I still have a question."

"Sure."

"Who stole the brass plate from the Park Service?"

"Melvin deVole," Mary replied.

"But why? And how did Mr. Mayhew get it?"

"We think," Mary went on, "that Black Jack Mayhew bought it from Melvin. We suspect deVole read the letter he stole from Ethel Jandrice and decided he could get more money from the Mayhews than from Kald, who is the most likely candidate for the one who sent him to Minneapolis in the first place."

"Mary's right," Tanner picked up the last tangled thread. Melvin was going to blackmail the Mayhew Corporation, just like Tommy planned to do, although with Tommy it was personal. Old man Mayhew was—is—still pretty sharp. He learned enough from Watt and the others dealing with deVole to put most of it together. And then later, when he figured out that Sarah and Tommy had been murdered, he decided to destroy their killers if he could get the information he needed. His detective got a lot of it right."

"This whole thing came about because some people worry too much about what others think."

Mary nodded in agreement.

"If you live on the edge of society, you frequently come to think everyone else has mostly evil intentions," Tanner said.

"Honor and a twisted kind of respect are very important to a lot of criminals. Remember when I said I was bothered by the randomness of these events?

"Kald was fronting for others in Chicago who thought that if Bob deVole was elected Illinois Attorney General, they'd have a special "in" at the capitol. So when the letter Ethel Jandrice found and Mary's inspection plate surfaced, they got worried."

"That's right," said Mary. "Kald figured he needed to do damage control, to quash any hint of scandal, even old scandal. Then things got out of hand. He caused the murders of Ethel and Tommy Callender and then Tommy's mother, Sarah. We still can't figure out why Sarah was killed. Circumstances spiraled out of control. She and Tommy and Ethel were ordinary people, the kind who don't seem to matter in the minds of manipulators like Kald and Roger Watt. But they didn't count on the power and rage of Black Jack Mayhew."

"Or on the persistence of a certain scuba diver." Tanner smiled and took Mary's hand. "Mayhew's nurse and Carole Ann must have been helping him keep track of things. When he began to realize that Sarah's disappearance at about the same time Tommy was killed probably only meant one thing, he hired an investigator."

"He loved Sarah very much. And he found a way to sort it out," Mary said. "But it's too bad he didn't show his love before she died."

Ella stirred in her chair. "It's awful. If everybody had just ignored that stuff, all those people would still be alive and Bob deVole would still be running for office. What happens to the others?"

"Not enough. Watt is out of a job as are some of the deVole people, I guess. There's just not enough proof of what we've told you to charge the others," Tanner said.

"But what about the *Amador*?" asked Vance.

Mary laughed softly. "We never found anything except the fork and the brass plate. I'm convinced there really was a special crate on board. And a list of names. But that probably disintegrated long ago. We'll never know for sure." She rose and went into the living room. "You know, it's also possible whatever cargo was there was found years ago by someone who never said anything. I don't care one way or the other. I'd like to spend the rest of the summer at home in Seattle doing next to nothing."

"I second that," responded Tanner. "I've a business to run, after all."

Vance and Ella took their leave and Tanner surveyed their packed luggage. "It'll be nice to get home," he said. "Have a little time on Puget Sound."

"Where would you like to go on our next vacation?"

Tanner grinned at Mary and opened the door for the cabbie who began to haul out the luggage. "How about somewhere peaceful, like the Adriatic?"